For Hazel Godwin, dearly departed,
but bubbling with life during the Bath years

CHAPTER 1

A World Heritage Site, the city of Bath was buzzing with people. Tills were ringing — or to be specific, credit cards were being swiped big time across readers. It was a wonderful sound. Hannah Driver was hearing something else.

'Murder, robbery and any other kind of mayhem must be kept at bay in this fair city, my dear girl; hence your appointment.'

Hannah — called Honey by those that knew her best, except her mother, who revelled in being different about everything — eyed Casper St John Gervais with incredulity.

'Crime Liaison Officer.'

'Yes.'

'On behalf of the Bath Hotels Association.'

'That's right.'

'Why me?'

'Your experience, my dear girl.' He sounded more like Noel Coward, the old-time actor he adored, than he usually did.

'I've never been a policeman . . . woman,' she corrected. The fact was, she was all at sixes and sevens.

Casper was still lecturing her. 'You know, my dear girl, how a city's reputation can affect tourism. Crime must be swiftly and effectively dealt with. Anyway, besides you having an interest in bed occupancy, I understand you used to work with criminals.'

Honey grimaced. 'I worked for the Probation Service — as a senior clerical officer.'

'Precisely my point.'

'Casper, that means I used to type social enquiry reports, a compilation of circumstances and excuses as to why the client shouldn't be banged up and the key thrown away.'

Casper had an aquiline nose, very thin at the bridge and widely flaring at the nostrils. When he fixed his gaze on her, his eyes seemed to close together, like a pince-nez perched on his nose. 'But you're all we have, my dear girl. No member of the Association has that kind of experience. And think of the good you could do . . . Hmm?' His eyebrows rose with his voice.

Honey glugged at her wine, nodded at fellow hoteliers and looked up at the ceiling and began counting the crystals on the chandelier.

One, two, three . . . fifty . . . How the devil was she going to get out of this? She hooked another drink from the table, where glasses of wine sat poised for the taking.

The Bath Hotels Association was holding their annual AGM. As chairman, Casper was to give a speech congratulating everyone on a splendid effort to attract even more visitors than last year and for sponsoring various hanging baskets and cultural events designed to attract even more. As usual the stuffy bit would be followed by a little party — quite a sizeable party, in fact. A well-known wine importer had supplied the drink, and a local caterer the food.

But Honey had done the unforgivable: arrived early and had to sit through the AGM. The bulk of the membership didn't arrive until the meeting was over. Perhaps if she'd arrived late someone else might have drawn the short straw.

A few glasses of Australian Shiraz helped alleviate her boredom. It also made her sleepy. Had she fallen asleep? She didn't think so.

'Thinking things over, my dear girl? Think of this: I guarantee that the Green River Hotel will benefit if you agree to this. Your rooms full, the clatter of cutlery on plates, bodies in beds and bums on seats.'

She started. Wiley old Casper had taken advantage of the situation.

Upgrading a few bedrooms at the Green River had left her with a chunky overdraft. Running a hotel in a beautiful city was no bed of roses. Unless you counted the thorns. Casper's promise had poured like honey into her ear.

'I guarantee to divert room occupancy your way.'

* * *

The rest of the evening passed in a blur. It hit hard and fast when she got home and told her daughter about it. Lindsey was eighteen but had the nous of somebody twenty years older.

'Relax. Consider the positive side. It could add a pinch of spice to your life. You need to get out more.'

Corners of her mouth downturned, Honey watched as Lindsey cleared the bar and locked up.

'Are you going nightclubbing tomorrow night?' she asked her, suddenly in need of diverting the subject.

Tomorrow night, Thursday, was Lindsey's night off.

Her daughter shook her tawny head. 'No. I'm going to a concert at the Abbey.'

'Pop?' Honey asked with a hopeful lifting of eyebrows.

'No. Medieval tunes for lute and lyre.'

'My, you are such a wild child. When I was eighteen . . .'

'You were irresponsible.'

'Who told you that?'

'Grandma.'

'She's a fine one to talk . . .'

Lindsey kissed her forehead. 'I'm off to bed. Now don't worry. Like I said, you could do with a little pinch of spice in your life. Who knows where it might lead?'

* * *

The little pinch of spice came at the wrong time. Honey loved auctions, especially when there were antique clothes up for grabs — underwear in particular. Today there was plenty. Tight lace-trimmed corsets, silky stockings plus early twentieth-century cami-knickers that barely covered what they were supposed to cover. Big knickers as well. The Victorians went in *big* time for *big* knickers. 'Mostly crotchless,' she'd stated to the rounded figure next to her who had held up a pair thinking they were some kind of tablecloth. 'Not a lot of people know that,' Honey added.

Collecting clothes from the past helped keep her sane. Musing over who might have worn those gloves, that button-up boot, that lace-trimmed chemise, made her forget that the laundry service had mislaid two-dozen tablecloths or that the honeymoon couple in room three had done irreversible damage to the bedsprings.

She had a small but interesting collection of lace mittens, silk stockings, garters, plus some very interesting underwear. Today she had hit the jackpot and would have gone one better, when Casper phoned. One arm half raised, she pulled out her phone with the other.

'Your first case,' he said. His voice sounded tinny at the end of the phone.

'OK,' she said, one eye on the auctioneer and the Victorian corset that was up for grabs: all whalebone and laces and made for a waist of less diameter than a modern thigh.

She was almost salivating.

'Where are you? Are you close by?'

Honey looked around her with furtive intent. Should she lie?

'The truth, dear girl,' said Casper reading her mind.

'I'm at Spencers' Auction Rooms.'

'Good. Be here by eleven thirty.'

Here meant his office. The phone went silent. He wasn't taking no for an answer.

Her head swivelled towards the auctioneer.

She waved at the rostrum.

'Gone! Sorry madam. You're too late.'

Blast! It had been such a pretty little corset — red satin, edged with black lace. Definitely French and very provocative.

'But not for you,' she muttered as she pushed her way through the dealers, the curious and the bargain hunters.

She glanced at her watch on the way out to the sheltered alcove and desk area where she had to settle her bill and collect her purchase. They were large, and so was the price. But then they'd been listed as having once belonged to Queen Victoria.

'Not for you, are they, hen?' smirked the cashier.

Alistair was huge, hairy and Scottish.

'Yep! I'm making a tent. The weather's going to be nice this summer.'

Once outside she shoved the Victorian bloomers into her Moroccan leather bag. A sliver of cotton knicker leg fluttered like bunting between the gaping leather.

The sun came out as she passed the Pump Rooms, turning the elegant facade the colour of honey. Inside a quartet was playing Handel. People were sipping tea made with real tealeaves and scoffing scones that oozed rich fruit jam and clotted cream.

The music drifted on the air, but did nothing to soothe her slightly savage breast.

Missing the corset rankled. Red satin! And over a hundred years old! Now, how rare was that?

Drat Casper St John Gervais! If he hadn't insisted she meet him at eleven thirty *precisely*, the corset would have been hers.

Ten years ago it might have fitted her. She smiled to herself. *Call yourself voluptuous, dear.* There again, wasn't everybody's waist way beyond the Victorian eighteen inches?

Bath city centre was busy, but it was June and only to be expected. Baskets bursting with geraniums adorned the fronts of offices, banks and shops. Wisps of variegated ivy and purple aubrietia fluttered from lamp posts. The elegant buildings forming Regency crescents and squares turned cowslip yellow when the sun came out.

Month after month the tourists flocked in from all over the world to gape at the Roman Baths, eat the massive buns on offer in Sally Lunn's Teashop and have their pictures taken in front of the Abbey, the Royal Crescent or at the end of Pulteney Bridge.

The tourists were the city's lifeblood, the fertiliser that had caused a raft of Georgian listed buildings to flower into hotels, restaurants and guest houses.

By the time she got to Hotel La Reine Rouge, an elegant edifice overlooking Pulteney Bridge and within walking distance of the Roman Baths, it felt as though she'd weaved her way through every nation in the world.

La Reine Rouge, Grade I-listed and oozing class, was even more elegant inside than out, thanks mainly to its owner-manager's exquisite choice and eclectic mix of antiques, colour and sophisticated lighting.

She patted the arm of a turbaned statuette, one of a gloriously crimson, black and gold pair guarding the entrance.

'Hi, chaps. Is the boss in?'

Neville, the eagle-eyed receptionist with bleached blond hair and wearing a burgundy waistcoat with a gold watch chain, answered her question.

'He's waiting for you, sweetie. He's got his manicurist with him. He's terribly tense you know what with everything that's been happening.'

She gasped. 'Happening? You mean he's broken a nail?'

He threw her a sideways sneer. 'You're a very naughty girl, Honey.'

His attention returned to the trio of white lilies he was placing in a tall, green vase. When they didn't fall the way he wanted, he picked them out and started all over again.

Honey flicked at a fleck of pollen that dared smear the eighteenth-century desk that served as the reception counter.

'Only when tempted. But then, Neville, I hear the same about you.'

Neville feigned coyness. 'Stop teasing me, Honey. You do it on purpose.'

The long case clock standing on a thick Turkish rug chose that moment to chime the half hour.

One of the lilies fell sideways.

'Bother!'

Neville's vocabulary was as delicate as his appearance.

Honey raised her eyebrows and couldn't resist a smirk. Neville grimaced.

'How much longer do you think he'll be?'

'As long as it takes, sweetie. Casper is something of a perfectionist, as well you know.'

Yes, she knew, and in knowing she looked down at her fingernails. The varnish was chipped. What else could she expect? Being the boss of her own hotel meant filling in when the dishwasher broke down or chambermaids didn't turn up.

Tucking her bag under her arm, she hid her fingers in her pockets and made her way along the thickly carpeted corridor and down the stairs to Casper's office.

The phone rang. Neville answered. 'Tea. Yes, of course, Casper. By the way, Honey is here.' A pause. 'Absolutely. I'll send her in.'

He put down the phone and nodded at her to go in.

At one time, the wine cellars beneath La Reine Rouge had stretched the whole length of the basement. After the builders had finished the basics, Casper had turned the area into offices for him and his staff. Hessian wallpaper, rich sienna in colour, was applied to the newly plastered walls. The furniture was a mix of minimalist settees, Georgian break-fronted bookcases and ethnic artwork. Oh, and clocks. Casper loved clocks. They were everywhere: wall clocks, grandfather clocks, grandmother clocks, skeleton clocks, carriage clocks, all ticking away together. They even chimed together. Casper insisted they all chimed together in unison. He hated untidiness.

'Honey. Come in.' His voice rang like the sharp chime of one of his clocks.

The manicurist was buffing the smallest finger of Casper's right hand. He waved the woman away once it was done.

'Another day, another finger job,' he said with a demure smile. 'I do like clean fingernails. Thank you, darling. Neville will settle the bill.'

Honey smiled to herself. Casper's patrician sensibilities prevented him from anything as plebeian as physically dealing with money.

He was sitting in a honey-coloured leather chair behind a mahogany desk that might once have belonged to Tennyson or Wordsworth. Casper loved items with provenance, a proven history and famous connections. He loved auctions as much as she did, though his preference was for mahogany chests of drawers rather than the cotton type with two legs that she favoured.

She smiled at him and brought on the flattery. 'You're looking as lovely as ever, Casper.'

'Thank you, my dear.'

Casper was the prima donna of the catering industry and adored flattery. He tried his best to sound like Noel Coward at the height of his success but looked like a rather late-middle-aged version of Randolph Scott.

While she stood there, he brought out a feather duster from a drawer and proceeded to flick it at the imagined dust the manicurist had left behind.

'I trust you've heard the news, so I'll not go into detail except to say that your services are required much earlier than one could possibly have anticipated.'

'Well, actually, I've been so busy . . .' She didn't get chance to explain that the dishwasher had thrown another tantrum or that a couple from Leicester had climbed out of the window that morning without paying their bill. She very much regretted not putting them on the third floor. That would have foxed them.

Casper was holding forth about the meeting of the Bath Hotels Association the week before.

'As you may recall, the meeting took a unanimous decision to appoint a crime liaison officer, someone who could deal with the police on their level and keep the rest of us informed. In view of your credentials, it was agreed that you were the right person for the job.'

'Yes, a little paperwork, a few meetings with the police and some room occupancy,' she added brightly.

'I think the problem brought to my attention this morning needs a hands-on approach.'

She felt her face tightening as her eyebrows rose up into her hairline.

'Hands-on? What exactly do you mean by that?'

Having secreted the feather duster in his top right-hand drawer, he used his elegant fingers to flick at an imaginary dust spot on his shoulder — too small a spot for Honey to see, even though she narrowed her eyes.

'I mean, my dear, that a little detective work would not go amiss. I think you'd be quite good at it — better than the police, in fact. You know how slow they can be.' His face stiffened with seriousness. 'I . . . *we* want results, Honey. Quickly.'

In her mind she saw herself knocking on doors just like the police did in their appeals for witnesses, hunting down muggers in their lairs. It could mean travelling to less salubrious areas in Bath or, heaven forbid, Bristol.

The tingle of excitement melted at the thought of confronting big bruisers with torsos the size of beer barrels.

'But Casper, I've got a hotel to run and I don't really think—'

'As you may recall,' Casper cut in, 'as members of the Bath Hotels Association, we agreed that crime was the greatest threat to visitor numbers. This honey-coloured city, this haunt of Jane Austen, Beau Brummel and . . . and . . .'

He looked up at the ceiling in his search for another famous name.

'Jane Seymour?' said Honey in an effort to help him out.

His brow furrowed in a deep frown. 'Did she live here? I never knew the Tudors graced us with their presence.'

'Not Henry VIII's wife. I meant the actress. You know — *Doctor Quinn, Medicine Woman* and Bond Girl? She used to live out at St Catherine's Court.'

He gave her a Paddington Bear type of stare, steely and cold. 'As I was saying, someone with your background—'

'I was nothing very—'

'There are perks, of course. You do recall me telling you that?'

Her jaw stopped where it was, her mouth half formed around a word.

'Yes. You did say so.'

Her heart thudded in her chest.

'As I outlined to you, it's only fair that the time you put into this should be recompensed in some way.'

He opened a leather-bound folder lying on his desk. 'I most definitely recall you saying that a block booking had been cancelled and you had rooms to let. Could you find eight rooms for more or less immediate occupation?'

Her voice resumed to normal service. 'When?'

'The tenth?'

'Just a minute.'

It was hard to keep breathing. Her fingers were all thumbs. This was a result, the type that put money in the bank.

Without thinking of the consequences, she heaved her shoulder bag onto the leather-topped desk.

'Off!'

Leaping to his feet, Casper reopened the right-hand drawer and brought out his feather duster. His face was a picture of wounded indignation. 'Do you realise this desk was once owned by Lord Berkeley?'

The feather duster had a strong enough head to sweep her bag onto the floor, but not before the nebulous knickers had spread over the desk.

Casper's raised eyebrows looked in danger of sliding upwards over his shiny forehead. He pointed a trembling finger. There were broad gaps between each word.

'WHAT . . . ARE . . . THOSE?'

Honey muttered vagaries about them having belonged to Queen Victoria and being a collector's item. 'Sorry, where the bloody hell is my diary!'

While she rummaged around the hidden depths of her shoulder bag, he fingered the voluminous knickers with disgusted delicacy. Eyes dinner plate wide, he held the waist strings between finger and thumb, peering through the centre of what must have been a singularly draughty garment.

'Sorry, Casper. I can't seem to find . . . Ah! Here it is.'

With a look somewhere between distaste and true-blue respect, Casper let the bloomers fall onto the desk, his delicate, white hands remaining at shoulder level.

He eyed them with disdain. 'What utterly dreadful items! They're big enough to form the mainsail of a racing yacht!'

'So what were those dates?'

Sighing as though life had become terribly difficult, he repeated them.

Honey checked her diary. The tenth had a thick, ugly line crossed through it. Someone had cancelled, and at this time of year she could have sold that room over and over again.

'No worries!' Her face was flushed. Her pulse raced. 'How many did you say?'

'Eight rooms. All singles, mark you.'

Singles! Only two-thirds of the normal price, but hey, beggars can't be choosers; and she was certainly a beggar, thanks to the upgrading of the attic rooms and an unsympathetic bank manager.

He passed her the letter and booking form. 'Here you are. As I said, I think it only fair that you should gain something from these extra duties. We must not allow crime to rise in this city as elsewhere in the western world. We have an image to maintain.'

'Not to mention a property portfolio and a lavish lifestyle,' Honey muttered, still scribbling in her diary.

'Exactly. People expect certain standards. Ambience, good service and a standard of personal safety one would associate with . . .'

He studied the ceiling as he searched for the right word.

'Disneyworld?'

He waved an arm and stabbed a finger. 'Exactly! Therefore, a crime liaison officer can only be a good thing.'

'Oh, I agree.'

Of course she did. Filling up eight rooms in one fell swoop was fantastic. The alternative would have been to accept lower-priced guests from the Tourist Information Office, who would come in dribs and drabs, stay for a night and be off to Stratford upon Avon, determined to see everything that was worth seeing in the space of three days. London, Bath and Stratford.

After folding the forms inside her diary, she grabbed the escaped undergarment and stuffed it back into her bag.

'So,' she said brightly, feigning absolute attention, 'who's been mugged, diddled or sold a duff budgie?'

A puzzled stiffness came over the face of the chairman of the Bath Hotels Association. Street cred and slang were low on Casper's need-to-know list. If anyone could truly look down their nose at you and make you feel you'd been peddling your body on the street all night, it was Casper.

'I'm not sure you're entirely aware of the seriousness of the situation.' His tone of voice was as sonorous as the clock in reception.

Honey felt warm. She'd made a good bid at auction, the dishwasher man should have finished repairing the blasted machine by the time she got back and the rooms she envisaged staying empty or selling cheap were full again. It was just a case now of doing this job for Casper.

'So what's the problem?'

The way Casper lowered his eyelids sowed the first seeds of worry in what had initially seemed a very fruitful morning.

'I'm afraid an American tourist has disappeared. Not from one of our more refined establishments, mark you. For some odd reason he chose to stay in a bed and breakfast on the Lower Bristol Road.'

Casper said the words 'bed' and 'breakfast' as though he were spitting out broken teeth.

'Are we sure of that? Couldn't he just have gone home early or done something unusual like visit Wales?' Wales was somewhere Americans went on a whim after discovering there were castles there.

'He left his luggage behind.'

'Oh.'

'And his passport.'

Steepling his fingers, he leaned forward. His tone was low, almost secretive. 'Let's look into this ourselves shall we — before we go to the police.'

'I don't think that's a good idea.'

That frown again. 'I insist.'

Of course he did, and if she didn't comply, those eight empty rooms would go unfilled.

She forced a smile. 'On reflection, I think you're quite right. I'll see what I can do.'

CHAPTER 2

Honey almost tripped over her own frown as she entered the Green River Hotel.

'What do I know about crime?'

Solving the crime before that funny little Belgian detective on TV, the one created by Agatha Christie, didn't qualify her to do it in real life.

Anna the Czech, a gem of a girl, was running reception. She'd obviously heard what Honey had said and was now eyeing her strangely.

'Everything OK?' asked Honey.

'Very good, Mrs Driver. Are you OK?'

'Yes. I've become an amateur sleuth.'

Anna looked perplexed. 'That is very nice for you. Does this mean the hotel gets an extra star?' Another star would look better on her CV.

'Not exactly.' She hunted for a simple statement that wouldn't confuse. 'It's more service in the community.' *Unwanted service*, she thought to herself. 'Oh. And I've bought Queen Victoria's bloomers.'

'Oh.' Anna didn't sound impressed.

Honey marched to the kitchen and was welcomed by the sound of the dishwasher gyrating with water. Great, that meant she could get on with a few things before paying a visit to Ferny Down Guest House, the bed and breakfast where the American tourist had chosen to stay.

She eyed the dishwasher with undisguised distrust. It was always breaking down.

'Done?' she asked Smudger Smith, her eccentric, soccer-mad chef.

'Done,' he said without looking up.

He was poking around in the tray of fresh meat just delivered by the butcher. He had a thing about marbling; steaks without the right amount of fat threading through them were only fit for the pet food trade, in his estimation.

The dishwasher continued to burble like a bonny brook.

Honey was happy. 'Right. I'm ready for anything.'

Smudger glanced over his shoulder. 'Your mother's here.'

'Except that,' she muttered, her feet already sprinting for the bar.

Her mother had her own flat at number two, Squires Mews, just behind the Theatre Royal. That didn't stop her turning up unannounced. Rarely did she muck in to help, and never with the washing-up — *I've just had my nails done, darling*. Her nails were perfectly shaped, perfectly shiny, unlike Honey's, which showed she often plunged her hands into soapy water; the dishwasher had a lot to answer for.

'Hannah!'

She was one of the few people who still called her Hannah, but only when she had something 'serious' to say.

Hoping to escape, Honey made the bar area just in time. The *tap-tap* of kitten-heeled shoes moved unrelentingly in her direction.

'Hannah, come out of that den of iniquity. I want to talk to you . . .'

'Sorry, Mother, but I have some important business on behalf of the Bath Hotels Association.'

The door at the back of the bar formed a quick escape route. Her mother never entered the bar. Although a Catholic,

15

she had a Methodist aversion to alcohol — probably because her husband, Honey's father, had had such a liking for it.

Lindsey was replenishing the fruit juices. She grinned. 'Grandma's heard about you becoming a private detective. She thinks you might get involved with a policeman and end up drinking in bars all night.'

Honey grimaced. 'I already drink in bars MOST of the night. I run a hotel, in case she hasn't noticed!'

'Grandma says she reckons you're no good at finding suitable men. She reckons she's going to find you one.'

Honey lowered her voice. 'Your grandmother's idea of suitable is someone with broad business interests and the personality of a hamster.'

Lindsey smirked. 'And yours is?'

Honey gave a waved her hand as if to say, *I don't know.* 'Broad shoulders?'

'A good starting point.' Lindsey's voice dropped to a whisper. 'Go on. Make your escape. I'll make the excuses.'

Honey kissed her soft cheek. 'Did I ever tell you that you're the best daughter in the world?'

Lindsey pretended to think about it. 'Only when I don't ask you for a pay rise.'

'That's my girl.'

'But you never call me that when I get back from clubbing at three in the morning.'

Honey threw Lindsey a long-suffering look.

'Mmmm!' She ruffled her daughter's tawny crop. 'Actually, I don't think you do it often enough.'

Lindsey had nerdy tendencies. She liked history, she read a lot and she went to concerts — not the twanging guitars of heavy rock, but the more melodious sounds of Bach, Schubert and especially medieval chamber music.

The door slid silently shut behind her, the car started first time, and although it was parked in a tight space, necessity honed her driving skills. She pulled out swiftly and headed straight for the other side of town.

Her stomach rumbled. Lunchtime had been and gone. The digital readout on the bathroom scales would reflect her abstention — at least she hoped they would, otherwise they were for the bin. Due to their damp environment, bathroom scales got rusty quickly, and they rarely gave an accurate reading.

It was midway through the afternoon, so the traffic wasn't too bad. She kept to the inner circuit road, skirting the city and sweeping towards the Wellsway then bearing right and immediately left onto the Bristol Road.

Heavy engineering works, scrap yards and devastation had once lined the road on the side fronting the river. They'd since been replaced by swank apartments in former warehouses, smart offices and landscaped car parks.

The other side of the road was unchanged — lined with Victorian villas, many advertising bed and breakfast.

Ferny Down Guest House was one of these. Hanging baskets full of purple, mauve and pink flowers hung from ground floor to guttering, obscuring the dirt-streaked facade of Ferny Down Guest House. A low wall divided a tiny front garden from the busy road.

The door was plastic, totally out of sync with the Victorian brickwork but easy to wash down with a damp rag. Honey made a mental note to table a discussion about the kerbside appeal of the city's guest houses at the next meeting of the Association.

She rang the doorbell, heard it echo inside.

There were other noises, but not the sort associated with someone coming to answer the front door.

Stepping back, she looked up at the windows. Like the door they had plastic frames and were double glazed to keep out traffic noise: so much for keeping things in period.

The door remained steadfastly closed.

Grunting sounds, the sort struggling men make when they're lifting something heavy, came from the alleyway between Ferny Down and the house next door.

Well, she didn't have all afternoon. Back she went, turning right then right again into the alley.

Three men were manhandling an old chest freezer out of the back gate.

'Careful with my fence. I only just put that up. Did my back in that did.'

Ah, thought Honey. That had to be the proprietor, Mervyn Herbert.

She trod to the side entrance, and there found Mervyn in all his glory — or rather not. Good looks and dress sense were not his forte. He wore a sleeveless pullover, quite the rage back in the fifties.

Overweight, but not obese, he had the worn-out look of someone trapped in a routine he didn't want to be in.

She called out to him. 'Mr Herbert? Can I have a word?'

She flattened herself against a side wall as the men carrying the rusty old freezer squeezed out through the gate.

Mervyn's bushy eyebrows beetled when he looked her up and down. 'You from the council?'

'No, I'm not.'

'Just as well. They're always around 'ere with their bleedin' clipboards. There's always something we're doin' wrong. Ought to get a proper job, the bleedin' lot of them. Interfering little knob'eads . . .'

He gave her another once over and looked pleased with what he saw.

'Then whatever I can 'elp you with, darlin'?'

Honey adopted her most professional manner and stayed pleasant, disguising her repulsion.

'My name's Honey Driver. I'm . . .' she paused. What was it Casper had called her? 'I'm the new crime liaison officer for the Bath Hotels Association. I came to see you about your little problem.'

For a moment he looked as though he wasn't sure what she was talking about.

Sensing he wouldn't be keen to air his carelessness in public — losing a paying customer — she mouthed the words, 'Your missing guest.'

'Oh. That. You'd best see the wife. Come this way if you like. Mind you don't trip.'

Once the freezer was on its way to the council truck, she edged her way around the path, carefully avoiding a pyramid of stones and what looked to be freshly planted alpines.

Mr Herbert jerked his head in the direction of a plastic-framed conservatory. Through the misted glass she detected a blob of colour moving in a chair and wreathed in cigarette smoke.

'She's in there. I'll leave you to it darlin', but if you need me, just 'oller.'

'Thank you.' With nimble speed she left him, heard him doing some hollering himself, shouting at the men handling the freezer.

''Ere!' she heard him shout. 'Go easy with that! Don't knock into my wall. Only just painted it. Bleedin' council!'

Mrs Cora Herbert threw aside the magazine she'd been reading and beckoned her over.

'You from the Association?'

'Yes. My name's Honey Driver. I own the Green River.'

'Oh. That posh job in Duke Street.'

Honey refrained from being apologetic; the Green River was hardly posh, and she worked as hard any guest house owner.

'I understand you wanted us to look into things before reporting your guest's disappearance to the police.'

Cora heaved her ample bust. 'Too right. Don't want the pigs sniffing round 'ere. We likes our privacy.'

Honey managed a smile that professed agreement. At the same time she took in the too-tight T-shirt and skirt, the black shiny tights and the impractical high-heeled shoes. Mrs Herbert was mutton trying and failing to be lamb.

'Nice name you got, though. Unusual. Are you American?'

'My father was.'

'I thought so,' she said, beaming from ear to ear. 'I bet you look like 'im.'

'I can't remember. He died when I was young.'

Cora's face crumpled with sympathy. 'Accident, was it?'

'You could say that.'

The accidental element was having met a twenty-two-year-old model at a business do. It was hardly an accident that he'd lusted after her, divorced Honey's mother, then dropped dead on his honeymoon. No drugs were involved. Viagra hadn't been around back then. His ambitions had not been equalled by his ability.

'Quite cosy in here,' said Honey after taking in her surroundings. The room reeked of tobacco and stale coffee, but being friendly was what sleuths did to take people off guard.

A half-drunk cup of coffee sat on the table. So did an ashtray containing cigarette stubs stained with pink lipstick.

'Cosy enough for me. It's my den where I can do what I bloody well like,' said Cora Herbert as if guessing what Honey was thinking, shooting her down before she made comment. 'Are you dry?'

'Sorry?'

'Do ya wanna cup of coffee?'

Honey eyed the half-drunk coffee again.

'No thanks.'

She got out her notebook and a pen — first requisite of a decent detective. 'So, the missing guest . . .?'

'Mr Bernstock. At least that's what he said his name was. But that isn't the name on his passport, nor the address he gave us.'

'Didn't you check his passport details against the address given when he checked in?'

Without so much as a bashful blink, Cora took a cigarette from a packet and lit up. Thankfully, she turned her head away when she exhaled.

'What for? He paid cash up front.' She shrugged. 'What the tax man don't see, he can't get his maulers on.'

'Ah!' Honey nodded.

'How long did he stay?'

'A whole week!'

Cora Herbert's tone was the oral equivalent of rubbing her hands together.

'Unusual for a bed and breakfast.'

'A guest house! We are a *guest house*,' Cora Herbert snapped, sending whorls of smoke escaping from her mouth.

'Sorry. Still — a good booking. Few Americans take that long to look round Bath.'

Cora shrugged her naked shoulders against the gleam of see-through plastic bra straps. 'Whatever. He paid and that was it.'

'So his things are still in his room?'

Cora made a hissing sound through her teeth. 'Ooow, no. I had to clear the room because I had bookings, you see. It's in storage. I'll have to charge him, of course.'

'Of course.'

Cora Herbert clearly let nothing stand in the way of business. Every penny counted.

'If he's still alive, that is.'

Honey threw her a look of surprise. 'I'm sorry?'

'Well, I can hardly charge him if he's dead.'

'Of course not.'

Honey rebuked herself for having misjudged the woman.

'I'll have to send the bill to his family.'

Back to square one!

Now burning only an inch or so from Cora's yellow-stained fingertips, the cigarette was stubbed out. A second or two, a little nail biting, and another one glowed red between sequined fingernails.

Honey's eyes flitted to the garden, wishing she was out there breathing fresh air.

She pulled herself back to the job in hand. 'Did he do much sightseeing?'

Cora narrowed her eyes against the rising smoke until they were just slits shaded by eyelashes caked with mascara. 'I suppose he did, though I didn't like to pry. I asked in a general kind of way, and he answered in a general kind of way.'

'Any particular places?'

'Well, the Royal Crescent, of course, and the Baths, but I think he went a bit further afield too. Came home by taxi three days running. Handed the driver roughly fifty quid each time. I know the driver. He's a regular pick-up and put-down. Busy Bee Cabs.'

Honey agreed that he must have been visiting some-where outside the city to attract that size of taxi fare: the American Museum at Claverton Down, or even pretty little Bradford on Avon? 'Its Saxon church is especially fine,' a Berkeley professor had told her. He'd also related a potted history of the Berkeley family and the castle situated halfway between Bath and Gloucester. He'd also mentioned the film *Pulp Fiction* and the phrase 'getting medieval on your ass.'

'And you're sure it was the same taxi driver and the same cab company each time?'

Cora nodded. 'The car was black. All their cars are black with a ruddy great bee on the side.'

'What about your husband?'

'What about him?'

The tone turned sour, the eyes hard as pebbles.

'Did he speak to Mr Bernstock?'

'Had a few words. Got riled with 'im 'cause he was always asking for crushed ice.' She laughed. 'The look on Mervyn's face when he was bashing them ice cubes with a rolling pin — enough to commit murder, they were. "Why can't he have bloody cubes like everybody bloody else?" he said.'

Crushed ice. Honey knew from experience that Americans loved crushed ice. It could be annoying when nothing else would do and other guests were making demands.

'Still, we aim to please.'

'Look, I know your husband's busy at the moment, but I would like a word when he's free.'

Cora got up and poked her head out of the conservatory. 'MER-VYN!'

'No chance,' she said, coming back in shaking her head in consternation. 'He's been 'elping the council blokes to

22

take that freezer. Must have got up a sweat and decided a few pints were needed.'

'He's gone to the pub?'

'Yeah.' Cora screwed up her nose and took another puff of her cigarette. 'It's an 'ome from bloody 'ome these days.'

Honey narrowed her eyes, partly against the damned smoke, and partly because she was making a mental list of all the questions she should ask. She wrote down his name along with a note to question the taxi driver should Mr Bernstock not turn up. She smoothed the page flat with her hand. This was all very satisfying and just a teeny bit exciting. Sleuthing was based on a process of elimination. Now what would those detectives on TV do?

'You said you put his things in storage. Can I take a look at them?'

Cora got up from her chair. 'Follow me.'

Instead of taking her to a secure lock-up as she'd expected, Cora led her to a cupboard beneath the stairs. 'There it is.'

Two holdalls, one smaller than the other but neither of them very big.

'Great!' She leaned forward meaning to drag the bags outside.

An indignant Cora stopped her. 'I don't want his stuff out here messing up my hallway. I've just vacuumed it and I've got guests coming.'

She said it as though she were the Royal Crescent Hotel and expecting a presidential cavalcade, rather than a gang of spotty backpackers on a tight budget.

Before Honey had chance to ask where she could take them, Cora pushed her into the cupboard. 'There. I can't shut the door without locking it, but you'll be all right. You've got a light. Give me a knock when you've finished and I'll let you out.'

Stephen King horror stories sprang to mind. She couldn't quite recall one about a mad landlady locking an unsuspecting amateur sleuth under the stairs, but that didn't mean it wasn't possible.

After settling her nerves and giving her thudding heart a severe talking to, she hunkered down and got on with it.

Nothing unusual about the clothes: typically non-iron stuff that anyone with any sense would take on a long-term vacation.

The flight documents and passport were in a see-through plastic zip-lock. That alone was worrying, though not unusual. Most people carried their passports with them, unless they had access to a safe. Only upmarket hotels had safes.

'So I would take my passport with me if I was staying in a place like this,' Honey muttered to herself. 'But you didn't . . .' Her voice trailed away. So why leave it? Unless he hadn't had time or unless something bad, very bad, had happened . . . The picture in the passport showed a chiselled-looking man with fair hair. Nice-looking. Not unusual, not surprising. His name was surprising, though. It was given as Elmer John Maxted, age forty-three, eyes blue.

'Hello, Mr Maxted,' she muttered, then frowned. 'Now why call yourself Bernstock?'

Her eyes flitted over a receipt for travel insurance and his given address — somewhere in California — then landed on the space reserved for occupation, fully expecting something mundane like 'accountant' or 'realtor'. Far from it!

Holding it up to the bare light bulb, she reread the details. Her heart skipped a beat.

'Let me out,' she shouted, hammering on the door. 'Let me out!'

No sound from the hallway on the other side of the door. Wherever Cora Herbert was, she wasn't close at hand as promised.

Honey dug her cell phone out of her pocket and tapped Casper's number.

'Casper. I know you won't want to do this, but you have to call the police.'

He mumbled a few excuses as to why he shouldn't and asked why she thought he should.

'Look, he's left his passport here . . .'

Casper questioned what was the big deal about that?

'Casper, no one leaves their passport behind in a bed and breakfast. But there's something else. His name's not Bernstock, it's Maxted, and he's a private detective.'

CHAPTER 3

'The police are making enquiries.'

'Is that all?'

'My dear girl, the man has only gone missing. And that, my dear, is more or less what was said to me. They said give it one more day. If he doesn't turn up then they'll put out a nationwide alert.'

Honey sighed. The case of the missing tourist had run up against the buffers. She was disappointed. This had seemed like a REAL crime case. The police had tagged it routine.

On top of that the weather forecast took a nosedive.

'It's June, for goodness' sake!'

The weather god took no notice of her outburst, and the rain started at five that afternoon.

Thursday was Lindsey's night off, and she was presently hogging the bathroom. The fallout from all manner of scented soap, shower gel and shampoo was drifting with the steam out of the bathroom window.

Honey was sitting outside beneath a 200-year-old canopy. Its metal roof, the original colour turned to the mottled green of aged copper, ran the length of the private patio. Clematis and other plants climbed the fretwork supports. The patio area it covered was further divided from hotel guests by bushes and more plants climbing over a sturdy mesh of wire and stone pillars.

Honey settled herself on a wooden bench. Like the roof, its framework was also made of iron and painted white. As she fondled the lion heads forming the arms, she wondered how long before her career in amateur detection would recommence.

The sound of running water coming from the bathroom ceased. Accompanied by a cloud of steam, Lindsey came out wearing a bathrobe and a towel around her wet hair.

'I suppose you'll be late tonight.'

'Tonight? Certainly not. Expect me at around three.'

'You said you were going to a concert.'

Lindsey's voice was muffled by towel and wet hair. 'Mother, I'm trying to appear wild. You want me to enjoy myself, don't you?'

'You're going clubbing?'

Lindsey smiled through fronds of wet hair. 'After the concert.'

Honey smiled. The young social scene in the city of Bath was second to none. Trendy wine bars rubbed shoulders with the Theatre Royal, pubs, restaurants and clubs that partied till dawn. Lindsey was part of that scene, but with reservations. Goodness knows where the culture vulture genes had come from.

'Anywhere nice?' Honey asked, trying to sound laid back and modern — even unconcerned. It was far from easy.

Lindsey rubbed vigorously at her hair. 'It depends on my friends.'

Who was she going out with? Honey sipped at her drink. Dare she ask?

'Three men friends,' said Lindsey before she had chance to ask.

Going to a nightclub with three men. Trying to sound laid back and modern flew out of the window. Mother Hen took over.

'Now look, if you must go clubbing, keep in a crowd and don't let these guys take advantage, and make sure you get a taxi home.'

'Taxis are expensive.'

A sense of déjà vu came over her. Her response was also familiar. 'I'll reimburse you.'

'Mum! Stop fussing. The guys are great pals. They're not going to rape me. Stop treating me like a child. I'm eighteen, for God's sake!'

Honey's mouth dropped as the truth dawned. 'Gosh. You sound just like me.'

Lindsey's eyes echoed the smile playing around her mouth. 'And you sound just like . . .'

'Hold it right there!' Honey held up her hand, palm facing her daughter. 'I apologise for sounding like my mother. Go out, get drunk, get laid, but don't bring any trouble home.' She kissed her daughter's cheek. 'Just take care of yourself.'

'I will.'

The old coach house they lived in was situated at the end of the long, paved courtyard to the rear of the hotel. There were two bedrooms downstairs, plus a bathroom. The upper floor that had once held hay and barley for the horses now boasted a fitted kitchen and a spacious living room. A stone fireplace graced one wall of the living room and two huge A-shaped trusses supported an exposed apex ceiling panelled in Canadian maple. The panelled ceiling was the reason Honey had created bedrooms on the ground floor and living space upstairs. The view was good. So was the ceiling when you were lying flat on your back, staring into space.

Kicking off her shoes, Honey lay back on the yellow leather settee and eyed with . . . affection? Yes, affection — her collection of corsets, silk stockings and beautiful garters festooned with ribbons, flowers and even tiny birds made of real feathers. Pride of place went to the copious bloomers. Like her other favourite items, the bloomers were safely framed behind glass and hanging above the fireplace.

Framing them had been done swiftly before an uninformed member of staff assumed the voluminous expanse of cotton was a tablecloth.

Honey grinned and raised her glass. Poor old Queen Victoria. She'd turn in her grave if she knew that someone could actually contemplate setting a plateful of English breakfast on her drawers!

End of the day. The best time. She poured herself a glass of wine. There was something about a good wine that made her see clearer, when in fact by reputation it should have made her thoughts fuzzy.

First, the question of Elmer Bernstock: was he merely missing? Was he here on a secret mission? Or was it simply that Mervyn Herbert had smashed one too many ice cubes and decided to smash in Elmer's head instead? On the other hand, perhaps there was some other reason that wasn't yet quite clear.

Never mind. At least her rooms were full. Dear old Casper had sent more business her way.

She toasted herself.

'Honey Driver. Five-star hotelier, world-famous beauty and renowned detective.'

A little over the top, but then . . .

'Give it time,' she said with a sigh and closed her eyes. She dreamed she was wearing a deerstalker hat, toting a magnifying glass and smoking a pipe.

CHAPTER 4

It was Saturday night, pouring down and gone one o'clock when Loretta Davies, Mervyn Herbert's stepdaughter, left the Underground Club, which was subterranean and close to the river.

'Getting a taxi?' shouted one of her friends, tottering on the edge of the pavement and hanging on grimly to her boyfriend, who was impatient to be away and screwing her in the privacy of some shop doorway.

'You must be jokin'. I'm skint now, ain't I?' The shouted reply was drowned out in the drumming of the downpour.

Whatever else her friend shouted back was drowned too. Both the girl and the young man faded into the darkness between the high buildings.

Loretta pulled the collar of her jacket up around her face as best she could. It was plastic, black and shiny. The rain hammered on it before running off in sheets like it would off a tin roof. The mac was also short, her skirt shorter and her black tights sodden from the thighs downwards. Wisps of hair clung wetly to her face and water dripped from her eyebrows.

Passing cars muted the sound of her bright-green Doc Martens splashing on the glossy pavements. Headlights glanced like the beams of a lighthouse through the teeming rain.

Streetlights and headlights lessened once she left North Parade. She kept the gardens on her right, aiming to make her way across the road near Bog Island, an old Victorian lavatory that some quirky soul had changed into a nightclub at one time, sadly now derelict.

Bending her head against the driving rain, she cursed the night. Her footsteps bounced off the walls in narrow alleys. At times it seemed like an army was following her — or at least one person, possibly more. She shivered inside her raincoat and dug her hands more deeply into her pockets, glad when she finally emerged into a rank of Regency houses.

Square panes in Georgian windows were shut tight around her and curtains drawn. Fewer cars flashed by, most sensible people already home in a warm bed with a warm body. Even the shop doorways were empty, fumbling couples defeated by the wind-driven rain, their novice explorations saved for another time.

Empty echoes, lonely streetlights and heavy rain: wetness and darkness took the night as their own. The rain hammered so hard and loud that she could no longer hear her own footsteps. She didn't hear his.

A shadow came alive.

She was startled when he stepped out in front of her until she saw who it was.

'You!'

Mervyn Herbert had deep-set eyes. His teeth were yellow. 'Nasty night.'

Loretta was far from pleased to see him. 'Mervyn, stop following me!'

He slipped a hand into his trouser pocket and brought out a twenty-pound note. 'Here you are. I expect you could do with it.'

She hesitated, her gaze bouncing between his face and the money.

She snatched it and stuffed it into her pocket.

'Thought you'd need it. You always did like a pound note, didn't you, girl?'

She didn't correct him and say that there was no such thing as a pound note, only a coin. The money always came in useful.

'I've got the car.'

His smile was wide. 'Come on, sweetheart. I'm only doing my duty as a loving daddy.'

'You're not my daddy!'

Her exclamation bounced between the buildings.

The light from a streetlamp picked out Mervyn's yellow teeth as he smiled.

'I'm married to yer mother — fer better or fer worse. So we're family. Anyway, it's a lousy night.'

The rain trickled into Loretta's eyes and down the nape of her neck. Could she cope with him? The rain increased and lightening lit up the sky.

Sure she could.

'Alright.'

She was still shivering when she slid into the front passenger seat of the five-year-old Ford 'family' car. Family! That was a laugh. Her mother told people she'd been a child bride. She could hear her now:

'My Loretta's seventeen. I know I don't look old enough, but I was very young when I had her. Only eighteen meself.'

Hogwash! Her mother had been well into her twenties, but denied herself those extra years, just as she denied the extra inches around her hips and thighs.

She fastened her safety belt as they pulled away. The rain was unceasing. The streets seemed empty.

The headlights of a passing car picked out a figure among the shadows. She sucked in her breath, saw him stare, then turn and run.

She jumped when Mervyn patted her knee. 'Everything all right, sweetheart?'

She smacked his hand away. 'Keep your dirty paw to yourself!'

She eyed the greyish complexion of the man sitting beside her. He'd made an effort to comb a few strands of hair across a hairless skull. The result was comical rather than complimentary. A sliver of hair slewed over his face. He pushed it back, a red blush of embarrassment creeping up his grizzled throat.

Loretta laughed out loud.

'Crikey,' she said, firmly asserting herself. 'You're getting to be a right slap'ead aren't ya!'

His knuckles whitened as his hands gripped the steering wheel more tightly. 'Saucy cow! One of these days . . .'

'One of these days what?' She laughed openly and loudly. 'You'll do what, Mervyn? Nothing! I'm not a little girl anymore. I can stick up for myself, and just you remember that!'

She gasped as his hand grabbed her knee more fiercely and painfully than before.

'You'd be surprised at what I'm capable of, sweetheart. There's more to yer old stepdaddy than meets the eye. And you want more money, don't you? You're always wanting my money.'

Getting the drift of what he was saying, she reached for the door handle. 'Let me out of the car!'

He opened his mouth and a cackle came out, like the sound dead men are supposed to make before they die. She wished that Mervyn Herbert were already dead. Better men than him were dead.

His hands were back on the wheel. She thought of opening the door and jumping out, but they were travelling too fast. Her tights were new. Her knees would be scratched.

Perhaps out of habit, or some vestige of memory, the old fear returned.

'Please, Mervyn. I'll do anything, anything . . .'

He grinned, his creased face a yellow gargoyle in the flashing glow of the streetlights.

'Yes,' he said, pausing to slick his tongue over his lips. 'Of course you will.'

* * *

The man who'd been following cursed. The stupid cow had got into a car. And not just any car, *his* bloody car! Bloody Mervyn Herbert.

The night was black and empty. Everyone was disappearing fast.

Fortunately he managed to flag down what must have been the only available taxi left in Bath.

'Follow that car!'

The driver, a young Asian wearing a white shirt and tie with a black leather jacket, beamed with disbelief. 'You're joking!'

Fingers thick as sausages grabbed his collar. 'No, I ain't!'

The driver stabbed on the gas too fiercely; the car skidded on the water-covered tarmac, careering from side to side as he fought to regain control.

Sweat glistened on the driver's forehead and he trembled as he followed the light-coloured Ford. It was now three cars ahead.

His passenger was impatient. 'Overtake! Overtake!'

Scared out of his wits, the taxi driver shook his head emphatically. 'No way! It's too narrow here!'

His passenger tried to grab the wheel. A car travelling in the other direction blew its horn as they swerved into the centre of the road.

'Please,' the driver shouted, his hands clammy on the wheel. 'We can't overtake here. It's too dangerous!'

Muttering an oath under his breath, the passenger slumped back in his seat. Ahead of them two cars went through a green traffic light. The next went through amber. The taxi stopped as the traffic light turned red.

The driver eyed his passenger from the comparative safety of the rear-view mirror. 'Where to now?' he asked, unable to control the trembling in his voice.

'Ferny Down Guest House. That's where they *should* be heading. It's on the Bristol Road. Do you know it?'

'Yes. Yes. I do.'

His eyes flickered nervously between the traffic light and the rear-view mirror. Late-night passengers troubled him, this one more than most.

The lights changed. The taxi moved forwards across the river and right towards the Lower Bristol Road.

Robert Howard Davies, lately of Horfield Prison, Bristol, made himself comfortable. He knew the taxi driver's eyes were studying him in the mirror, no doubt wondering whether he'd get his fare or not.

That depends, thought Robert, disgruntled because he'd got so close to reacquainting himself with his daughter. Still, no harm in going to see the wife, and God help Mervyn Herbert if he wasn't there when he arrived. There'd be some explaining to do, and he wasn't in the market for accepting excuses. Never had been. Never would be.

CHAPTER 5

One day, one whole twenty-four hours, had passed and Elmer Maxted was still missing.

'Casper says you need to go down there and liaise,' said Neville over the phone.

'I was thinking the same thing. Whether I want to or not, I have to tell the police all I know.'

There was silence. Neville must have placed his hand over the phone. Honey guessed that Casper was giving orders.

He came back.

'Casper says you're to try and keep a lid on things.'

'At the same time as assisting them with their enquiries?'

Again, silence.

'That's right,' said Neville on behalf of Casper.

'I can't make it for an hour or so. My receptionist is out sick.'

Again the delayed response.

'We'll send help.'

'Thanks. I appreciate it. How come Casper's indisposed?'

The response was swift, the tone one of shocked surprise.

'Casper *never* answers the phone while soaking in the bath.' The connection was severed.

Although it was Sunday morning, sauntering along to Manvers Street police station wasn't a problem as long as the promised help turned up. On the contrary, it was a welcome break.

Checking guests out flew by. One hour later she was brushing her hair, straightening her white cotton shirt and checking the seams in her tights. Yes! Tights. She always wore a skirt on Sunday. Wearing tights added to her feelings of lost femininity. Tights were functional. There was nothing sexy about tights.

Today had turned out exciting again. Nothing and no one could upset her mood — with the exception of her mother.

'I'm going on a cruise this summer.' She leaned closer. 'I'm going with a man friend. His name's Christopher Jordan, and he's a really charming man.'

Her mother scurried along behind her like an especially tenacious Jack Russell. 'Men are such good company. You should get yourself one.'

Honey swung left behind the reception desk. Undeterred, her mother leaned on the countertop. 'I think I was telling you about my dentist. He's got a friend with a very nice little business . . .'

'I thought he might,' said Honey with impatient reticence. She stabbed at the 'escape' key on the computer.

Susan, their regular receptionist, had phoned in sick. Honey had been expecting it. Lindsey had given her all the details. 'Lovesick! Swept off her feet by a handsome young man from Hungary. His name is Peter. He works at the Redcar and he's moved into the bedsit below Susan.'

International relations were bound to happen. This meant that if their days off didn't coincide, one of them fell sick. Today was the young man's day off. Hence, Susan was suddenly sick again, which meant Honey was dealing with reception and was trapped. Mother had pounced.

Blonde coiffeur, bedecked with expensive jewellery and wearing a silk trouser suit, her mother leaned on the reception desk. Her apricot lipstick matched her outfit.

Honey took shallow breaths in an effort to cope with the cloud of expensive perfume that fell over her.

'I've arranged for you to meet him in the Roman Bar of the Francis this evening at seven.'

'I can't go.'

'Why not?'

'I'm working.'

'Lunchtime then. I'll rearrange it for twelve noon.'

'Mother!'

'Don't shout.'

'I didn't shout, I merely protested.'

A husband and wife from Sydney chose that moment to check in, complete with three suitcases.

Honey took her time checking them in and giving them their keys, fliers and special offers on local attractions. The plan was that her mother would grow impatient and disappear. She didn't.

'Look, Mother . . .'

Jeremiah Poughty, Casper's very close friend, came breezing through the double doors. His fingers brushed over the brass handles as though he were checking for smudges.

'Casper sent me. I understand you're a trifle short-staffed, my darling. So here I am. Lately of the hotel trade, but I do remember which buttons to press.'

'So what are you doing, nowadays?' said Honey, purposely turning her back on her mother.

'I've got a stall in the Guildhall Market. It's called Rice, Spice and All Things Nice.'

'There now!'

Honey looked suitably impressed.

Unfortunately, so did her mother.

Gloria clapped her hands. 'There! You can go on your date and enjoy yourself.'

'No. This is for this morning only. I have an errand to run for the Bath Hotels Association. I'm working tonight.'

Honey sent the ergonomically designed, and very uncomfortable, receptionist chair sliding on its wheels as she got to her feet.

'He's sent the details to the police by messenger,' Jeremiah went on, sliding the chair back into place.

'If that's the case, I can't understand why he hasn't gone along himself.'

'He's not one for men in uniforms,' Jeremiah said, as though he'd read her thoughts. 'Reminds him of the bad old days when you only had to smile at another man and a policeman appeared. Now,' he said, leaning threateningly at the computer screen, 'no need to explain the system to me. Once you've used one, you've used them all.' He began enthusiastically entering the Australians' details into the appropriate box on the screen.

Honey grabbed her overlarge bag and slung it over her shoulder.

Her mother followed her to the door. 'Why are you going to the police station?'

Determined that everything should run smoothly in her absence, Honey ignored the question and addressed Jeremiah. 'There's a party for lunch coming in at twelve.'

Receiving no reply from her daughter, Gloria aimed her question at Jeremiah. 'Why is she going to the police station?'

Jeremiah was still taking in the orders Honey was throwing at him.

Exasperated, Gloria Cross slammed her hand down on the desk.

'Why is my daughter going to the police station? What has she done?'

Those guests sitting in the comfortable settees around the reception area, waiting for taxis, teas or their checkout bill, fell to silence. Curious eyes turned in her direction.

Honey played to the crowd.

'They're accusing me of planning to bury my mother under the patio. I told them it wasn't true, of course, and that I'd much prefer to drown her in malmsey, but they didn't believe me. Said they didn't think anyone would ruin good alcohol unless they were batty!'

'You are batty!' said her mother looking thoroughly annoyed.

The guests grinned, chuckled and exchanged knowing looks.

Honey threw a swift thank you to Jeremiah who merely nodded and proceeded to tidy up the whole online booking system and the paperwork around him. He also threw a disapproving look at the flower arrangement. Like Neville he was very good at arranging flowers. Her efforts were not to his taste.

Getting to the door had been easy enough compared to getting out of it. Her mother wasn't giving up *that* easily.

'Right. So you're off to the police station on official hotel business. That shouldn't take long. From there you can make your way to church.'

'Mother! I don't do church.'

Too late. She was already tapping out a number on her cell phone, a determined jut to her chin and a no-nonsense look in her eyes. 'Right. Father Anthony's expecting you.'

'I'm not Catholic.'

'Well, I think you should be.'

'My father wasn't.'

Her mother crossed herself. Becoming a Catholic had come late in life — once all the divorces were behind her.

'The service finishes at twelve. No need to hurry back. That nice poof in reception will take care of things until you get back.'

'Mother!'

Honey shook her head. Her mother didn't know how to spell *politically correct* let alone apply it. She was one of the old school and the words she used in her youth were still the ones she used now.

As she approached North Parade heading for Manvers Street, she began questioning Casper's generosity in sending over to help out. Casper could be very nice when he wanted to be. At other times he could be downright ruthless.

On her way there she plucked out her phone and opened the address book. Casper answered almost immediately.

'Thanks for sending Jeremiah over.'

'Oh! Is that where he is?'

Honey frowned. 'You didn't send him?'

'I asked him to pop over and assist you. He wasn't keen and murmured something about me using him as a stopgap. He's obviously changed his mind.'

'It's very much appreciated.'

'No doubt.'

* * *

It was a busy Sunday morning at the cop shop. The chalky smell of dried out paint and well-worn carpet came out to meet her. So too did the tinge of Jeyes Fluid each time the toilet doors opened in the foyer.

Once the desk sergeant had booked her in, she was told to sit down and wait.

'I think you should know that I'm here on behalf of the hoteliers of the city and I don't really have much time . . .'

'Take a seat,' he said without looking up from whatever it was he was doing.

No choice. She sat and studied the people waiting for attention.

Irate ex-motorists relieved of their vehicle by some mindless bozo who had fancied his chances at the Grand Prix over Brassknocker Hill. Grand Pricks were more like it, the cars mangled by now and dumped in some roadside ditch.

A crusty, complete with tangled dreadlocks, foetid smell and a scrawny dog, was demanding the return of his untaxed, uninsured and un-roadworthy vehicle.

An American tourist wearing a tartan cap and matching Bermudas waited while the desk sergeant took down his particulars.

'What I can't understand is how they knew we were tourists,' he drawled. His Bermuda shorts were bright red, his shirt hailed from his last trip to Hawaii, and the flat cap sitting like a pancake on his head was Stewart tartan. Obviously a golfing man.

Judging by their age, marriage had still been in fashion when they were young. The woman Honey took to be his wife slumped in the chair next to Honey.

Rolling her eyes, she whispered, 'I told him not to make himself conspicuous. But would he listen? "I'm not changing my style for anybody," he tells me.' The woman shook her head dolefully. 'Style it ain't, I told him.'

Honey smiled. 'Beauty is in the reflection in the mirror. We see gravity taking its toll, and your husband sees Steve McQueen. It's a man thing.'

'You got it!'

A door marked 'private' opened suddenly and a man wearing a black T-shirt and stone-washed jeans appeared.

His gaze swept over the waiting room and finally landed on her. She looked back.

Judging by the casual clothes and the stubble on his chin, he was attempting the 'rough-diamond' look. Looking hard was important when you were less than six feet in height. Strong hands added gravitas.

A policewoman lurked in the shadows behind him, glaring over his shoulder. Honey met the look and recognised green-glazed jealousy.

'Hannah Driver?'

'That's me.'

A waiting room full of curious eyes watched her cross the floor.

It was kind of like being on stage. But this was all real. All the senses kicked in. She was close enough to smell what remained of his aftershave. Three days or so since he'd shaved, but the pong was still there.

'I'm Detective Sergeant Steve Doherty.' He looked her up and down. 'So you're Bath's answer to Miss Marple.'

Sarcastic!

'Not quite. I don't knit or do crosswords, and neither do I frequent vicarage tea parties.'

Contempt flashed in his eyes. He didn't want her here. His surliness travelled to his tone of voice.

'Well, that's a disappointment. But then, amateur snoops come in all shapes and sizes.'

'So do cops. I thought you'd be taller.'

For a split second his gaze fell to her 36Cs. He smirked. She guessed what was coming.

'Being of average height has its advantages.'

If looks could have killed, she would have sliced his head off, but he didn't give her time.

'Through here.'

He jerked his thumb in the direction of the shadow in uniform and the corridor behind him.

The interview room was exactly as she'd expected — plain walls, desk, a few chairs and, of course, the tape recorder. Someone had lately run riot with a sweet-smelling aerosol, alpine flowers by the whiff of it.

Doherty flicked a switch on the tape recorder. The usual words were said, the date and location. Next came the personal details. 'This is Detective Sergeant Doherty. Interviewee is one Miss Hannah Driver . . .'

'Mrs.'

Doherty flashed her an impatient look. '*Mrs* Hannah Driver. Also present is Detective Constable Sian Williams. Right,' he said sitting back in his chair, 'tell me your involvement.'

'I prefer to be called Honey.'

'As in Honey Bee?'

She treated the comment with her own brand of contempt and ignored him.

'Well,' she began, feeling like a suspect in some cheap television detective series, 'I have been appointed by the Bath Hotels Association to liaise with the police regarding any crime connected with tourism . . .'

'Yeah! I understand that,' said Doherty. The fingers of his right hand fiddled with the pen protruding from his left breast pocket.

Her first impression of him lingered. What he said next confirmed it.

'That kind of stuff out there,' he jerked his head indicating the waiting room beyond the wall. 'Muggings, theft and diddling the exchange rate — anything that upsets the tourist industry. Must keep up our squeaky-clean image, mustn't we, or the Yanks won't be coming back. That would affect your bank balance. You and the rest of the hospitality trade.'

She sprang to her feet. 'Don't be so bloody condescending!'

He sprang to his feet. 'This is a cop shop not a bloody tea shop!'

Clearly he didn't want to deal with the likes of her, but ditto — neither did she.

They were like bookends, glaring at each other across the table.

'Look, I've got a chef that's threatening to slice out the butcher's entrails over the standard of the steaks, and a mother who's likely to get herself made into pies if she keeps trying to fix me up with dog-eared divorcees and bog-standard bachelors. Can we get this over so we can *both* get back to work?'

Doherty blinked once. She sensed a subtle change.

'Sit down!'

He sounded serious. She sat down.

Doherty sat sideways in his chair, eyeing her out of the corner of his eyes.

She copied his stance. If he noticed her mockery, he gave no sign of it.

'This bloke disappearing. I don't like the sound of it. I don't like it at all.'

It wasn't what she'd expected him to say. She leaned forward, her eyes in danger of popping out of her head. 'You think he's been murdered?'

He leaned forward too, lower arms resting on desk, hands clasped just inches from hers.

'I don't have a clue. Even private dicks go on mystery trips.'

Honey frowned. 'So what's happened? What is it you don't like?'

Doherty grimaced. 'I've been appointed as your official contact within the police force. Chief constable's orders. I'll do my duty, but I'm not happy about it. I thought you should know that.'

Honey sat back in her chair. 'Really? Well, with your natural interpersonal skills, I can see why they gave you the job.'

The sound of a stifled snigger came from Detective Constable Sian Williams.

Doherty scowled. 'Shut that!'

The policewoman's pink lips wobbled a bit before coming under control.

Something was not quite right. Honey narrowed her eyes and threw Doherty a piercing look. He looked surprised, either because he hadn't expected such a response or he liked the look anyway.

'So why the hell is that thing on?' She stabbed her finger at the tape recorder.

He shrugged.

'It doesn't work. I just turn it on for the hell of it. Didn't unnerve you, did I?' One side of his mouth lurched upwards into a lop-sided grin.

Honey got to her feet. 'You're taking the mick! Well stuff you, Doherty! You may have time for fun and games, but I do not! I have a business to run and it depends on tourism, which, I might add, pays your wages!'

The smirk changed into a smile and the blue eyes twinkled.

He held up his hands in surrender. 'Look, I'm sorry.'

'You're not taking this seriously.'

He nodded at the policewoman indicating she make for the door. It closed behind her.

Doherty's eyes danced over her again, and Honey folded her arms in a way that shielded her bosom. 'I should never have taken this job,' she muttered.

Doherty looked surprised. 'You mean to say you didn't want to develop a long-lasting relationship with a crime fighting member of your local constabulary? Even one as good-looking and available as me?'

She cocked an eyebrow. 'Don't flatter yourself. I wasn't exactly spoilt for choice either!'

She didn't go into details of why she'd accepted the role. What would the likes of an unshaved, hard-nosed copper know about business?

He pursed his lips, folded his arms, kept a steady gaze. 'Can we start again?'

She considered telling him to get lost, but the shrewder side of her nature stopped her. Casper had promised her fiscal reward. Filling her rooms to capacity and every table in the restaurant ordering three courses plus the best vintage wine was one hell of a carrot to dangle in front of her.

'So! What about this Elmer Bernstock/Maxted or whatever? What are you going to do about it?'

Doherty laid his hands flat on the desk and studied his fingernails. 'So! He was a private detective,' he said thoughtfully.

'Was he here on a job? Have you checked?'

'Yes. We have checked, and no, he was not here on a job. He was on vacation according to his office: tracing his family tree, so I was told.'

Honey frowned. So why use an alias?

Doherty gave his own answer to the unspoken question in a voice that was a fair impersonation of Humphrey Bogart.

'These private dicks have a sense of the dramatic. They've been watching too many cop shows on TV.'

Honey eyed him accusingly. 'You're not going to investigate, are you?'

He leaned forward, and a waft of aftershave came with him.

'No. Shall I tell you why?'

'You don't have to, but I guess you will anyway.'

'I'm guessing he's met some dishy broad and gone off to taste a last sip of the sweet honey of life. So what if he doesn't make his flight? Flight or a bit of fluff?' He leaned back in his chair, hands clasped behind his head and a dreamy look in his eyes. 'I know which I'd choose. Yep. That's my theory. A taste of honey. That's what he's found.'

She waved a dismissive hand. 'Very poetic, but I think you're wrong.'

He spread his hands and winked. 'That's it, sugar.'

Blue eyes and dark hair. It shouldn't be allowed. Her lips slid into a smile without warning. She managed to wipe it off before it reached full bloom.

'I'm not going to encourage you.'

She got to her feet.

'So what are you going to do, sugar?'

She paused by the door. 'I think I'll pay another visit to the house of a thousand ashtrays.'

He grinned. 'Cora Herbert. I know her from of old before she got married and acquired a guest house.'

'A hooker?'

'Well, she was no Jane Austen, that's for sure. You're wasting your time. Go back to your hotel. Do what you do best and leave the law to me.'

Honey rested her hand on one curvaceous hip and held her head to one side. 'You didn't want to work with me and you still don't, do you?'

His expression clouded. 'It's nothing personal.'

'No,' she said, 'and it won't ever get that way.'

* * *

Sian came back after Honey had left, her stockings making a rustling sound as she slid one leg over the other. She folded her arms across her uniformed chest and grinned at him.

'You enjoyed that more than you thought you would.'

He stretched his arms above his head and flexed his muscles. 'Take that grin off your face.'

'She's an attractive woman.'

He spun to face her and pointed an accusing finger. 'Not another word, Williams. I still think this hotel nonsense is all a bloody waste of time.'

She cocked one eyebrow. 'But she might make it more palatable?'

Doherty smirked and a lock of dark hair fell onto his forehead, matching the stray whorls that clung to his neck.

Sian Williams went weak at the knees. Most women, her included, couldn't help falling for his rakish charm.

His smile was enough to leave her panting for more. Last night his voice had poured into her ear like thick, dark treacle. She'd scored, but knew from Doherty's reputation that she wasn't the only one.

Steve Doherty was smiling to himself and whatever thoughts he was thinking were strictly private.

When he spoke, she knew he wasn't really speaking to her. He was advising his inner self, telling it just what to expect next.

'Leave it with me. A little of the old Doherty charm and she'll forget all about being Miss bloody Marple. She'll be putty in my hands. I guarantee it.'

CHAPTER 6

On her next visit, Cora Herbert had insisted that Honey take Elmer Maxted's stuff away.

'I can't have it blocking up my storage facility,' Cora had said indignantly, an unlit cigarette jiggling at the corner of her mouth.

Honey grimaced at the memory of the dusty, dirty cupboard beneath the stairs. Describing it as a storage facility was stretching credibility.

There was no real reason why she couldn't oblige. She had a small room behind reception for guests' luggage and two more bags wouldn't make any difference.

Once they were in situ, she couldn't resist taking another peek.

After checking there was no one hanging around in the brown-carpeted hallway, she closed the door behind her. Although she'd checked through things while shut in under Cora Herbert's stairs, she'd done it in a hurry. Now she had time to take things a little more slowly. Who knows what she might find?

She took out his passport, flight tickets and official documents and took them into her office and her private safe.

On studying the flight ticket, she noticed the return date was only two days hence.

Two days until he flew home? He should be making plans to go right now, checking railway and bus schedules or making arrangements to drop off a hire car — if he'd ever had one.

And there was something else. If Elmer was tracing his forebears, why no birth, marriage or death certificates, or even a half-completed family tree?

She couldn't suppress the shiver that ran down her back. Neither could she throw off her first instinct — that Elmer Maxted was dead. Murdered. But how and by whom? And why?

A sudden vision of Mervyn crept into her mind like a bad dream. It was pure speculation that he could have something to do with it. The fact was he gave her the creeps. She'd known a few creeps in her time but that didn't mean they'd committed murder. Still, that old saying about first impressions was a good starting point.

The hospitality industry consisted of sixteen-hour days, seven days a week. Public holidays, like Christmas, Easter and the height of summer, were their busiest times of the year.

Even during the normal times, she rose at dawn and didn't fall into bed until the early hours of the next day. Tiredness led to short tempers. Had Cora or Mervyn snapped and done something stupid? She thought about it. Cora? No. The woman wouldn't win Hotelier of the Year, but the only murdering that went on in their guest house was probably the burning of sausages at breakfast time.

The door to the office was well oiled, so she didn't hear Lindsey come in.

'Mother! What are you doing?'

Honey nearly jumped out of her skin. 'You nearly gave me a heart attack.'

Lindsey was wearing her gym kit, her navy-and-white bag slung over her shoulder. She grinned. 'I wouldn't do that. Not unless you've left me a fortune in your will. I might chance it then.'

'I suggest you speak to your grandmother on that score.'

Honey's mother, Gloria Cross had had three husbands. All of them had been millionaires, including her own father. When he'd shoved off back to Connecticut with a trophy wife, her mother had sued for settlement, got it, got a new millionaire and drank a toast to her former husband's memory when he'd died in bed on his honeymoon.

'A fitting end to a man who loved women,' she had said.

Lindsey looked over her mother's shoulder. 'What are you up to?'

Honey sighed and began tucking the passports, papers and flight tickets back into the plastic bag before placing all of it into the safe. Just before finally turning the key, she paused, her eyes again falling to the date.

'There's a disparity between the booking he made at Ferny Down Guest House and his return flight from London Heathrow. Where did he intend going between those two dates?'

Lindsey shrugged. 'Perhaps he was going to stay on at Chez Greasy Spoon a few more days.'

Honey thought about it then shook her head. 'To book in for a week at a bed and breakfast in Bath is unusual in itself. Most tourists aren't that specific — certainly not in an establishment like Ferny Down. It caters for the lower end of the market.'

'We're not being snobby here, are we?'

'Realistic!'

Lindsey nodded. 'Sure.'

She was as aware as her mother that certain tourists staying in certain establishments had particular travel plans. Depending on budget, one or two days sufficed in each place they visited.

'But there are always exceptions.'

Honey waved the airline ticket. 'He was flying home two days from now. That doesn't leave long for travelling anywhere. A day at most. The last day would have been set aside for travelling to the airport.'

Lindsey, who Honey sometimes forgot was only eighteen, agreed. 'Most people travel up to London the day before.'

Honey fluttered the tickets against her mouth as she thought things through. She raised her eyes and met Lindsey's equally dark ones. 'That means he would have left for the airport tomorrow.'

'And what else?'

Honey slid her eyes sidelong. 'He was researching his family tree, and yet there are no birth, death or marriage certificates in his luggage. I find that strange.'

Lindsey sighed and looked at her watch. 'He's been murdered.'

'Do you think so?' Honey's eyes widened and a mix of fear and excitement tingled in her ample bosom. The possibility had entered her mind, but surely there was no hard evidence. Had Lindsey spotted something she hadn't?

Her daughter's response swiftly deflated any chance of enlightenment.

Lindsey grinned. 'Or maybe he just went for a long walk. I'm too busy to think about it, really.' She glanced at her watch again. 'Oops! Must get changed. I've a bar to open.'

'Where do you get your energy?'

Lindsey kissed her mother's cheek. 'I inherited it from my mother, along with her good looks.'

Honey studied her muted reflection in a glass-fronted cabinet.

Lindsey wrapped a loving arm around her shoulder. 'See,' she said, her head resting against that of her mother. 'We're more like sisters than mother and daughter. So tell me, did you meet any good-looking policemen?'

Honey opened her mouth to deny the fact. Doherty popped into her mind.

'Mother, you're blushing.'

'No, no, no, no, no. It's my age.'

Looking amused, Lindsey stood by the door, a glint in her eye and her brown legs smooth and shiny. 'You may be my mother, but you're also a woman. I think it's time you lived for yourself, not for me. Have a slice of romance, Mother. You deserve it.'

Honey gaped. When Geoff died in a boating accident, Honey had promised herself that she would put Lindsey first in everything. For that reason she'd shied off permanent relationships. She'd seen the problems they could cause. She'd never voiced that promise, so it came as something of a surprise that Lindsey was aware of her sacrifice. And now?

Like a thickly iced cream slice, Doherty came to mind again. She smiled to herself. Naughty, but nice.

Once she was alone, Honey dragged her thoughts back to the missing tourist. Cupping her chin in her hand she stared out at the blank wall beyond the small window. If they had murdered him, where would they bury him?

She shook the thoughts from her head, zipped up the bags and shifted them into a far corner. He'd just gone walkabout. Perhaps he'd met some old relative while tracing his family tree and was making up for lost time.

As she shut the door behind her and prepared to check in a nice couple from Ontario, another thought crossed her mind. Would a man seriously searching his family tree leave the paperwork behind? Perhaps that might explain there being none in his luggage. But if that were the case, why leave his passport and everything else?

She shook her head. Her mind was in overdrive.

The Canadians waited patiently while she came back down to earth.

'We have a room booked in the name of Whittaker,' said the nice, middle-aged man.

Plastering a smile on her face, she entered their names on the system, checked their passports and handed them their room keys, menu cards and a map of the city.

'There's plenty of information in the folder in your room,' she added, 'but don't hesitate to ask if there's anything else you require.'

They thanked her before moving off, and Daniel — porter, handyman and a native of Croatia — helped them with their luggage.

* * *

Doherty could help himself no longer. He picked up the phone and dialled.

'Hi there! I was wondering . . .'

'So was I,' replied Honey. 'If Mr or Mrs Herbert had murdered Elmer Bernstock, Maxted or whatever his name is, where would they bury him?'

'That wasn't what I was going to ask you.' He could barely disguise his disappointment.

Honey carried on as though she hadn't heard him. 'I suppose if you were looking for a body, you'd dig the garden up first, wouldn't you?'

Steve Doherty prided himself on being a bit of a ladies' man. So why wasn't she listening to him? He was about to tell her to forget it, when an idea occurred to him. Humour her. Make her think this really was going to be a serious case.

He cleared his throat. 'I've had second thoughts about this case and a few possible theories. Can we meet for dinner and talk about it — you know, away from interruptions?'

'You do think he was murdered!'

Doherty felt himself drowning in her rapture. It wouldn't be in his interest to contradict her, so he didn't.

He smiled in that secretive way he'd practised in front of the mirror, the sort of smile Bogart used to use. Left-hand corner of mouth lifted, right-hand corner turned downwards.

'Let's just say I have a hunch.'

'I'm all ears. Beats washing dishes, hands down. How about the Zodiac?'

Steve patted himself on the back. What a clever dick he was! 'Great. What time?'

'Sometime after midnight, say about twelve thirty?'

Steve covered the phone with his hand as he swore. Wanting to have her to himself had backfired. The Zodiac was a bar and steak restaurant beneath North Parade. Its entrance was on one side of the street. A set of narrow steps led down to a barrel-roofed cellar that swept out beneath the road. At the other end a glass covered archway looked out over North Parade Gardens. Laid out in the eighteenth century, the gardens were below the level of the road.

A lovely spot, the green lawns plastered with tourists by day sitting on the benches, rubbing their bare feet and swearing not to go on any more ghost walks, Austen walks and tours of the Roman Baths.

The Zodiac didn't open until nine o'clock at night and didn't shut until three in the morning. Hence it was popular with the city's hoteliers and publicans, their only free time being between midnight and dawn. *Like vampires*, thought Steve, *they only come out at night.*

Steve visualised his duty roster. On duty until ten tonight, and on again at six tomorrow . . .

'OK,' he said. 'I'll be there.' He pulled his face out of shape as a thought occurred to him. Sian Williams would be on duty with him tonight, and a bird in the hand . . .

Honey made things easy for him. 'But not tonight. Not this week in fact. How about Friday week?'

His whole body relaxed. That was when the roster changed. At least he'd get a lie-in the following morning. And Sian Williams would be on a different shift. Best to keep women divided. It kept them interested.

'Suits me fine.'

* * *

There was no one hanging around in reception except for Mrs Spear pushing the vacuum cleaner. She was singing along to whatever she was listening to on a personal stereo that her daughter had given her years ago. She refused to use a mobile phone, so it was all she had.

Honey gave her a wave. She didn't notice.

A totally frameless conservatory, an extravagance she'd never regretted, led off the reception area. Through its unsullied glass she could see the top of the abbey, the mansard roofs and the tall chimneys framing the green hills circling the city like giant arms.

This was the view that tourists came to see, so why had Elmer Maxted stayed in a budget guest house? His luggage was expensive, and although private detectives were portrayed as dirt poor in TV programmes, it wasn't necessarily true.

Her thoughts were interrupted.

'Honey! Honey, darling!'

She recognised the voice of Mary Jane Jefferies, who'd been a resident of the Green River for years.

Wearing a pink caftan over equally pink trousers, the tall woman floated towards her waving a copy of the Bath City bus timetable.

'I have a problem,' she said, taking hold of Honey's shoulder and steering her into the sitting room. 'Or rather, I think you have a problem,' she said, her voice dropping to not much more than a whisper. 'Take a seat.'

Honey found herself obeying instantly. That's how it was with Mary Jane. The sort of conversation they were about to have would come as no surprise. Mary Jane was a doctor of parapsychology — a ghost goddess, as she'd explained to Honey when they'd first met.

Honey had been dumbstruck. Yes, she knew the place was old and it creaked and groaned through the night, but then, didn't all old buildings do that? It wasn't old like Stonehenge or the Roman Baths. The outside was imposing but promised comfort; the large, oblong windows glowed amber with inner light at night and by day sparkled in sunlight. The décor was fresh and fitting for the age of the house. Honey had no trouble sleeping between its aching walls. What was 200 years in the great scheme of things?

It was old by American standards, Mary explained, and left it at that. Sometimes, perhaps because Honey was a relative newcomer to the hotel in comparison with Mary Jane, it seemed that the tall, lanky woman actually had more right to the place than she did.

As Mary Jane chattered on, a retired university professor from Connecticut strolled past the window, her mother walking beside him.

Hopefully they'll elope together.

The sound of her mother's voice drifted through the window. 'Families used to stick together, and marriage was for life . . .'

And this coming from a thrice-married woman. Honey almost choked.

'About this problem,' Mary Jane was saying.

'More than one problem, I think,' Honey murmured, a jaundiced eye following her mother and the professor until they were safely out of sight.

Her mother loved meeting hotel guests and did her bit to help out, though nothing remotely physical. She regarded herself as the official social secretary of the Green River Hotel, a bit like those she'd met on cruise ships. Her mother went on lots of cruises.

At least it kept her out of the kitchen. Gloria Cross had learned first-hand that Head Chef, Smudger Smith was likely to reach for the meat cleaver if she interfered in his domain. Honey had backed him up. Good chefs were hard to come by. Interfering mothers were two a penny.

Mary Jane broke into her thoughts. 'I told her she was mistaken. He doesn't come from that side of the house. He always comes out of number five and walks along the landing. Mrs Goulding is trying to say that he's coming out of the closet and chasing her around the room. Well! It's nonsense. All wishful thinking and a figment of her imagination.'

Honey stared at the tall, gaunt woman sitting beside her as she tried to get the drift of this. 'A man is chasing her around the room?'

'Sir Cedric! She reckons he's coming out of her closet, when both you and I know very well that he lives — or rather materialises —from the closet in room twelve.'

'I see.'

It sounded wacky, but Honey had got used to it. Mary Jane was in her late seventies and claimed she knew all there was to know about the afterlife and the spirits residing there. That's why she had returned to the Green River time and time again then finally made herself a permanent fixture. According to her, the Grade I Georgian building was much favoured by the spirits of the departed. She particularly liked Sir Cedric, the eighteenth-century gentleman who resided in the closet in room twelve, the room she insisted on residing in.

She listened patiently. 'Have you seen Sir Cedric lately?'

Mary Jane looked hurt. 'Well, no. But that doesn't mean he's deserted me. After all, I am his great, great, great, great grandniece.'

And there's the rub, thought Honey. Not for the world did she wish to upset Mary Jane, but surely no one actually *owned* a ghost, even if they were related. But it was pointless trying to tell her that. It was best to humour her.

Mary Jane had long ago made it plain that there were rules for those who had passed over. By the sound of it, she'd written the book.

'Don't worry,' said Honey, patting Mary Jane's liver-spotted hand. 'I'm sure she's just imagining things. And as you point out yourself, Sir Cedric wouldn't desert you in order to take up with a perfect stranger.'

Mary Jane's crumpled face unfolded. 'No! Of course not. There's the family honour at stake! I told her that, but she dared question whether Sir Cedric really was one of my ancestors. I told her straight that I'd traced the family tree myself. And not just on these internet sites. Check the facts. The best source are the records written centuries ago – parish registers for instance.'

Honey's ears pricked up at the mention of tracing family trees.

'Mary Jane,' she began. 'Isn't it true that a person needs birth certificates and all that stuff if they're tracing their family tree?'

'Best to have that, though if you've got gaps in your knowledge there's always specialists willing to give you a hand. Not just computer nerds, but experts with local knowledge.'

'There are such people?'

'Of course. A little information — some bits of family gossip and hearsay can go a long way.'

'Where's the best place to start tracing a family tree if you happen to be an American?'

Mary Jane's twinkling blue eyes twinkled a bit more. 'It varies. But I can tell you where I started. Are you going to do yours?'

Honey shook her head at the same time as hearing her mother's voice and the patter of her footsteps out in reception. She shuddered. 'I'd rather not know.'

Mary Jane's eyes held a glassy look as though the other world she believed in had superimposed itself onto the real one.

'As I've already said, parish registers are good for on the spot information. So is the local registrar of births, marriages and deaths. More reliable than those online registers, I think. If you want to get down to the real nitty gritty, best thing is to contact the relatives.'

Honey dragged her worried eyes away from the sounds in reception. 'Could you do that for me? I could give you some basic information. The name's Maxted.' She frowned. 'It doesn't sound very Bathonian or even North Somerset, but it's all I have. What I'd really like to know is if an American named Elmer Maxted has contacted anyone about tracing his family in the last few weeks.'

Face bright with enthusiasm, Mary Jane nodded. 'I'll get on to it right away. Now,' she said, fumbling for a pen in her purse, 'in your case the best thing I can do is to interview your mother . . .'

'No. You misunderstand. I told you. It's not for me.'

She saw the surprise, even disappointment, on Mary Jane's face.

'Oh!'

Honey dropped her voice to a whisper and leaned close. 'This Mr Elmer Bernstock I mentioned, alias Maxted, has gone missing. He was researching his family tree.'

Mary Jane was unfortunate enough to have slightly protruding eyes; now they were more than slightly protruding. 'You don't say!'

'Do you think you could help?'

Mary Jane's response was diametrically opposed to the low-key Philip Marlowe approach. She looked like a fizzing firecracker about to explode.

'Ye . . . sss,' she hissed, the word elongated because she was trying so hard to suppress the exhilaration that coloured her face and made her eyes glow. 'I know just what he would do. First, he would speak to Bob the Job.'

She saw Honey's puzzled look.

Mary Jane explained. 'He's the first port of call in this city if you're looking to trace your pedigree.'

Eyes flickering towards reception and her mother's advancing footsteps, Honey gave a casual nod.

'I have to go now, but I'd appreciate you making enquiries.'

Mary Jane was scribbling Elmer's name on the back of the bus timetable. 'If he's a serious player, Bob will know all about the guy.'

I'm sure my daughter would love to hear about your research of the Pilgrims' Trail.'

As her mother's voice came closer, Honey began her dash for the French doors.

'Well, I really don't think I've got the time just now . . .'

A male voice. The professor was stalling — thank God!

'Leave this with me,' Mary Jane was saying as Honey backed out through the doors and into the garden.

The pages of magazines on a table near the door fluttered on the incoming draught.

Mary got up and shut it. She said something from the other side of the glazed door that Honey couldn't hear. She guessed from the movement and shape of her mouth that she was telling her to have a nice day.

'I will,' she called back, waved and ran.

Somewhere in the city was a taxicab that had ferried Elmer Maxted around before he'd disappeared.

Cora had told of a black Ford with 'Busy Bee Cabs' emblazoned in red on its side. That, she decided, was as good a place as any to start.

CHAPTER 7

Devotees of Jane Austen and all things Regency thronged through Bath's elegant crescents and leafy squares. Some narrowed their eyes in an effort to blank out the traffic and pretend that Mr Darcy was striding the pavement, resplendent in tails and overly tight trousers.

Those keener on cameras than books snapped pictures of each other leaning on lamp posts or posing outside McDonald's, burger in hand. Many used their phones to snap, but that was how the amateurs did it. Real photographers used a camera.

The Australians made for a decent brew in a reasonably priced café. The Americans did the tours at lightning speed, determined to get as much value as possible from their transatlantic flight.

This morning those looking over the parapet towards Pulteney Bridge were somewhat subdued. Something had happened that attracted everyone's curiosity, something that certainly wasn't on the tourist trail.

Uniformed police were filtering people around the blue-and-white incident tape fluttering around the steps leading from the road and down onto the towpath.

The river thundered over the weir, throwing up clouds of foam and filling the air with spray.

Steve Doherty narrowed his eyes at the span of Pulteney Bridge, its stone piecrust gold. The rain had cleared. Licked by the early morning sun, the crescents, parades and avenues of Bath tiered upwards like steaming slabs of honey to the crisp blue of the sky. What a spot! All blue and gold on postcards sent home to Mom in Illinois or Auntie Meg in Alice Springs.

He was down on the towpath examining the body. Above him the curious watched in hushed silence until an incident tent hid the crime scene from view.

Flanders, the scene-of-crime officer, a man with pale eyes and even paler skin, gave him the low down.

'Been dead a while. Look at him. Reminds you of a . . .'

'Stilton cheese,' Doherty interrupted, knowing he was going to comment about the effect of blood congealing in the veins thanks to the absence of a heartbeat and the pull of gravity. 'I know, I know.'

Flanders's pallid features took on a dejected look. He so loved flaunting his knowledge, especially if it meant he could make someone sick with the details. It was easier to make young constables sick. More difficult with seasoned detectives.

Doherty had burst his bubble on the first count, but he wouldn't on the second; Flanders was pretty sure of that.

The man had been found fully clothed with a sack covering his head. Flanders carefully removed the sack. The side of the man's head was caved in.

'Blunt instrument,' he said flatly. He'd probably seen hundreds in his life but had long ago giving up counting.

He picked up a transparent evidence bag.

'See this piece of wood?'

Doherty scrutinised it. The wood was old and weathered.

'Part of a door,' said Flanders, warming to his subject. 'It had a number on it. See?' He pointed to the faint indentation on the wood. 'A nine or perhaps a six. It was lodged beneath his armpit. Look at this place.'

Doherty looked along the embankment wondering what he was supposed to see.

'Not a scrap of litter. No rubbish. The council clear things up very quickly so neither the river nor the towpath are littered. The portion immediately lodged in the armpit is quite dry – which suggests to me it lodged there on dry land or close to it.'

Doherty frowned and thought it through. There were eddies along the river thanks to the weir. Some were strong enough to fasten anything thrown into the bank.

'In the absence of anything else it was used to push the body further out into the water, but it got stuck.'

'It's a possibility.'

In an effort to cope with the grim probabilities, Doherty's attention strayed to a group of office girls — leggy, lovely things and young enough to be his daughters.

'Give you a full report later!' Flanders puffed once he'd reached the top of the towpath steps and was only a few steps and a few more puffs from his dark-green Citroen. Nearby a traffic warden checked her watch, pursed her lips and clenched her jaw. This morning her routine and her tally were sharply curtailed and she looked pig sick about it.

Doherty dragged his gaze away from the office girls before barking out orders to the assembled team. 'Come on, lads. We've got work to do. Let's be having you. I want it swept with a toothbrush if need be. No skimping, and no moaning about bad backs and cups of tea.'

One of his team chose that moment to lean over the wall and spray the towpath with a shower of whatever he'd had for breakfast that morning. The office girls groaned and began to disperse.

Flanders kept on about the piece of wood.

Doherty refused to be impressed. 'So what? The river's high. There's always flotsam and jetsam floating about.'

'Do you want me to throw it back in?' Flanders smirked.

'Just get on with the search.'

Flanders bowed to his job, his white plastic jumpsuit crackling as he carried out the last rites as far as a cop is concerned: going through the deceased's pockets.

'No money on him, no watch, just a white mark where it used to be. A dead-cert mugging.' His probing fingers hesitated. 'Hello, hello! What have we here?'

Flanders held up the Amex credit card so he could more easily read the name. 'Elmer John Maxted.'

'You don't say!'

'I do.'

Thoughts whirling, Doherty watched as it was slid into yet another transparent evidence bag. Turning away, he took out his phone and scrolled down the numbers until he got to hers.

She answered after the fourth ring. It sounded as though she were in a hurry.

'Hannah — Mrs Driver? This is Detective Sergeant Doherty.'

'I'll ring you back.'

He frowned at the phone. It wasn't the response he'd been banking on. He'd been about to eat humble pie. Blow her. It could wait.

CHAPTER 8

A row of taxicabs waited on the rank alongside Bath Abbey. A few of them were of the old-fashioned London black cab variety, like a row of shiny-backed beetles queuing for a meal. The others were smart saloons of various colours. Only Busy Bee Cabs proclaimed their trade in red lettering along the sides.

After making enquiries, she was directed to a man named Ivor Webber, a stocky Welshman of West Indian descent.

'He's the one who got the fat fares last week,' someone told her. 'Bloody Welsh Tafia!'

Ivor was sitting in the driving seat of his cab sipping at an elderberry crush and reading what looked like a copy of *Mein Kampf*.

'Sorry to interrupt you,' she said, bending down close enough to see that he really *was* reading Hitler's one and only attempt to woo the world with the written word.

Ivor flipped his sunglasses back onto his forehead. 'Where to, lovely?' He closed his book and placed it on the seat beside him.

Honey jerked her chin in its direction. 'An unusual title.'

His teeth flashed in a healthy white smile. 'Well, there you are, lovely. I'm an unusual man. I like to form my own opinions, you see? It attests more reasonably to my intellectual growth. Now, where can I take you?'

'Nowhere.' She leaned on the door. 'Just a question. Do you remember an American you picked up from Ferny Down Guest House?'

His amiability was undiminished. He threw back his head and slapped the steering wheel.

'You mean good old Elmer. Wish I had a few more like him in a week: a generous tipper 'e was. There's not many of them nowadays, what with the exchange rate and all that.'

Sensing a good start, Honey carried on. 'Must have been some long journeys. Where did you take him?'

'Here and there.' Ivor maintained a happy expression.

She fancied the smile was a permanent fixture.

'Pretty far, I hear.'

He nodded.

Honey brought out her notebook and pen. 'So, where exactly?'

His smile melted. 'You the fuzz, lovely?'

'Now what makes you think that?'

The wariness of a man who hasn't always been upright and law abiding came to his eyes. 'Instinct, lovely, just instinct.'

She decided to come clean. 'Look. He's gone missing and his relatives are wondering where he's got to.'

OK, so it wasn't 100-per-cent true, but a little white lie about worried relatives wouldn't hurt, surely?

Ivor showed the whites of his eyes. 'Is that right, lovely? Well, I never. I took him to a few places. Bit of sightseeing. Usual stuff like Bradford on Avon, St Catherine's Valley, Lacock even — you know, the place they use on a lot of those historical dramas on television and film and suchlike.'

Honey nodded appreciatively. This was going *so* well! 'You sound as though you like history,' she said.

'I do, but not that fancy-pants, heaving-bosom stuff. You can keep your Jane Austen. I prefer World War Two myself. See?' He held up the offending tome. 'Not so much the military and political side, though that of course is interesting. I like to investigate how it started, you see? The thinking behind it. Just in case. You know what they say about history, don't you?'

Honey didn't bother to tell him she knew very well; he was going to tell her anyway.

'History repeats itself,' he said with the air of a man who'd spent a lot of time analysing world politics while awaiting fares.

Her phone rang again. She thanked him before turning away to take the call. This time it was her mother.

Her voice was thin — not exactly wavering and weak, more wavering and worked on.

'I fell down the stairs, dear.'

Honey raised her eyes to heaven — or at least as far as the pigeons squatting around the fancy bits on the abbey roof. It was the way her mother said 'dear' that raised her hackles, and falling down the stairs had nothing to do with it.

'Mother, you've done this before.'

'It's my age, dear. One gets very tottery as one gets older. I need you here.'

Honey gritted her teeth. 'That wasn't what I meant.'

'Oh dear! I feel quite faint.'

Yet again her mother had played the guilt card. Her instinct told her that she'd probably only tripped down one stair and that if she phoned Lindsey she'd get the truth. Her sense of duty made her head for home, but she had an inkling her mother had an ulterior motive for getting her there.

CHAPTER 9

It was gone midday and Lindsey was on reception when she got back. She looked extremely businesslike, a pen in one hand and a pile of invoices in the other. Her eyes slid sidelong in the direction of the lounge.

'Grandma's in there. She's got a man with her.'

Honey hunched her shoulders questioningly and not without an element of apprehension.

Lindsey mimicked the same action. 'I've no idea who he is. A would-be candidate for my mother's affection?'

Forearmed but wary, Honey followed the smell of fresh coffee.

Her mother was semi-prone on a settee, bandaged ankle resting on a stool.

Someone was sitting on a chair opposite her. They looked to be in close conversation.

Her mother saw her and looked up. 'So! You came back to see how I am.'

'You look good.'

'My ankle doesn't.'

'I suppose it could be better.'

'You bet it could!'

Normally she avoided the men her mother chose for her. On this occasion the set of his shoulders and the casual demeanour attracted her attention. She forced herself not to give in and faced directly forward.

Her mother didn't leave things there.

'Hannah? This is John Rees.'

'Mother, I can't stop . . .'

Her first inclination had been to throw a killer look at her mother and a contemptuous one at the man she'd found for her. Instead she found her brittleness melting away.

'Hello.'

'Hello.'

'John's just opened a bookshop in Rifleman's Way. He's from Kansas.'

John took her hand and shook it firmly. 'Originally from Kansas. I live in San Diego nowadays. Or rather, I did. Now I live here. In Bath. Best little city in the world.'

His voice was like silk. His hair was light brown shot with just a little white at the temples.

'Well, that's . . .'

She was about to say how nice that was, when the first notes of Beethoven's Fifth throbbed against her chest.

'My phone,' she said, inwardly groaning as she plucked it from her bag.

Making sincere excuses, she backed towards the door.

She recognised the rough-diamond copper's voice. 'I thought you'd like to know; we've found Elmer Maxted.'

'Great!'

Her eyes strayed back to John. He was tall and lean and had a merry look in his eyes — not at all the dusty professor or accountant sort her mother kept digging up. For once this could be fun. And she had time now, didn't she? The case of the missing tourist was all but over, wasn't it?

It wasn't.

'He's dead. Murdered. I need to talk to you.'

Drat! Honey placed her hand over the phone. Her smile flew like a bird to gorgeous John.

'I'm sorry. I have to take this call, but if you'd like to leave your details, perhaps we can get in touch. Unless you'd like to wait.' She bit her lip. Business and pleasure were colliding here. Normally business would take precedence, but John had a certain look about him . . .

'Honey? Are you still there?'

The sound of Doherty's voice seeped through her fingers.

Reluctantly, she bent her lips back to the mouthpiece. 'Sorry, I just had something to arrange.'

'Can you meet me at this place he was staying at? What was it again?'

'Ferny Down Guest House on the Lower Bristol Road.'

'That's it. I'll see you there.'

'Sorry,' she mouthed to the delectable John Rees. She wriggled her fingers in a wave at her mother.

'What about my ankle?' her mother called after her.

'Ask Chef for a bag of frozen peas.'

She tried to phone Casper to see if he'd heard the news. He was out of the office and never, ever used a cell phone. She tried Neville.

'Not a clue.' He sounded snappy. The pair rowed infrequently, so his indignation had to be about something important. She made the mistake of asking him what the matter was.

'He wanted harvest beige in reception and I wanted blush pink.'

Not that important, then. 'Heavens! Who won?'

'He did.'

'So where is he?'

'I don't know.'

'Oh, come on. Casper tells you everything. You're his bosom buddy.'

She sensed the stiffening on the other end of the phone. 'Not all the time! Sometimes he's in a world of his own. No consideration. None at all!'

Casper was aloof, superior, elegant and efficient; she'd never known him to be secretive.

'Tell him . . .'

Neville interrupted. 'I suggest you tell him yourself!'

The connection was terminated with an angry click.

So Casper had secrets. So did a very large number of Bath's slightly superior population. She wondered at his response once he knew that their missing American had turned up dead.

Her mother had got to her feet. 'Are you staying for lunch, dear?'

She seemed steady enough and there was no mention of spraining her ankle or feeling faint.

Honey looked over her shoulder into the lounge at John Rees. He was finishing his coffee. She was sorely tempted, but Doherty and a dead body awaited her. She shook her head.

'I can't.' She threw a smile in John's direction. 'Duty calls. Another time, perhaps?'

'Sure. I'll make a note of your number.'

For the second time that day she was in two minds. Lunch with a charming guy or suffer the ashy fumes of Ferny Down Guest House, courtesy of Cora Herbert. Curiosity overwhelmed temptation. She couldn't resist. Murder was taking precedence over pleasure.

On passing through reception she remembered Jeremiah Poughty. Lindsey traced his number and asked him if he knew where she could find Casper. He told her.

CHAPTER 10

Casper St John Gervais appreciated balance and having things in perfect order. He also found it mesmerising just how quickly one minute flowed into another. That's why he collected clocks. Clocks were one of the reasons he visited Simon Tye. Simon was as at home with the underworld of a small city as he had been with a large one. In London he'd upset the wrong people — which is why he'd headed west and opened a clock shop.

Tye's Timepieces was tucked away in a bow-fronted shop down a set of damp green steps. Only crumpled pavements and a mass of wandering tourists separated it from the sticky aspect of Sally Lunn's Teashop. The shop had been there for years and specialised in Bath buns dripping with butter, and tea served loose leaf in old-fashioned teapots. To mention teabags was sacrilege.

Casper paused before pushing the door open. Already his heart was beating faster. What would he find inside — Simon Tye, of course. But what gems of mechanical chronology would he have there to tempt him?

'Get a grip,' he muttered against his impeccably knotted tie.

He smoothed his hair back from his forehead to help calm his nerves. Once properly under control, he pushed at the door.

An old-fashioned doorbell clanged overhead. Mechanical whirrs, taps, ticks, scrapings and dull thuds filled the air. So did the pungent but pleasant cloy of beeswax and linseed oil. No matter how hard he attempted to maintain his self-control, something akin to passion clutched at his heart.

Brass, mahogany, oak, maple and marble decorated with French Ormolu — the clocks surrounded him, their ticks and their chimes as sweet as words of love to his keen ear and knowledgeable mind. Instinctively, he knew there was something special for him here.

It was set on a chest of drawers with a serpentine front and hanging brass handles, as fragile as fine string. Simon always did have a way of showing things off to their best advantage. 'Presentation is what matters, guv,' he always said. He was right. The honeyed glint of the satinwood emphasised the ice-cold perfection of white porcelain. It was brilliant, four feet wide and three feet high, Dresden figures grouped around a china-faced clock figured with brass.

He ran his fingers over the beautifully defined muscles of the crisply carved shepherd. 'Divine,' he breathed.

'You wan' it?'

Like a grinning satyr, Simon Tye's face appeared over the top of the clock, one bony elbow close to the porcelain shepherdess who leaned nonchalantly against the round barrel of the clock face.

Casper stepped closer, his eyes taking in every intricate detail: the shepherd, a lamb flung around his shoulders; the shepherdess, a crook in her dainty hand, her skirts piled like a pumpkin between her narrow waist and her graceful little ankles. Sheep and lambs gambolled before them and graceful naiads held the clock above them on porcelain ribbons.

It was gorgeous, and there were myriad questions he'd like to ask about it, but he had calculated the price. 'It's very nice, but not the best I've seen.'

He was lying, and could see from the shopkeeper's face that he knew it. Never mind. He would brazen it out.

Simon grinned as though he were looking through him and knew the truth. He looked almost part of the clock itself, yet a lot less beautiful. Wide mouth, almond-shaped eyes and a straggly mass of blue-grey hair that hid a hunk of reddened gristle and a gaping hole — all that remained of his left ear. That's what came of grassing up blokes in the East End of London. No wonder he'd headed west and opened up a clock shop.

'I knew you'd want it the minute you saw it, Mr St John, sir.'

Casper licked the dryness from his lips. Damn the man! He tried to ignore the smile that was spreading across Simon's face like melting cheese. To hell with it! Unable to resist, he reached out and trailed his fingers over the gleaming glaze. A thrill shot through his body. He breathed deeply before he asked the first question.

'Dresden?'

'Dead right!' Simon's smile was unaltered. He seemed to be enjoying Casper's discomfort. 'Made for the Paris Exhibition years and years ago. Brilliant, ain't it?'

Casper squirmed inside but, hells bells, he certainly wasn't going to take it all without giving some out.

'Did you get it legally, Mr Tye?'

Simon looked hurt. '*Mr Tye*, is it? Are you tryin' to throw me off balance, get the better of me an' 'ave it away for nix? It was a legitimate purchase. Cross me 'eart.'

He made the usual sign on his narrow chest in the place where his heart might have been.

Casper took advantage. 'So?' He lifted his eyebrows questioningly.

'To tell you the truth, I bought it off a lady who brought it 'ere in her car. Said the 'ouse was cluttered with stuff and she needed the room. Took a song for it, she did — though, I shouldn't be telling you that.' His eyes narrowed.

Casper shook his head and tutted reproachfully. 'What sort of person would want to get rid of a lovely thing like that?'

'A woman who don't like too much dusting, I s'pose. Though, mind you, she didn't look the type that got 'er 'ands dirty too often.'

'No taste,' said Casper, his eyes fixed on the clock.

'No shame,' echoed Simon.

'How much?' he asked, the words spitting from his mouth as though he had no control over his tongue at all. He wanted this clock.

Triumph shone in Simon's watery grey eyes and slinked in shiny wetness along his wide, flaccid lips.

'I could get seven at auction.'

'Hundred?' said Casper hopefully.

'Leave it out. Thousand,' Simon retorted, feigning insult.

'Exorbitant!'

Simon's eyes were pinpricks in narrow slits. 'No it ain't, and you know it ain't.'

Casper laid a well-manicured hand across his chest. His heart was racing like an express train. It was now or never. He braced himself to forego the temptation. He even made a half-turn towards the door.

Alluringly, the clock began to chime its lucid siren song — heavily seductive to a clock collector's ear.

He stared at it, aware that Simon was watching him like a hungry hawk, his fingers thoughtfully tapping at his bottom lip, scratching at his chin. But his eyes stayed fixed on Casper's face.

His self-control wobbled like a jelly and finally toppled. 'I'll give you five.'

'Well . . .' said Simon thoughtfully. His eyes were hooded. He was looking downwards so Casper couldn't see how delighted he was. 'Let's say five and a half, shall we?'

Not to be outwitted, Casper fixed his gaze on Simon and set his jaw in a firm, determined line. 'Let's say five thousand, two hundred.'

Simon chuckled and shook his head. For a moment Casper was almost panicked into raising his offer. He forced himself to hold out though his mouth was as dry as the bottom of a birdcage.

'It's a deal!' Simon spit on his palm and reached out.

Casper declined to shake hands. 'Fine. I'll get it collected,' he said before the brass bell jangled and the door edged shut.

Wonderful day, he thought to himself, smiling at the world that eddied and flowed around him.

A coachload of German tourists was taking photographs of the flowers, the edifice of the Guildhall, the entrance to the Roman Baths.

He beamed at them as the more professionally minded of them set up their shots, checked their lighting and posed their portraits.

He smiled with satisfaction. This year would be a very good year for the city and for Hotel La Reine Rouge.

The day was a good one and remained so — until he sauntered into his favourite restaurant.

The Saville Roe served all manner of seafood, nestled beside an alley of polished cobbles just behind the Theatre Royal. Panelled walls alleviated by the use of white damask tablecloths and silver-plated cruets gave it a rich, gothic-style ambience. The clientele were well heeled, and at lunchtime businessmen outnumbered tourists. He was shown to his usual table in the far corner. A menu card and wine list as white as the table linen were brought within a minute of him sitting down.

Just as he was deciding between a goat's cheese and salmon concoction and slices of sea bass flambéed in pear juice, the waiter brought him a cordless telephone.

'For you, sir,' said the handsome Italian as he handed him the phone.

It was quite usual to receive calls at his favourite haunts by those that knew him and also knew of his distaste for mobile phones.

For a brief moment he eyed the proffered receiver with something close to disdain. He was also slightly miffed that his habits had become so, well, habitual that people knew where he could be contacted.

Never mind, he told himself as he accepted the call; you've had a good day. It's June and the sun is shining, business is good and you've had a stroke of good luck.

Then Honey spoke and told him about Elmer Maxted. Suddenly the June sky dulled to November.

CHAPTER 11

It became obvious to Honey from his attitude that it wasn't Doherty's idea that she should accompany him to Ferny Down Guest House.

'I don't see the point,' he told her bluntly.

Dealing with the public had well prepared her for characters like him. Identification was instant. Grumblers, groaners and disgruntled Dr Jekyll types who began their complaints with, 'I'm not one to complain, but . . .'

And they would grumble, but in the next instant were as sweet as sorbet.

Likewise, there were two sides to Steve Doherty. His social side wanted to do more than embrace her; his professional side wanted her out of his way.

He adopted a glum look as he drove, an unmistakable grimness seizing his mouth as the disgruntled grumbler took over.

She stated what she thought was the matter. 'You were told I had to come along.'

He fidgeted in his seat. 'The chief constable thinks he might get more media coverage with you on board. He likes having his picture in the press.'

He said it through gritted teeth.

Honey couldn't help grinning.

'Never mind,' she said, patting his hand. A cold hand. Cold hands, warm heart? 'You've been ordered. I've been ordered — well, more or less. So let's leave it at that and get on with it, shall we?'

He grunted something. She couldn't tell what.

'I'll take that as an affirmative.'

There was nothing for it but to settle comfortably into her seat and eye the passing scene.

Doherty sat silently beside her.

'The flowers look lovely this year. I like pink and mauve together, don't you?'

He took his eyes off the road long enough to glance at her.

'Mrs Driver, this is hardly the time to be noticing flowers.'

Maintaining her smile and her bright disposition, she tilted her head sideways so that a sweep of hair blanketed her right shoulder.

'It's a question of keeping things in perspective. Flowers are like music; they soothe the nerves. That's what I'm here to do. Think of me as a flower.'

'What?'

Yes! A response! The car swerved towards the centre reservation, earning a blaring horn and a two-fingered salute from white-van man.

Showing no sign that she'd noticed, Honey carried on.

'You're like a stone: steadfast. Ask Mrs Herbert lots of questions. I'm the fragrant flower that calms her nerves.'

Doherty shook his head in disbelief.

'So!' Honey went on. 'You're going to arrest Mrs Herbert?'

'I didn't say that.'

'But you're not discounting it.'

'That depends on the evidence and her answers to my questions.'

Doherty's square chin turned squarer. She sensed his confusion, personal and professional colliding behind the resolute exterior.

'I doubt that she did it, though she is a criminal — of sorts. She should be locked up just for her choice of clothes and make-up. And pollution. She smells like an old ashtray. Now that's criminal!'

'Yeah, yeah, yeah,' said Doherty as he turned off the engine. 'Right. Now, there's a few questions I've got for you, flower.'

Honey pointed at her chest. 'Me?'

'Yes. You said that her old man was manhandling a chest freezer out of the back gate when you first visited.'

She nodded. 'That's right. The council truck was waiting outside to take it to the recycling plant for degassing before it's crushed.'

He stroked his chin thoughtfully. 'Is that so? Are you sure about that?'

'It's an environmental thing they have to do.'

'I wonder whether they've crushed it yet.'

'I thought you found Elmer in the river.'

'We did.'

'So why . . . ?'

'I want it checked.'

He made the call before they got out of the car.

The flowers in the hanging baskets were wilting slightly. Honey wondered whether Mervyn was the one who was supposed to look after them. Not necessarily, of course. It could be Cora, but she was down in the dumps and had forgotten, perhaps. Not surprising.

His expression was deadly serious as he rang the doorbell. Comprehension regarding Honey's innuendos blinked into his eyes when Cora Herbert answered the door. Her black-rimmed eyes landed on Honey.

'What? You again!'

'It's me,' Honey said, trusting her smile would override Cora's hostility. She needn't have worried. Her attention swerved to Steve Doherty. A deep intake of breath ballooned her bosoms.

Her sense of style hadn't altered one iota. She was wearing a cropped black top and chequered skirt with a ragged

81

fringe around the hem. Her eyes were heavily outlined. A gold droplet dangled from her pierced belly button. Her flesh was white like dimpled bread dough. The gold droplet heaved in and out as though it were gasping for air.

If Doherty had been the cream and she'd been the cat, he would have been all lapped up by now.

She was straight to it. 'And you are?'

Doherty took a sidestep. Partially shielded by Honey, he flashed his identity card.

'Detective Sergeant Doherty. I need to speak to everyone who lives here.'

Cora gushed the information. 'Me, me husband and me daughter.'

Doherty's chin shot forward when he nodded, his jaw almost resting on her shoulder. The stubble rippled as his mouth moved.

Honey watched it move. Funnily enough, it was exactly the same length as two days previously. It occurred to her that he trimmed it to just the right length in an effort to make exactly the right impression.

'Just the three of you?'

'And guests when we've got any. Mind you, I can always find room for a nice-looking bloke like you.'

Doherty's right eye twitched, but he held his nerve.

'Fine, then I need to speak to you, your daughter and your husband.'

Thick with mascara, Cora's eyelashes flickered like the wings of tiny bats.

'Our Loretta's up in her room. Merv isn't here.'

Honey recalled Cora telling her where he usually spent his quality time.

'Perhaps if you could tell me which pub . . .'

Her interference was not welcome. Cora glared and her tone turned as cold as frozen fish.

'He's not gone to the pub. He's gone away. He's allowed to go away, isn't he? God knows but we work hard enough, put up with enough . . .'

Aware that her attempts at flirtation had flopped, the belly she'd attempted to hold in relaxed into its natural pudding shape.

'For goodness' sake,' she muttered, 'it's only a tourist gone on a mystery tour! That's my opinion, anyway.'

Doherty's face set like quick-drying cement.

'Mrs Herbert, today a body was pulled from Pulteney Weir. We believe it to be the body of your former guest, a Mr Elmer Bernstock, also known as Maxted. We would like you — or your husband — to make a formal identification.'

This knocked the wind out of her sails. Her botoxed bottom lip hung puffy and quivering. Her eyes stretched to prominence in the podgy, pallid face.

Still wary of Cora's intentions, Doherty let Honey take the lead.

'Right,' she said. 'Can we come in and discuss what you know?'

Cora nodded and retreated into the green-and-white hall.

Honey recalled the fug in the conservatory and prepared to take small shallow breaths. To her relief they were shown into the guests' lounge instead. A 'no smoking' sign was prominently displayed on the mantelpiece. The room had a more pleasant smell than the conservatory by virtue of a can of air freshener — lilies of the valley, by the whiff of it.

Cora Herbert didn't offer them tea or invite them to sit down, but they did anyway. Cora perched on the arm of a chair immediately opposite them, like a vulture deciding whether to fly off or stay and pluck their eyes out.

Steve Doherty got out his notebook and a smart-looking pen. 'Right!'

Honey eyed him sidelong. Murder had made him a serious man. All the same, he appeared to make himself comfortable. Honey sensed he was far from that.

She noticed he was making a list on the pad and ticking things off — far too slowly for her liking. Overwhelming urges to know *everything* and *at once* took hold of her. She found herself counting the seconds he was taking to ask the first relevant question.

It was obvious that he was terrified of Cora Herbert. But for goodness sake, he was a policeman. Weren't they brave, fearless and bold?

Start! Go on. Start!

He didn't. So she did.

'Can you tell me who was here the last time you saw the man you knew as Mr Bernstock?'

Policemen were usually forceful — or at least they were on television. Steve Doherty looked almost relieved that she'd taken the lead.

Her reply was aimed directly at Doherty, at the same time smoothing her skirt suggestively over her thighs.

'There's Mervyn, of course, and my daughter, Loretta.'

'How old is she?'

'Seventeen.' Her smile was weak, but her simpering spilled out, unhindered by recent events. 'I had her very young you see . . .'

The door to the lounge creaked open. The truth bounced into the room.

'I'm nearly eighteen and Ma isn't as young as she makes out!'

The rectification came from the heavily made-up girl poking her head around the door. Her blonde hair was streaked with three shades of copper. Her earrings were big enough to swing on and she wore six rings on her right hand alone.

Doherty nodded a greeting and turned back to Cora. 'Right . . .'

Waffler, thought Honey, and took the advantage, directing her question at Loretta.

'The man you knew as Mr Bernstock is dead. Did you have anything to do with him while he was staying here — you know, general stuff like saying hi in the morning and how's the weather?'

She could feel Doherty's resentment burning into the side of her head. She ignored him.

Loretta's earrings made a tinkling noise as she folded her arms beneath her pert breasts. Definitely six rings on three fingers of each hand and one on each thumb; none on her index fingers.

She was wearing a red sweater with a keyhole design over her cleavage that left nothing to the imagination. Like her mother, her belly button was pierced.

Like mother, like daughter.

Loretta shrugged in the petulant way of all teenagers. 'I didn't have much to do with him meself. He chatted to Mervyn a lot. They used to booze a bit in the den.'

Cora smiled at Doherty. 'I don't think this nice policeman has got any more questions for you, Loretta.' She turned back to the girl, her expression hardening just a teeny, weeny bit. 'I'll be along shortly to make yer lunch, love.'

Honey saw the contempt in Loretta's eyes. Teenagers sometimes looked at their parents like that and took a while to grow out of it. All the same, she sensed discontent, even an air of secrecy.

Honey carried on regardless. 'Come on, Loretta. Perhaps there's something you might remember that could help us.'

'Yes. That's right,' said Doherty. He was doing his best not to sound aggrieved.

For her part, Honey was trying not to stare at Loretta's skirt. If it had been much shorter, she would have seen her dinner. *If my Lindsey wore a skirt like that . . .* But Lindsey wouldn't. She preferred longer skirts even though she had a dancer's legs.

Doherty was asking Loretta when she had last seen her father.

'He's not my father.'

'Loretta's dad was my first marriage,' Cora explained with a weak grin to them and a warning look to her daughter.

All she got in return was a look of pure contempt. She answered.

'The other night when I heard him talking to Mr Bernstock was the last time I saw him — or heard him, more like.'

There was something in the careless way she shrugged again that set the alarm bells ringing — at least for Honey. She glanced sidelong at Doherty. Did he have teenage children? Perhaps not, or none that he was in touch with. He hadn't seen that telling slide of the eyeballs that was meant to show casual indifference but in fact meant something entirely different. He was asking her questions. Honey knew beyond doubt that whatever Loretta said, she'd be lying.

'You overheard what was said?'

'Yes. They were in the kitchen. Mr Bernstock had asked Mervyn for ice.' A wicked grin crossed her face. 'Mervyn hated having to get crushed ice. Not that it was any big deal, wrapping cubes in a tea towel and bashing them to smithereens. Is it true he's dead?'

Doherty nodded. 'The man you knew as Mr Bernstock is dead, yes.'

Loretta's eyes lit up. 'Bludgeoned to death? Could it have been done with a rolling pin? Old Merv is a dab hand with that rolling pin. That's what he used to crush the ice.'

'You little bitch!' Cora sprang to her feet. Fingers like claws reached for her daughter's throat.

Honey got in between them. 'Now, calm down!' She frowned at Doherty. 'So, how was he killed?'

'We're not sure yet,' said Doherty. 'Once we have the details of the post-mortem, I can . . .'

Honey was losing patience. 'Can we get to the point, please?' Both the policeman and the teenager looked surprised. A cloud of sickly sweet perfume emanated from the trendy teenager when Honey addressed Loretta. 'What were they talking about?'

A thunder-faced Cora butted in again, her lips quivering slightly. 'She's just told you. Mervyn was crushing some ice. That's all.'

'No! You said they were talking,' said Honey, fixing her gaze on Loretta and refusing to take notice of the sour looks Doherty was throwing her way. 'Now, to my mind that means after the ice was crushed. Is it possible that the man you knew as Mr Bernstock had his own bottle of whisky? Quite a few Americans buy their own to save on bar prices. Could he have asked Mervyn to sit down and have a drink with him?'

Loretta began fiddling with a wispy strand of hair caught around her earring. 'Yes. They were. I could tell they'd had a drop by their voices. It echoes a bit in the den anyway.'

Honey pounced on this extra bit of information. 'The den? What den? I thought they were in the kitchen.'

Loretta studied her fingernails in a nonchalant, cocky kind of way. The polish looked black or at least dark purple. 'They were in the kitchen first, getting the ice, and then they went into the den. Mervyn was showing him his watch collection.'

Honey's ears pricked up even more. She could feel Doherty's eyes on her, but didn't look his way. Things were beginning to get interesting. Casper had enrolled her for this job and collected clocks. Mervyn collected watches. Was it pure coincidence or was there some kind of connection?

CHAPTER 12

Mervyn opened his eyes but saw nothing. Everything was dark and his head ached. The dryness on his tongue was like iron filings, and for some daft reason he could smell something that reminded him of Christmas.

With each breath the sack covering his head was sucked up into his nostrils and on into his nasal passages. What with that and the gag around his mouth, it was becoming difficult to breathe. A sense of panic overwhelmed him. He was going to die. Not comfortably, perhaps not even quickly, but slowly suffocating, struggling for even the slightest morsel of air.

No! No!

He tried to remember exactly what had happened, but all he could think of was Loretta. Everything began and finished with her. Even in this, his worst nightmare, the thought of her nubile body assuaged his fear. Eventually his fear won the battle.

What was he doing here?

Mentally, he retraced his movements. Somehow, he couldn't move forward from Cora's first husband giving him a beating. All he'd done was give Loretta a lift home. He'd tried to explain that it was raining, but to no avail. The blows still fell hard and fast.

That was when he'd made the decision to leave. If that moron was walking free and easy, then he was off. For good! First get some money together . . .

Something about that gelled in his brain. Money! Sometime after that he'd arranged to meet someone, but for the life of him he couldn't remember the guy's name or why he'd arranged to meet him.

His clothes were chill and damp against his skin. He knew he'd sweated a lot. Now he was cold, terribly cold. One shiver came quickly after another. If he hadn't been gagged his teeth would have chattered.

He tried moving his arms, flexing his fingers, squirming against the ropes that bound his wrists.

Suddenly he became aware that someone was there. The footsteps were muffled because of the sack over his head. He tried to lift his head, to roll away.

He never saw the hand that killed him. He saw only the wasted years of his life flashing before his eyes before even the memories drained away along with the blood and bits of brain.

* * *

The cellars were deep, one tier on top of another. A thin scum of orange silt covered the cracked concrete and dented cobbles, a result of those times when the river was swollen, the lower levels flooded.

It was like that now, slippery and smelling of river mud and untreated effluent. Coke cans and plastic shopping bags bobbed around just below the ledge that dipped into the river. This was the very lowest cellar, and slowly, with the passing of the years, the river was claiming it as its own.

The body had softened and was faintly marbled by virtue of resident bacteria. He'd covered the head with a small sack so he didn't have to look at the staring eyes. The sacks were readily available. He used them frequently for other, less gruesome things.

The rest of the body was wrapped in a length of polythene that crackled when he lifted it up. The man wasn't light, but not too heavy either. Carefully so as not to slip, he carried Mervyn Herbert down the last flight of steps. There was a strong current in the river, a welcome result of the earlier rains. Water thundered over the weir.

On the opposite bank he could see ranks of sodium streetlights winding through the darkness. Spots of reflected amber light danced on the racing river.

There were no lights on his side, only the black square shadows thrown by the circling colonnade above. The night was his, as dark as his mind.

Gently, still holding on to his precious piece of polythene that had once covered a mattress, he let the body slide into the water. It bobbed about a bit, clung to the bank as if unwilling to leave him.

Beneath his breath he cursed. With the help of a torch he searched behind him for something to poke the body away from the bank and into the main stream.

What had once been a door lay cobwebbed and rotting against the wall. Just as he'd done before, he tore a piece of rotten plank from it, green paint clinging in odd patches over its rough surface.

With the fingers of one hand, he gripped the crumbling door lintel overhead. In the other he held the piece of wood. Still holding on to the flaking masonry, he reached out and poked at the body until it was safely carried away by the current. Then, carelessly, no longer interested in the bloated flotsam he had consigned to the water, he flung the plank in after it.

Unafraid and uncaring, he watched it ebb into the black night and black water. What was it to him? What was anyone to him, except for one notable exception, the one person he loved more than himself?

The rush of water and a slight bumping sound made him look back again.

The body had returned, the current pinning it against the riverbank.

There was no option but to drag it back onto the slime-covered flagstones. It had to be got rid of, but where?

He sat down and thought about blame and throwing the police off the scent. Blame and guilt. He knew a lot about them and about loss and restitution, making things up to those you loved.

An idea came to him. Suspicion fell initially on close acquaintances in a murder case. So, if the body was found in the right place . . . ?

CHAPTER 13

One thirty. Smudger the chef was complaining about the butcher again.

'I swear to you, it's rubbish. Trust me. Let me tell him that if he don't up 'is standards, I'm for chopping out his liver!'

Honey rolled her eyes. How was a woman to cope? A batty chef *and* a mad mother.

Her mother was rabbiting on about a very upright and uptight type she wanted her to meet. 'You must meet him, Hannah, darling. I'm sure you'll get on like a house on fire.'

'Mother, I can arrange my own dates.'

Her mother shrugged. 'Doesn't seem that way to me.' Digging her painted nails into Honey's shoulders, she flipped her round to face her.

'Tell me the truth, the whole truth and nothing but the truth. Do you have a man friend?'

'Yes.'

'Yes?' Her mother sounded incredulous. She clapped her hands and looked extraordinarily happy. 'You do? Who is he?'

'Just a guy.'

'That's his name?'

'Jeremy.'

Her mother frowned. 'I don't know him, do I?'

'Right. You don't know him. Now do excuse me, mother. I need a word with my head chef . . . Smudger? You will not threaten the man. If he fails to deliver decent meat, then he doesn't get his money. Savvy?'

Smudger grinned cheekily. His sandy-coloured hair curled out from beneath his tall chef's hat. 'Great! I can't wait to see his face when I tell him to stick it.'

'No!' Honey wagged a finger at him. 'That isn't what I said. Just insist that he keeps his standards up, or else . . .'

'I chop him!'

A gleaming meat cleaver waved with gleeful anticipation.

'No! Smudger, pain comes in many forms. A light bank account hurts more than a knife wound!'

Smudger looked disappointed but accepted her judgement.

'And for my next trick . . .' she muttered to herself, heading out of the kitchen.

'Right. Mother.'

Taking hold of her mother's elbow, she wheeled her away from Smudger's realm and into the conservatory.

'Doesn't the garden look lovely?' she said, pressing her up against the glass.

Her mother glared back at her. 'Don't try to fool me, Hannah. You don't have a boyfriend, do you? You were lying.'

'Yes.'

'Well, I've got one for you.'

'I don't want one.'

The conservatory looked out over an enclosed garden. The trees had grown high and wide, obliterating the view of other buildings.

Her mother looked puzzled, her lips parted as though there was something she wanted to say, but she wasn't quite sure how to phrase it.

Faced for once with silence, Honey took the bait. 'So, tell me about him.'

'He's a widower.'

The vision of the gorgeous guy she'd seen standing beside her mother at the beginning of the week flashed into her mind. Somehow she hadn't envisaged him as being a widower.

Giving herself time to digest this, Honey banged on the window at Mary Jane, their resident professor of the paranormal, and waved. Mary Jane was practising her tai chi and managed to include a slow wave among her movements.

Accompanied by her mother's listing of reasons why she should meet this man, Honey continued to watch Mary Jane's sinuous arms rolling and wafting outwards, one leg slowly raised, one little twist of her spine.

'OK, he's a bit of a steady Eddie, but I'm sure he's the right man for you.'

This last sentence sunk in. 'I'm really surprised. He didn't strike me that way,' said Honey.

'But you haven't met him yet.'

The vision shattered.

'What?'

Her mother smoothed her corn-coloured tunic as she settled gracefully into a chair. She looked pensive, a slight frown creasing her professionally plucked eyebrows. 'You haven't met him, dear.'

Honey frowned. Was she missing something here? 'But he was here the other day. You said he was a bookseller. His name was John Rees.'

Her mother looked nervous for a moment, but it wasn't long before her natural brazenness took over. 'Not him. I meant Edgar Paget. He's my dentist. And a very good one,' she added with a toothy smile, as though that in some way recommended him as a potential suitor.

Time to escape.

'Mother, I don't think I can take to a guy who makes a living from peering into peoples' mouths.'

'He's not just *any* dentist! Private patients only. And very expensive.'

Honey turned her back on Mary Jane, who had just entered into the final movements of her daily routine.

Folding her arms across her chest, she glared at her mother with a mix of disbelief and confusion. Was her mother trying to get her to notch up the same number of marriages as she'd gone through?

'So this bookseller. What was he here for?'

'To organise a book fair. He wanted to make a booking. I just got talking to him. He seemed very pleasant.'

Honey's jaw dropped. 'A booking?'

'Yes, dear.'

'So why didn't you pass him to reception?'

'Because he asked to see you.'

Honey sighed. 'I'll have to phone him.'

Her mother looked taken aback.

'So what about my dentist — Mr Paget?'

'No!'

Her mother rarely frowned. *It causes wrinkles, dear.* But her heart-shaped face became elongated as her chin dropped. The resultant wrinkles wouldn't have looked amiss on a bloodhound.

'Hannah, you can be so ungrateful at times. I don't know where you get it from.'

Honey's thoughts were still on the gorgeous bookseller. 'So what happened with John Rees?'

'He couldn't wait. Had to go. There's no need to panic. He said he'd call back . . . and he left his card.'

Honey headed for reception, her mother scurrying along beside her, and rummaged among the bits of paper in a basket marked 'file'. Everything that didn't have a home — which included the calling cards of salesmen selling disposables — went into the 'file'.

'Have we had a booking for a book fair?' she asked Deehta, who usually came in to cover on Tuesdays and Thursdays, but could often be persuaded to fill in when needed.

'No.' Deehta shook her dark head vehemently. When it came to efficiency, Deehta was top of the pops. Honey had no recourse but to believe her.

There was no sign of a business card marked 'bookshop'.

'Never mind,' Honey said once she was satisfied that her filing tray was its usual, uninteresting self.

Mary Jane, apparently finished with her tai chi session, called out.

'We need to talk,' she said in a hushed rush of a voice, as though secrecy and speed were paramount.

Needing solace after her brushes with Chef and Mother, her first inclination was to say that she was too busy. But Mary Jane's animated features changed her mind. By now her mother was heading for home, perhaps to call her dentist. The date with her daughter wouldn't be happening.

'I know where he went,' said Mary Jane. 'That guy who went missing. I know who he was asking about and where he went.'

Honey took hold of Mary Jane's bony elbow, hauled her into her private office and shut the door. 'Tell me!'

'He enquired about a family called Charlborough.'

Honey frowned. 'Do you mean the wealthy Charlborough family of Charlborough Grange?'

Mary Jane's face wizened into a question mark. 'Do I?'

'They live out at Limpley Stoke.'

Mary Jane's face brightened. 'That's the place. That's where he went.'

It added up. Ivor had taken Elmer to the church at Limpley Stoke, though he hadn't mentioned Charlborough Grange.

'Were the Charlboroughs part of his seeking out his family tree?'

Mary Jane's earrings, colourful parrots swinging on a perch, rattled as she shook her head. 'Oh, he couldn't say. He wasn't specific, according to Bob.'

'Presumably he would have been looking for the parish register. Isn't a parish register a mine of information?'

'He sure would,' said Mary Jane. 'That's one thing you can say about the church, they certainly kept tight tabs on everybody.'

CHAPTER 14

The alarm woke Honey just after 11 p.m. A quick shower, fresh make-up and hair dried. A search through her clothes. Jeans, a black T-shirt and pearl earrings. Casual but classy, she decided, after a brief glance in the mirror.

On the way to meet Detective Sergeant Doherty, she passed the taxi stand and looked for Ivor's car but couldn't see him. After Mary Jane's revelations, she wanted to find out more about Elmer's visit to Limpley Stoke.

The night air was still and cool. The lights of the city obliterated the blackness of the river, which was running high and fast and didn't look its normal friendly self. Possibly there'd been heavy rain upstream.

Doherty had mumbled something about sharing information. Well, that would have to be taken with a pinch of salt! Never mind the professional liaison. She sensed a personal liaison would be much more to his liking.

As she descended the steps to the Zodiac Club, she considered whether she should tell him about Elmer having been in touch with a man named Bob the Job. Crazy name, but it went with the territory. People hoping to find fame or notoriety in their background were a bit crazy, often devastated when they find their ancestry contains nothing more than generation after generation of farm labourers, housemaids and crossing sweepers — the blokes who swept away horse droppings. Lindsey had told her about that.

Right! She was going out to meet a policeman. Should she tell him where she *thought* Elmer had gone, or should she check out this Bob the Job guy? Better still, she'd get Ivor to confirm it once she spotted him on his cab stand. Until then she would also keep it to herself.

The Zodiac was a private club situated in a huge cellar that ran beneath the hotel and out under the road. A set of narrow steps led down to the entrance. The steps were not lit. It was like descending into a black hole and the smell of damp was strong.

On ringing the bell, a small slot opened. A pair of eyes looked out and a muffled voice asked for her name and whether she was a member.

'It's me.'

The eyes opened wide in recognition and the door opened. The smell of garlic prawns and sizzling steaks fell over them.

'Good evening, madam!'

'Good evening, Clint. I think that's the first time you've ever called me "madam".' She looked him up and down. 'Nice suit.'

As he smoothed the front of the black evening suit, Clint, her part-time washer-up, grinned from ear to ear. Despite the spider's web etched into his skull and the gold earring, Clint looked very presentable — and slightly menacing. In fact, ideal for the job.

'I got it at the Oxfam charity shop. Not bad, is it?'

'No. Not bad at all. Should last you a while, as long as you don't go washing up in it.'

His grin stretched across his face. 'I won't be doing that. Serving in me mate's shop is me daytime job, washing-up is early evening, and this is my night-time job.'

'So when do you sleep?'

'When I can. Got to have a social life, ain't I?'

'You certainly do.'

And all for cash, thought a bemused Honey. It occurred to her that he could be making more money than she was, enjoying a better social life and paying no tax.

'Look,' she said. 'I'm expecting a guest. His name's Steve . . .'

'Doherty. Yeah.' His grin collapsed into a stiff grimace. 'The dude's already here.'

There was no point asking him how come he knew a member of the local constabulary. She could guess, but Clint was Clint, and his business was his own.

Threading her way through the smoke brought to mind old black-and-white movies, clubs where shady characters clustered in dingy alcoves. The ceiling was barrel-vaulted and the walls bare stone. Down lighters picked out swirls of blue smoke drifting from the sizzling steaks being grilled in the kitchen. Apart from them, the lighting was minimal, if not downright scarce.

Steve was propped up on the counter of the bar. A space had opened up around him once news of his professional standing had travelled. Isolation didn't seem to worry him. His eyes were everywhere but stalled once they landed on her.

'Drink?' he asked, shifting his stance and digging his hand into the pocket of his black leather jacket.

She ordered a vodka and tonic. 'With ice and lemon,' she added.

He took the money from his pocket. No wallet, she noticed. A cautious man. She wondered where he kept his credit cards.

'Are you hungry?' he asked.

She shook her head while eyeing the clientele, noting who was there relaxing after hours. Hotel and pub managers, plus those who owned and ran their own hotels — and worked bloody hard in them.

Steve looked at her admiringly. 'Cheers!'

They clinked glasses.

Honey glimpsed the glint of a gold bracelet on his right wrist. His hair was too densely coloured for a man of his age. Doherty wasn't taking middle age lying down. She wondered whether he realised that he had something in common with Cora Herbert. Men were vainer than women.

'So,' she said after taking a generous sip of vodka and tonic. 'Have you informed the relatives?'

'He doesn't have any. Apparently, there was a sister, but she died just a few months ago.'

'So he went travelling to get away?'

Doherty shrugged. 'I suppose so. Who knows? They reckoned he was well into doing research. Tracing ancestors was the latest thing. Before that, it was haemophilia.'

She frowned. 'The bleeding disease?'

'That's the one.'

Her frown remained. 'Why haemophilia? Out of general interest or something to do with his family?'

'Search me.'

Still wondering at that, she finished her drink. He insisted on buying her another.

Do I deserve another?

Weekends were hard in the hospitality trade: the world and his wife came away on weekend breaks, and the locals were out for wining and dining. Add that to the huge influx of tourists at this time of year, and it was a punishing schedule.

You bet!

'OK.'

It came to her suddenly that they were in competition with each other. He wanted all the glory in cracking this, and so did she. She hadn't thought about it before, not when the job had first been foisted on her. But now? Something was stirring. Unfortunately for Steve, it wasn't passion that had coloured her decision to meet him, but curiosity, a drive to find out exactly what was going on. That was the reason, she told herself, but still her eyes kept sliding sidelong. Steve Doherty was only average height but had a good body, strong rather than stocky.

She shook the thoughts from her head.

'Bubbles,' she explained on seeing Steve's quizzical expression. She cleared her throat. 'Are there any clues?'

'Minor things. A piece of wood jammed into the side of the deceased. The river's full of debris following heavy rain. But it was interesting. There was an indentation on it where a number used to be. Could have been a nine. Could have been a six.'

'Depending on whether you're Australian.'

She laughed at her own joke.

Doherty had a blond moment. He didn't have a clue — or perhaps just no sense of humour.

She took it slowly. 'Upside down. A six if you're upright and living in the northern hemisphere, and a nine if you're Down Under.'

'Very funny.'

He gave a weak laugh.

No sense of humour, she decided, but then, on reflection, it wasn't a very good joke.

Doherty went straight into the facts. He had a sack over his head. Not a big sack. A small one. It had a smell. Not a nasty smell. A nice smell.'

He said it as though only he knew its significance.

Honey nodded appreciatively as though she understood. But why should she? A sack was a sack, was a sack. And the smell? Hemp, surely?

'Hemp?'

'Spice.'

She noticed how quickly he had spoken, giving away information that perhaps he shouldn't. She sensed him looking at her. Decided it was her turn to speak.

'And he was never in the freezer?'

He shook his head. 'No. We checked the city dump. It was still there waiting to be de-gassed and whatever. It was empty and there were no traces of a body having been in there.'

Just as she'd guessed, it wasn't long before he got onto personal things.

'So! I take it you're divorced.'

He had a hopeful look in his eyes.

She shook her head. 'No. He died in a sailing accident.'

'I'm sorry.'

I'm sorry. That's what everyone said. But she wasn't. Racing and delivering sailing yachts had taken precedence over her and Lindsey. The more impassioned he'd got with his sport, the less they'd seen of him. It didn't help that most of the crew he'd hired had been women. *They bond well and do all that I ask of them.* You bet they did!

The usual questions followed.

'Any children?'

'One. Lindsey. She's eighteen.'

'Get on! You don't look old enough.'

'Very kind, but I've heard it before.'

'I meant it. Does she look like you?'

'No. She looks like her father.'

She knew he was making small talk and that he didn't really want to know what Lindsey looked like at all.

He nodded sagely, as though she had said something very profound.

She asked him about himself. He told her he was divorced — something she'd already guessed — and that he'd moved to Bath from London.

'To make a new start,' he added. 'Got fed up with the pressure of work in the Met.'

He told her he was renting a flat in Lansdown Crescent, but was looking to buy. 'When I can find something affordable.'

She knew where he was coming from. Bath was expensive. Many of the well-proportioned Grade I and II Georgian houses, horrendously expensive to maintain, had long ago been divided into flats. But their elegance was undiminished and their interiors were furnished with suitably expensive antiques. Nothing in a really good location came cheap.

She let him make headway until she finally judged the time was right to make her excuses. Carefully avoiding a puddle of spilled drink, she gathered her navy-blue satchel from off the bar.

'I'm cooking breakfast in the morning.' It wasn't strictly true. Dumpy Doris, a woman of dumpling roundness with arms a sumo wrestler would be proud of, cooked up a cardiologist's nightmare — fried sausages, fried eggs and fried bacon. It was said that even the cornflakes would be fried if Dumpy Doris had her way.

He offered to walk her home.

'No,' she replied, as Clint, his eyeballs bouncing between Doherty and Honey, opened the door.

'It's no trouble.'

'It's no distance.'

Doherty threw a backward glance at Clint before the door slammed shut.

'I know him.'

'Everyone knows Clint.' She hid the ensuing grin as she began her ascent up the steps to the road.

She didn't want to know what Clint did when he wasn't working for her; she didn't want to know what offences Doherty might have charged him with in case she couldn't bring herself to employ him ever again. Best let sleeping dogs lie. When they got to a certain age, automatic dishwashers were notoriously unreliable. Clint was not.

'Are you sure you'll be all right?' he said once they were up at pavement level.

'Fine.' She nodded. 'It's not far.'

'No,' he said, taking her arm. 'I insist.'

'Will you frogmarch me if I refuse?'

'Possibly. You know us cops: brutal, insistent — but cute.'

'Shouldn't you add conceited?'

'I can't see why.'

Bath didn't have the typical night-time smell of a big city — the stewed traffic fumes, the dank river and heat rising like dust from concrete buildings. Set like Rome in a sweeping valley surrounded by tree-topped hills, its lawns and well-kept flowerbeds lent a spring-like freshness to the air. The mellow walls of ancient buildings glowed in the borrowed gleam of well-placed lighting. Even at this hour the streets had a safe feeling about them, as though the ghosts of the past stood sentinel over those treading its cosy alleys and broad thoroughfares. Late-night revellers wending their merry way home raised a hand, called and waved goodnight.

Pulteney Street flew straight as a dart from the centre of the city to the Warminster Road. Green River was close to the very end, tucked away down a cul-de-sac.

Doherty sniffed the air. 'I love this place. There's something timeless about it. It looks beautiful, even at this hour. It's sacrilege that we're talking about a murder case. It shouldn't happen here.'

'That's Casper's belief.' Hence lumbering me with the job of crime liaison officer, she thought, but kept her mouth shut.

He hadn't mentioned much about the murder tonight, though goodness, she was grateful for the details he had given.

'Almost there,' she added, her footsteps slowing. She stopped and faced him. 'Look. You don't need to come any further.'

She smiled as she said it. No, she did not want him to see her to the door. The windows would be black, the minimum of light falling from the reception area; everyone would — or should — be in bed. But that wasn't the real reason. Like a lot of seniors, her mother was a light sleeper, and she had opted to stay overnight. Questions would be asked. She'd prefer them not to be.

She turned swiftly away before he had a chance to kiss her. She wasn't ready for it. Not just yet.

'Goodnight.'

'Goodnight.'

He sounded disappointed, perhaps even hurt. She glanced back to ensure he had indeed strolled off towards Lansdown Crescent and his bachelor pad. His form, his shadow and the sound of his footsteps faded into the night.

Walking on tiptoe was never going to be easy. The flag-stones skirting the cul-de-sac were uneven and badly worn from centuries of use. Her steps slowed the closer she got to the hotel entrance. At last, once she was sure he was gone, she stopped and turned round.

The night breeze was cool as water against her face.

Counting to ten she waited, then slowly, still with her heels held barely off the ground, she retraced her steps. She heard a car and presumed he'd got a taxi. Certain she was right she increased her speed, then paused as her fingers felt something in her pocket. Why was she bothering to walk to the taxi rank? Ivor Williams had given her his number.

Taking out the card, she held it to catch the gleam of a streetlight, took her phone from her pocket and dialled the number.

Ivor answered.

'How's the book going?' she asked.

'Too busy for reading at present, lovely. What can I do to help you?'

It was obvious by his response that he didn't recognise her from their previous meeting.

'It's the hotel lady that was asking questions about Elmer Maxted. I suppose you've heard the news.'

'Yeah.' He sounded horrified. 'Poor bloke. Who would have thought it, eh?'

She counted off all the bits of information she'd come across. Was Bob the Job for real or was he as imagined as the ghost Mary Jane insisted came out of the closet? Was her information likely to be pure fabrication?

Here goes, she thought to herself.

'When you drove him around, remind me, did you ever take him to Limpley Stoke?'

'Sure. He wanted to visit the church. Took his time, of course. Wanted to meet the vicar, you see. Had things he wanted to ask, so he said.'

She breathed a sigh of relief. Her confidence returned.

'What sort of things?'

Ivor paused before his words began again in that very Welsh, singsong way. 'Well, I can't say for sure, mind you, but it was something to do with family.'

'His family?'

'Yes.'

'And he stayed there quite a while?'

'Three days in a row.'

'Three days!'

She couldn't help sounding surprised. Why would anyone, even the most ardent sightseer or family historian, want to spend three days peering into old, dusty archives? Surely, he couldn't have spent all that time in the company of the vicar? She asked Ivor.

'He saw the vicar on the first day. I saw them talking. But not after that. He just went into the church and walked around the gravestones and all that. Took some time, that did. I waited until he came out and we went sightseeing. Not that he seemed that interested. He was quiet when he came back. Doing a lot of thinking, you see. Finding out about your ancestors can be a bit daunting, you know.'

After thanking Ivor for his help she put her phone away and turned for home. So Mary Jane's friend was right. There was no mention that he'd actually visited Charlborough Grange and introduced himself to the family. According to Ivor he'd gone no further than the church and its grounds. Would searching through the archives take three consecutive days?

That, she decided, was a question that had to be answered.

The hotel was in darkness. Loud snoring drifted out from the settee in the room just behind reception. The night porter was (almost) on duty.

She took off her shoes.

'No point trying to creep in, Mother.'

Honey jumped, and Lindsey's head bobbed up from where she was lying full stretch on a brown leather chesterfield.

'I wish you'd stop doing that.'

'Scaring you or waiting up for you?'

'Both.'

Honey eased herself onto the settee beside her daughter. 'Are you spying on me?'

'Yes. You're such a virgin when it comes to men.'

'Excuse me?'

'Don't remind me that I'm your daughter et cetera, et cetera. I mean, you haven't indulged for a while. That's why I've got to look out for you.'

'Lindsey, I've only been out for a drink.'

Lindsey reached over and made a lengthening motion from the tip of her mother's nose. 'OK, Pinocchio.' She huddled forward, her face, even in the gloom, glowing with interest. 'So! Tell me what he's like.'

'Who?'

'The policeman. And don't try and look so innocent. Grandma was dusting in the dining room and overheard your conversation. She put two and two together.'

'There's nothing to it.'

Lindsey gave her a 'Who do you think you're kidding?' kind of look.

Honey held her head to one side and looked at her daughter. 'Are you always going to be looking out for me?'

Lindsey nodded.

'Correction. Spying on me.'

'Yep.'

'I thought so.'

CHAPTER 15

She wasn't thinking of sacks; in fact, she wasn't even thinking of the murder when she took a shortcut through the Guildhall. Her mind was open to possibilities. In fact it was like a great whiteboard on which the problem is detailed in green felt tip and all the connecting factors are entered around it.

Her thoughts roamed free. There was plenty of room for them here in this place. The Guildhall Market was a magical place where stalls dealing in antiques jostled with those selling a wide variety of cheese, garlic sausage and dried flower arrangements.

She sniffed the air, enjoying the mix of fragrances and the way it cleared her head.

Suddenly she breathed in the unmistakable tang of spices. *A sack smelling of spices.*

She looked round in the hope that she might find the source of the smell, perhaps a suspect. Stupid really. Was there likely to be a sign saying 'Get your small sacks here: Ideal for placing over the head of your victims?'

When she saw where the smell was coming from and the stallholder, she smiled: Jeremiah Poughty, the very same who had taken over reception on orders from Casper.

She could tell by the look on his face that he wasn't missing the hospitality trade one little bit.

Cloves, cinnamon, bay leaves, turmeric and a host of other scents filled her head and cleared the very minimal excesses of the night before. There was a clichéd exoticism about them: a hint of the east, Persian markets, the Alhambra and an overindulgence of the senses.

It was all for sale under a sign printed in garish red letters on an apple-green background which screamed HERBS AND SPICE AND ALL THINGS NICE.

Jeremiah waved before beaming a wondrously white smile at a woman customer. She was giving him aggro.

'What's that one?' The woman's voice had all the enchantment of iron filings.

'Turmeric, honey.' Jeremiah settled one hand on his slim hips. They were tightly clad in tan suede trousers. He wore a matching waistcoat festooned with embroidered flowers all down the front over a peasant-style shirt. His lipstick was purple and his complexion was as shiny and brown as a conker.

'And that?' The woman poked her finger at another small sack and sniffed.

'Paprika, *dahling*.' He nodded a greeting to Honey. 'Looking for something exotic to spice up our life, are we?'

The woman did not appear to notice that he was talking to someone else. She pointed a podgy finger.

'Pretty colour. Got much taste?'

'Lots, honey.'

The woman frowned and shook her head.

'I'm not sure. I normally only buy such things when uncontaminated by human hand. Preferably in plastic bags and on a supermarket shelf. Are your hands very clean?' asked the woman, her small eyes narrowing in her pudding face.

Jeremiah threw her an indignant look. 'If you want something in plastic, go trot along to the supermarket. Everything on this stall is *au naturel*.'

Jeremiah was committed to all things green and free trade and free love, and everything else that didn't come pre-packaged and with a hefty price tag. But that didn't mean he suffered fools gladly.

The woman took on a shocked expression, wrapped her sheepskin coat more tightly around her body, then shuffled off to the next stall.

Jeremiah recovered quickly. 'Win some, lose some. Oh well. There's great demand for what I sell.'

As stalls went, Jeremiah Poughty's wasn't a bad one. It was a well-stuffed pitch — wooden shelves at the back filled with sacks of vibrant-coloured powders, beans, nuts and other items she didn't recognise. Bunches of herbs, thyme, parsley, fennel and sage hung in bunches overhead. Some stuffed in between looked questionable.

'Jeremy, can I ask you something?'

His eyelids fluttered nervously. 'Sure. But if it's a date, I'm not your type.'

She smiled. 'No, and I'm not yours.'

She looked over his stall and upwards at the sign, face spiked with amusement.

'Nice little spot, Jeremiah. Herbs, Spice and All Things Nice.'

Suddenly Jeremiah was all teeth, wide mouth and floating hands. 'Spice adds a little colour to your cooking — you should try some.'

The words came rat-a-tat-tat out of his mouth.

'It's mine and Ade's.' He nodded towards his partner, who was wearing a green T-shirt, matching silk scarf and trousers too tight for decency. *Like an unripe banana*, thought Honey.

He smiled briefly by virtue of the fact that he was bagging up half a pound of dried beans for a crusty with three rings in his nose and the usual uniform of ragged parka jacket, half-shaved head and well-fed dog.

'I will. But not today.' Honey dug her thumbs into the waistband of her jeans. Designer, of course. Bums and thighs were a nightmare without a good cut.

'On the house.'

Honey grinned. 'Can I put this in my mother's curry?'

'What you do to your mother is your affair. It's a free sample — we give it to other customers too.'

She eyed him quizzically. 'Just how heavily spiced is it?'

Jeremiah laughed. 'I told you. Purely legit, dahling thing.'

Honey took the brown paper bag and slid it into her bag.

'Go on,' he said. 'What do you want to ask me?'

'About these sacks . . .'

The necks of the sacks containing the spices were rolled over, revealing the brightly coloured contents. Honey fingered them thoughtfully.

'They're just sacks,' said Jeremiah with a nonchalant shrug. She noticed his eyes slide sidelong to his partner.

'One of them was found covering the head of the man they dragged from the weir the other day.'

Jeremiah gasped. 'He was murdered?'

'He was that. The sack over his head smelled of spices.'

'How terrible! Poor man! Suffocated with spices.'

'And hit over the head with a blunt instrument.'

She wasn't sure either by his expression or tone of voice whether he was being facetious or strangely enraptured. She didn't know him well enough to judge but felt obliged to burst his bubble.

'You know I'm crime liaison officer for the Bath Hotels Association, don't you?'

He looked at her askance. She'd taken him off guard.

'He was killed three days ago. Saturday night sometime.'

'Saturday night is music night, not a night for murder.'

'Where were you last Saturday?'

His features froze for a moment. Then he laughed nervously. 'You're just joking. You can't really ask me questions. You're not a policeman, dahling.'

She raised one questioning eyebrow. 'A sack smelling of spices? You've got loads of them here.' She spread her hands, indicating tier upon tier of small, filled bags.

'A friend of mine who *is* a police detective would be interested in hearing that.'

'You wouldn't!'

'I would.'

His eyelashes fluttered darkly over his cheeks. Honey was sure they were made of nylon. As he leaned closer, the smell of his perfume obliterated that of the spices. 'I was out with someone,' he said softly. 'You won't say anything will you?'

Honey fixed her eyes on Jeremiah's partner, who was still serving. 'Who were you with?'

His tongue swept along his bottom lip. 'I really couldn't . . .'

'Perhaps I should ask your friend.' She made a sideways move. From behind his counter, Jeremiah followed her like a mirror image.

'No! There's no need.' He glanced over his shoulder.

Ade, Jeremiah's partner, was now talking with the young man from the coffee stall.

'Andrew Charlborough. I was with him.' The name came out in a rush of breath.

Honey frowned. She wasn't often amazed at what people with status and money got up to in their spare time. She'd seen Andrew Charlborough at a number of auctions. They were hardly on nodding acquaintance, but she'd judged him as an upright, respectable citizen, the sort that's in bed by eleven with a good book and a devoted wife.

'You mean the antiques dealer?'

Jeremiah nodded. 'And before you jump to the wrong conclusion about the man, I was invited to give a quote for some plants he wanted. A bloke who works for him and sometimes delivers for us asked if I'd be interested. He introduced us, said he was interested in large tropical plants.'

'So why wouldn't you want your partner to know?'

Jeremiah chewed at his lip. 'I kept the deal to myself. And the money.'

Honey's mind was already darting elsewhere. Elmer's head had been covered with a small sack smelling of spices.

Jeremiah dealt in spices supplied in small hessian sacks. 'So what happens to the sacks once they're empty?'

Jeremiah shrugged. 'Mostly I give them away. Or chuck them. Some people buy by the sack — the big customers, that is.'

She eyed him speculatively.

He wasn't long interpreting her look.

'I have not a killing bone in my body!'

You can't detect a murderer just by the looks of him. Just because he denies the fact doesn't mean anything either. She'd hedge her bets.

'Can you provide me with a list of regular customers? The bigger buyers?'

Jeremiah shrugged his narrow shoulders. 'There's only a few. Shipping orders ain't our style. Half a pound here, a pound there for most of our customers.'

Honey fixed her gaze on Jeremiah's face. 'Please. It would be a great help.'

Recognising he had to put himself out, Jeremiah sighed and nodded. 'I'll do what I can.'

CHAPTER 16

The next morning, showered, breakfasted and perky, she phoned Doherty.

'Any developments?'

'No.'

To say he was not forthcoming was putting it mildly. Well, two could play at that game.

'OK. So I won't tell you what I know. See you.'

'Hang on there!'

She smiled. *I won't show you mine unless you show me yours.*

'We're tracing his movements. We've spoken to the taxi driver who ferried him around.'

'I guessed you would. I hear Elmer was interested in the Charlborough family. Do you know them?'

'I've heard of them. What's the connection?'

'I think they figure somewhere in his family tree. It's possible that's why Elmer went to the church. He was checking out the parish register.'

'Whoa right there. That line of enquiry is a dead end. Elmer was taken there and back by the taxi driver. He didn't go missing in the grounds or thereabouts. We found him in the river, which means he must have been killed somewhere in the city. Mrs Herbert did say he went sightseeing there, and on the night he disappeared he went out quite late.'

Honey bit her lip in a half-snarl. He had a point.

'So there you are,' he crowed. 'That's the way it was. We have a witness who overheard Elmer arguing with Mervyn Herbert. She also gave us a very good description of his car.'

'So Mervyn Herbert is the chief suspect. You're still looking for him?'

'Ah! Yes.'

He asked her out again. She said she'd take a rain check. It wasn't that she wasn't attracted to him; she was. It was nerves. Plain and simple.

* * *

As if there wasn't enough to do in running the hotel, her mother had stopped over and was hounding her about having carpet laid over a truly lovely stone floor. 'Look, Franks Carpets are doing a great deal . . .'

'Mother! You're talking about a listed building and an original floor.'

'A stone floor is no good for arthritis.'

Honey muttered under breath. 'Keep going and you could end up beneath it.'

She looked for a quiet alcove where she could check the new menus — Smudger liked to change them every three months — and having her mother breathing fire over her shoulder did nothing to help her concentration.

Lindsey saved her bacon and brightened her day.

'That nice bookseller is here to see you again,' she said as she flounced past, a litre of Gordon's gin in one hand and a bottle of Glenfiddich in the other.

Honey stopped what she was doing. 'Is he?'

She shoved the menus into a folder for later.

Her mother pounced. 'I think a green carpet would be nice.'

'That rather dishy bookseller is here, the one you introduced me to the other week.'

Her mother frowned. 'A bookseller? Do you think I would introduce you to a bookseller? You know there's no money in selling books. It's a mug's game. Besides, he's American.'

'Dad was American.'

Her mother made an odd sound. She'd been caught out and was reluctant to face the consequences. Honey escaped.

Mary Jane waylaid her on her way to greet John Rees.

'I need to make arrangements to hold a séance,' she said. 'Do you know of anyone whose loved ones have passed over who might be interested in attending? Older people in particular take great comfort from it.'

Honey turned round just in time to see her mother beating a fast retreat across reception.

'Mother! Mary Jane would like a word with you.'

Her mother came to a giddy halt. It wasn't often she got trapped into doing something she didn't want to do. She was usually the trapper.

Mary Jane's lucid voice rang across reception. 'Gloria, my dear . . .'

Honey exchanged a secretive smile with her daughter, who had just emerged from the bar.

Lindsey shook her head. 'Granny won't be pleased.'

'Never mind. It'll keep her occupied for an hour. Now, where have you put my visitor?'

'Prince Charming awaits you in the lounge with a cup of coffee,' said Lindsey, then smiled as Honey unconsciously tidied her hair as she passed an ornate Georgian mirror.

'I wonder, is he really Prince Charming or a frog in disguise?'

'You won't find out until you kiss him.'

John Rees had delayed her plans to drive out to the church at Limpley Stoke, but even a girl pushing forty has to have fun.

His hair was sandy, his face slim, and warm hazel eyes danced with humour behind his frameless spectacles. He removed them when she entered and stood to greet her. It was old-fashioned and oddly touching. She half expected to look down and see that her sensible skirt had turned into a crinoline or something that warranted a bustle.

Her smile was one of genuine welcome. 'Mr Rees. I'm so sorry I missed speaking to you when you last called. There was a misunderstanding. I thought your being here was my mother's doing.'

One side of his face seemed to rise in amusement, his eyes twinkling as though he'd read her mother just like . . . well, a book.

Feeling a trifle nervous, she rubbed her hands down over her hips and offered to pour another coffee.

'No. Thank you,' he said.

Making the effort to sound the professional hotelier, she tucked her skirt beneath her as they both sat back down.

'So! What can I do for you?'

'I want to hold a book fair.'

Green River had a very handsome conference room overlooking the park at the rear. Conferences and wedding fairs brought in good revenue. Why not a book fair?

'I think we have exactly what you're looking for. Our conference room holds sixty people . . .'

'No,' he said. He raised his hand, his palm facing her like a stop sign. 'You misunderstand. I'm holding a book fair at the shop. I run themed evenings complete with wine and cheese and whatever. I pick a theme, you see. I select the books covering that particular subject, and objects featured in those books. For instance, I've done a modern art theme. The books were on modern art, so I asked local artists to lend me their paintings for the evening — price tags included.'

Honey wasn't quite sure where this was going, but hazarded a guess. 'You're going to use hotels as a theme? Haute cuisine perhaps?'

Honey felt a shiver down her spine. What if the epicureans attending were niggardly with praise and slated whatever dishes the Green River produced? Smudger didn't take criticism well. He got huffy easily, and it was her that had to contend with his moods.

'I favour a Victorian theme for my next event, and that, of course, will include the clothes of the era. Not the big crinolines and stuff like that, I don't have the room. But smaller things: gloves, mittens, hats . . .'

'Underwear?' said Honey as Queen Victoria's voluminous undergarments, currently displayed behind glass in an ebony frame, came to mind.

'Exactly,' he said. 'Just enough to set the scene. And then I'll select the books to go with it.'

Honey nodded. The fact that she wasn't going to earn anything out of his fair wasn't important. But something else was.

'Am I invited?'

He smiled. 'That's what I wanted to ask you. Would you come?'

Feeling as though she was somehow floating up to the ceiling, she smiled back. 'Of course I will.'

CHAPTER 17

Casper St John Gervais enjoyed the good things in life. He took pride in running a superbly furnished and well-run hotel. He adored cashmere sweaters, tailor-made jackets and trousers, but nothing could compete with a pure cotton shirt made by a skilled Indian gentleman in Saville Row, London.

His exquisite taste extended to his surroundings. His hotel had graced in-flight brochures, *Hidden Hotels of the World* magazine, and was frequented by the rich and famous, confident they would receive excellent service and absolute discretion.

He didn't live in the flat down in the basement, but in a gem of Georgian architecture, one of the impressive twenty-four that made up the Circus, a ring of mathematically produced elegance from the fevered brain of John Wood.

As with many Georgian houses, the ceilings were high and the windows large. The Georgians had excelled in letting in as much light as possible in the days before Edison lit up the whole world and invented the electricity bill.

The paintwork was finished in traditional colours; the furniture was even more elegant than that in his hotel. Gilded mirrors reflected the star-bright quality of the chandeliers, prisms of light flashing outwards.

Thick Turkish rugs hushed his footsteps. The only other sound was the incessant ticking of his clocks. His home was full of them.

He was sitting admiring his latest purchase when the front doorbell rang. Sighing, he put his single malt onto a silver coaster to avoid marking the small piecrust table near his chair, then walked along the passage to the front door. He opened it to find Simon Tye standing there.

'Did you smell the cork out of the whisky bottle?' he asked casually.

'If you're offering, I'm accepting,' said Simon, and without being asked swept past him, striding through the hallway purposefully.

Simon was oddly quiet as Casper poured the whisky.

'Enough?' he asked, raising the glass so Simon could inspect its contents.

Simon's eyes were fixed on the porcelain clock, his brows furrowed as if he could see some flaw in it that he had not seen before.

'Don't say the vendor who sold it to you it wants it back,' said Casper as he handed him the drink.

'No,' said Simon. 'But her husband does.'

Casper raised his eyebrows quizzically.

Simon glugged back a good portion of whisky. 'It appears she never had permission to sell it.' Simon clutched his glass with both hands and looked totally embarrassed. 'I'm sorry mate, but Charlborough wants it back.'

Casper was all attention. 'Charlborough? Do you mean who I think you mean?'

Simon nodded. 'Yes, the same bloke who bid against you for the Chepstow longcase up at Marlborough in the summer.'

Casper took a slug of whisky. So did Simon.

'He reckons he's goin' to sue if he don't get it back.'

Casper caught the caginess in the sidelong expression Simon threw him.

'I told him I sold it to you.'

Casper groaned as he slouched back in his chair.

Simon nodded. 'Sorry, mate.' He began to dig in his pocket. 'Here's your money. In cash.'

Simon only dealt in cash. Nothing wrong with that as such, but . . .

Casper eyed the bundle of fifties Simon placed on the table. They looked grubby and therefore beneath his fastidious ideas of cleanliness. He would get Neville to gather them up, or otherwise use the pink washing-up gloves kept in the kitchen drawer.

'I'll take it now if you like, though you'll have to help me.'

'I don't do lifting,' said Casper with a shrewish pout and gazed blankly into space. The thought of letting the clock go too quickly gave him great pain. Perhaps he could persuade Charlborough to let him keep it. He'd offer him more, double what he'd paid Simon Tye. It was certainly worth a try.

Simon shook his head. 'No,' he said, resolutely reading Casper's mind. 'It has to go back.'

Casper sighed, and although there was still plenty in his glass, he set it dumbly down on the table.

'You can count on me to make arrangements.'

* * *

His second visitor that night helped the situation along.

'I've come to make my report,' Honey said, breezing in more joyfully than Simon Tye had done.

She told him what the taxi driver had told her.

'Couldn't you get in trouble for withholding information from the police?'

Honey shrugged. 'Sergeant Doherty has his own theories. He's adamant that the victim was murdered close to the river. I must admit, he does have a point.'

'He's trying to hit on you?'

She refrained from blushing. 'Something like that. Anyway, I thought I'd go along and ask the vicar what our American friend had found out about his family tree.'

She looked surprised when Casper stated he would go with her.

He sighed heavily. 'Two birds with one stone, my dear girl. We both have quests to fulfil.'

CHAPTER 18

The Warminster Road winds up a hill out of Bath passing substantial Victorian villas with far-reaching views over the meadows dipping down into the Avon Valley. Like a blueprint from history, a canal and a railway line run alongside the river. Together they spanned the centuries that constituted the Industrial Revolution.

Further out the villas are replaced by modern detached houses, and further out still the sunlight twinkles through battalions of trees bordering the roadside.

The road to Trowbridge branches off to the left, under a railway arch and into the village of Limpley Stoke. Some way up the hill in the older part of the village, the church nestles among houses of its own age, built in the years of the Stuart kings.

Casper had outlined the story of the clock and insisted they first return it before she made her enquiries of the vicar. He'd phoned Charlborough and offered more money, but had been refused. His mood was sullen and it was a fairly silent drive.

It was no trouble for Honey to alter her prior appointment. But Casper was a picture of resentment. He was brooding on the fact that he had to travel at all. That woman! That bloody Charlborough woman had upset his equanimity. He wished her ill. *No*, he thought, changing his mind. He wished her dead.

* * *

Pamela Charlborough had come back from Spain under duress and she was dead brassed off about it.

If her husband Andrew hadn't discovered she'd sold the clock she would be back out there now lunching in one of the smaller but more select quayside restaurants in Puerto Buenos, rubbing shoulders with the owners of luxury superyachts. As it was, her personal bank account was sadly lacking, replenished only if her husband chose to do so. Furious as he was about the clock, there was no chance of that, so she was back in England and bored stiff.

'I needed that money. You're such a skinflint.' Her comment and request for more money had been ignored. 'You care more for that clock than you do for me.'

Annoyingly he'd agreed with her.

She paced the conservatory, an old and elegant structure erected by some Victorian antecedent of her husband Andrew. The man should have been named Midas but was more formally named Reginald. He'd spared no expense on this particular monstrosity. The place was filled with a wide variety of tropical plants from all over the world. The profusion of greenery was almost beautiful, but there was a wild carelessness about it. The plants were huge, thick-leaved affairs, forming a jungle under glass. Rather than being a pleasant place to sit shaded by dotted palms, the overabundant foliage throttled the huge structure.

There were two views from the conservatory. To the rear were massive greenhouses full of even larger tropical plants. Huge leaves pressed against the glass as if trying to escape from the dank humidity that prevailed inside. She'd gone in there once. Once was enough.

From the other end of the conservatory she could look over the drive and the wide steps that led up onto the parapet to the front door. She sighed. The drive was empty and she was lonely. Oh, for a bit of red-blooded male company.

She took a red leather address book from her handbag, opened it and ran her finger down the letters of the alphabet, stopping at the letter 'P'. With one well-manicured finger-tip, she flicked the book open at that page and smiled at the entry. She kept the book open, picked up her phone and dialled. It rang for a while then was answered. The sound of his voice made her go weak at the knees.

'Well, hello,' she purred. 'And how is my favourite little pussycat? Due for some well-earned leave yet? Spain is still very warm, you know, and there are regular flights from the local airport.'

The response on the other end of the line was negative. Her smile stiffened. Expensive heels of exquisite shoes tapped the tiled floor and her smile faded.

'You haven't got time? For me you should make time.' She gritted her teeth until her lips felt stretched and dry. 'Don't worry about it, darling. After all, you're just a number on my list — just as I am on yours. One of my older numbers, of course. Adios, amigo!'

She snapped the phone shut then flung it as far as she could.

'Damn you!'

It bounced off the back wall and disappeared into the greenery. The sound of car tyres crunching on gravel made her look towards the drive.

A car she didn't recognise. Some company might be entertaining. Any diversion was welcome.

CHAPTER 19

'I smell money,' said Honey.

Her eyes took in the fudge-coloured stone, the lead-paned windows set into stalwart mullions of creamy-coloured stone. Elizabethan?

'Old money,' corrected Casper, suddenly breaking his silence. 'Enough of it to allow Sir Andrew to do more or less what he wanted in life. Started off conservatively enough: Eton, Cambridge, the army, followed by some acting and then the writing of his memoirs.'

'About his time wearing tights?' asked Honey with a grin.

'Don't be facetious!'

He ducked slightly so that his gaze could sweep unimpeded over the elegant facade. 'Apparently the place was in danger of falling down back in the fifties. Annoyingly gorgeous now!'

Honey noticed that Casper kept his eyes averted from the clock draped like a beautiful woman on the back seat. Her car of course. He'd made perfectly reasonable excuses as to why they couldn't use his.

'Darling, mine's a two-seater. Isn't yours one of those people carrier contraptions?'

She'd gritted her teeth. No. It wasn't. But the clock needed its own seat. Of course they'd have to use her car.

Casper slammed the car door as if banishing the timepiece from his mind.

Looking distinctly unhappy, he clumped up the mossy steps to the next level of gravel.

Italian terracotta pots lined each tread and terrace, from which fell a froth of straggling lobelia, nasturtiums and variegated ivy.

The front door opened as if by magic, and there was Andrew Charlborough, a military-looking man of white hair and strong features. The ruddiness of his complexion was typical of a man who'd served in the army, climbed mountains and tramped through the jungles of Borneo. Not too good on an actor, perhaps, but his bone structure was good.

He wore a powder-blue sweater and matching trousers. A crisp white shirt collar emphasised the rugged features of a man who spent a lot of time outdoors.

He glanced swiftly at his wrist. The gold strap of an expensive wristwatch glistened.

'You're late.'

He addressed Casper, turning away once the words had been snapped.

Unfazed and mildly respectful of gentry, Casper replied, 'Do accept my apologies, old boy, but due to circumstances beyond our control—'

'The traffic was heavy,' added Honey, irritated by Casper's flowery language.

Charlborough barely glanced at her. Again he addressed Casper. 'Have you brought it with you?'

'Yes indeed, though the thought of returning such a wondrous object weighs heavy on my heart.'

It sounded like Shakespeare, but wasn't. Honey raised her eyes heavenwards. Casper was doing everything to impress except licking the man's boots.

Charlborough was unmoved. 'Bring it in here.' He turned away. Casper looked as though he was about to blow a gasket.

'I do not hump!' he said, both hands resting on his silver-topped walking stick.

Honey looked down at her shoes in an effort to hide her grin.

'My butler and his wife are off today,' said Charlborough, his expression unaltered. I'll see if the gardener and someone else can lend a hand. You'll have coffee while I arrange things.'

Casper grabbed the chance to have a nose around, just as Honey knew he would. One more chance to ogle his beloved clock.

They stepped into a hall where the walls were lined with heavy oak panelling and the floor thick with the rich colours of ancient oriental rugs. There was a dark-green tapestry along one wall where a hunter sat on a pale horse, his dogs and retainers around him. A falcon perched on his wrist. Against the tapestry and set on a long Jacobean table with barley twist legs was a display of eighteenth-century silver. It was an incredible collection, handed down, Honey guessed, rather than purchased.

Above a stone mantelpiece sat a skeleton clock, its workings suitably protected beneath a dome of Victorian glass.

'Such exquisite items,' breathed Casper, his eyes shining with delight. 'Absolutely exquisite.'

Honey glanced around at a profusion of clocks, all showing the time of 2.35 p.m.

Honey checked her watch. They were quite correct.

Casper gave it one last try. 'I came here to see if we could not come to some understanding. I'm willing to offer more than your wife was paid for the clock.'

Charlborough paused and eyed him as though he were considering the depth of Casper's pockets.

Pretty deep, thought Honey. La Reine Rouge must be worth in excess of four million, and Casper's private residence was one of the few in the Circus that had not been converted into luxury apartments. Even so, compared to Charlborough Grange it was peanuts.

'Haven't I seen you at Sotheby's?' Andrew Charlborough directed his question at Casper.

Casper visibly grimaced. 'We've bid against each other on a number of occasions.'

Irritated by Casper's ongoing toadiness, Honey asked if she could use the bathroom.

Charlborough indicated a corridor of panelled wood and more tapestries running off the main hall.

'Take that passage, turn right then left at the end. It's on the right.'

She heard Charlborough tell Casper that they would talk in the study.

After ogling and using the Delft-tiled bathroom, it was time to play 'hunt the study', a place Elmer Maxted might not have gained access to. It has to be off the reception hall, she told herself, and began trying a few doorknobs. Some were locked.

'Can I help you?'

She started. A man of around thirty stood next to her holding a tea tray. The thick carpets had smothered the sound of his footfall. Of muscular build, he looked pleasant enough, if a bit young for a butler.

She smiled. 'I'm a bit lost.'

He smiled politely. 'Follow me. Andrew asked me to bring tea to the study. I presume that's where you should be.'

She wondered at his familiarity, calling Sir Andrew by his first name.

'Are you a member of the family?'

'I've been here for some time,' he said, which didn't really answer anything. 'I suppose you could say I was. But I get paid for being here.'

His smile was disarming.

'In here.' He indicated a door. She opened it.

The study was as impressive as the rest of the house. Rich spines of old books lined packed shelves; there was a white-marble fireplace of a later age than the house and an overmantel above it of a later age still. The clock was of black marble, round and nestled on a mock carriage of gold ormolu and decorated each side with fat-bottomed puttees.

Bunches of carved grapes wound in fertile splendour up and around the huge mirror hanging above the mantelpiece. Honey mentally assessed its height at around eight feet, and it was about the same across.

There were a few pictures on the wall: black-and-white snaps and one or two coloured. Family shots, a wife, a child. And later, just a young man — the child grown-up, perhaps? But no wife. No woman at all.

Sir Andrew appeared with Casper and did not acknowledge the young man who'd brought the tea, who left with as much deference as he'd entered.

'Would you like to pour?'

Honey realised Sir Andrew was directing the question at her.

Sexist, but she was here on a mission. Let him think her biddable. Ha!

'Um. Yes.'

'Shall we get down to business?'

Charlborough went to where three decanters sat on a silver tray. He began to pour himself a drink. He didn't offer them one. Casper and Honey exchanged contemptuous looks. Tea for them, brandy for him. If Casper was put out, he didn't show it.

The class system is alive and kicking.

'I admit to being disappointed,' said Casper as Andrew Charlborough seated himself behind a desk that was almost big enough to be a dinner table.

'My wife had no business selling the clock.'

'Are you sure you won't reconsider . . . ?'

There was an awkward silence, during which she allowed her gaze to drift. She got up and paced the perimeter of the room.

'Had quite a career in the army, sir?' She nodded at another line of photographs that covered a good few feet of panelling. They were black and white, unmistakably in foreign parts and full of smiling soldierly faces. Most of those pictured looked boyish. Charlborough, who she just about recognised, looked more head-boyish and a touch superior.

'Indeed, yes. Great days. Great boys.' Charlborough's jowls drooped with nostalgic sadness.

He was on his second glass from the decanter. No further mention had been made of refreshments. And there would be none.

'Do you know Jeremiah Poughty?' She adopted her sweetest voice. 'West Indian parents, born in Gloucester, now runs a spice stall in the Guildhall Market.'

'I've never heard of the man.'

'He deals in spices and plants. You invited him here to talk about plants, I think.'

He shrugged. 'Perhaps I did. I don't recall the name.'

'You might recall what he looked like. He's very . . .' She paused for the right word. There was only one. 'Colourful! Both in skin tone and clothes. A bit of a peacock, you could say.'

Charlborough remained as cool as his powder-blue sweater, but there was a blip of something approaching alarm in his steely eyes.

'Oh yes. The plants. I don't handle the domestic side of running this place. Anyway, what's that got to do with my clock?'

'Nothing really, except that the sacks . . .'

Casper interrupted. 'Look, I'm sorry about this, we really have taken up too much of your time, but if you should ever reconsider . . .'

'The clock is not for sale — at any price! And now . . .' The glass was slapped down.

Honey recognised the sign for goodbye. Sir Andrew had had enough.

He pressed a buzzer fixed to his desk. 'Mark will show you out.'

The young man who'd brought the tea reappeared.

Honey eyed the black T-shirt, the tight-fitting jeans. He smelled slightly of oil.

131

'Please,' he said, indicating the open door.

Honey slipped through followed by Casper.

'So you're the butler,' she remarked once they were out in the corridor.

'Hardly,' he said with a tight smile as he accompanied them to the main entrance. 'Trevor's away visiting relatives. I'm the back-room boy. I take care of anything mechanical but I'm just filling in until he gets back some time tonight.'

Casper pouted all the way down the steps to the car. As he walked, he swung his silver-topped walking cane.

'Watch out,' said Honey, ducking to one side. 'You look as though you're about to bash someone with it.'

'That man! Why couldn't he indulge his wife a little, let her sell the clock and spend the money at will? I could swear, I really could!'

He slumped in the front seat and slammed the door.

'Bugger, blast and sod it.'

Honey got behind the driving wheel and turned the key. 'No swearing Casper. We're off to see the vicar next.'

CHAPTER 20

A downcast Casper opted to stay in the car.

'Walk it off,' Honey said to him.

He glowered.

She persisted. 'A bit of fresh air will do you good.'

'I don't want to be done good! I want that clock!'

'Children,' she breathed quietly, and headed for the arched and ancient entrance to the parish church.

The interior was very dim by virtue of its narrow Saxon windows. The walls were whitewashed but looked ice blue by virtue of the light diffusing through stained glass.

A woman arranging flowers told her where she could find the vicar.

'Through the chancel and down the steps to the crypt.' She pointed a skeletal finger tipped with bright-pink nail varnish. 'He's got an archive down there.'

Apart from her painted fingernails, the woman seemed a sensible sort. She wore a flowered dress and lace-up shoes. Her eyes darted about as swiftly as her nimble fingers. She looked her up and down in the same way as her mother.

'You could do with wearing something warmer. Cold as death it is down them steps — though only to be expected, I suppose. It's only a skip and a spit from the crypt.'

Charming. What better way to spend a warm spring day?

'Don't worry. I'm quite resilient.'

Stone steps led down into the chantry: cold air met her at the bottom and she shivered.

The Reverend Reece Mellors was bending over what could only be a parish register. It was huge, big enough to make a tabletop — a coffee table, at least.

'Reverend Mellors?'

He looked up.

She beamed warmly. 'I'm Hannah Driver. I rang you.'

'Of course, of course. Good afternoon!'

His voice ricocheted off the cold walls. His hand swallowed hers.

She'd expected a pasty-faced vicar with horn-rim spectacles and a vague look in his eyes. Instead she was confronted with a tall man who had to stoop beneath the vaulted roof. Black was the best way to describe him: black hair, black eyes, black bushy eyebrows, and dressed in black. The blackness contrasted eerily with his pale complexion: like Count Dracula, she thought, and found her gaze fixing on his mouth when he spoke. No sign of fangs.

'I spoke to you about an American tourist, a Mr Elmer Bernstock, though he may have used the name Maxted.'

The vicar's smile lifted his saturnine features. 'Ah yes. Interesting chap. Couldn't quite get out of the habit of using a pseudonym. He told me both names and that he had his reasons. He also swore me to secrecy as to which was his real name. I had no problem with that. In my opinion, I think he liked the excitement of having two names. I can't think of any other reason for him doing so.'

Well, this was something. Perhaps the vicar was right. There was no secret to him using two names. It was just the habit of a detective's profession.

'Were you of any help?'

'Oh, I think so, although he had done quite a bit of groundwork himself.'

'I wouldn't have thought either of those names would be very common around Bath.'

'They're not. He wasn't tracing his own kin. He was tracing his wife's, and even then only by marriage. His wife's sister married Sir Andrew Charlborough in this very church.'

'Is that so?'

Now this was interesting.

'That is so.' His finger traced a relatively late entry in the parish register.

'She died about twenty years ago.'

Honey recalled the photographs: black and white of Charlborough and his lady and child, then a later one of a young man, the child grown into manhood.

'And the son? Is his name and birth date listed?'

The Reverend Mellors slammed the book shut. 'Not in this one.' He reached for another hard-covered book. 'His baptism would be in here.'

She watched as he rustled through the pages.

'Ah! Here it is. Lance Charlborough was baptised eighteen years ago.'

Honey's thoughts returned to the photographs of the handsome young man. Some had been fairly recent. And his mother had died twenty years ago. She was just about to point this out, but Mellors beat her to it.

'Not his birth date, you understand,' said the vicar, having noted the expression on her face. 'That would be in that book,' he said, patting the former epic tome he'd been perusing.

'Aren't baptisms or christenings usually done within a few weeks or months of birth?' she asked him.

He pursed his wide sensuous mouth when he nodded. 'Usually. There must have been some reason otherwise. Perhaps they were abroad at the time. Sir Andrew did serve in the army, I believe.'

'Did Elmer have children?'

'No. I did ask him — you know, out of interest, as one does in the course of a conversation. He said something about his wife having had an inherited disease, so they'd chosen not to. Apparently, she died some time ago. He's alone now.'

It was on the tip of her tongue to ask him to look up Lance Charlborough's birth date, when the woman who'd been arranging the flowers called down the stairs.

'There's a phone call for you, vicar, from the bishop. I took it in the study.'

'I'll be right there.'

He grinned ruefully. 'Sorry about this. I quite often put my phone on divert so I can take it on my mobile, but Mrs Quentin puts her trust in God, not modern technology. She picks up the receiver within the first three rings.' He sighed. 'Oh well. Sorry about this.'

'Never mind.'

'I'll look it up for you and give you a call. Shouldn't take too long. Is that all right with you?'

'Of course.'

Mrs Quentin, the swift-moving flower arranger, escorted her down the aisle to the church door — a bit like a wedding in reverse.

'The vicar's a bit lax when it comes to security,' she said in rushed tones as though impatient to get back to her flowers. 'But I like to make sure that anyone who comes visiting is properly shown off the premises.'

Honey knew all right. Women like Mrs Quentin didn't need a computer-based diary when it came to recalling who had visited, where they'd come from and what their intentions were. The naturally nosey had a ten-megabyte memory installed at birth.

Honey asked the obvious question. 'Do you recall an American who came checking out his family tree?'

Mrs Quentin nodded. 'Mr Maxted. He came here three days on the trot poring over the old registers and asking questions. He snooped around a lot. I caught him behind the church. That was when I realised he wasn't just interested in his family tree,' she said, her voice falling into a disdainful hush. '*She* was there. I saw her out back on t'other side of the fence. Hussy, she is. Lady Charlborough, indeed. No lady her! The first Lady Charlborough — now, she was a lady. But that one!'

A woman! Was Elmer having an affair?

'Did you happen to overhear what they were talking about?'

The red lips pouted with disdain. 'Certainly not! I am not in the habit of listening in on private conversations!'

Honey mumbled an apology.

'Besides, they were talking normally, not like that man who came along after him that day. Scruffy-looking individual he was. Perhaps that's unfair. Not so much scruffy as pallid and bland. And loud. T'were a wonder they didn't come to blows. The American were none too happy with him, I can tell you.'

The sun had warmed the coldness of the crypt from Honey's back, but a fresh chill ran down her spine. The description was familiar. So, Mrs Quentin was Steve Doherty's witness. Dare she ask?

'You didn't catch a name, did you?'

Mrs Quentin shook her head. 'No. But I saw his car.'

It was hard not to cross her fingers and wish or shout hallelujah, but Honey contained herself. 'You don't happen to remember what make or colour of car?'

The powdered cheeks puckered into a knowing smile. 'I does indeed! One of them cars that keeps the lights on all day. And it was dark blue. And an estate. Let's see, it begins with a 'V' . . .'

'A Volvo?'

'V for Volvo. That's the one!'

Honey resisted the urge to skip all the way back down the churchyard to her waiting car.

'Home,' muttered Casper, who was laid back in his seat, his hat pulled down over his eyes.

'Not yet,' said Honey, hardly able to control her excitement. 'I think our American might have been having an affair with Charlborough's wife.'

Casper peered out from beneath the brim as she swung the car away from the kerb.

'Steady on, old girl.'

Accelerator stabbed to the floor, they were off down the road heading back to Charlborough Grange.

'I declare I am utterly wearied by all this detective work,' muttered Casper. 'I only asked you to liaise with the police, not run the case.'

'I never do things by halves, Casper.'

He waved a hand in surrender. 'Please yourself. But don't expect me to go back into his superior presence. He is not the type I would wish to include even on my 'B' list of acquaintances.'

'Never mind him. Now listen to this, Casper. According to the vicar, Elmer was Sir Andrew's brother-in-law by marriage, but not the present marriage. The first marriage.'

'You're suspecting familial skulduggery,' he said profoundly. 'Or might I suggest that you hope it is.'

'Do I sound as though I do?'

'Yes. Like a bulldog. You have sunk your teeth into this bone and you're not letting it go.'

'There's more. One of the women who does the flowers in the church heard Elmer having an argument. Guess who with?'

'Go on. Tell me,' Casper said wearily, the brim of his hat bouncing on his nose.

'Mervyn Herbert!'

'Ah! We have our murderer.'

'We would if we knew where he was. According to Mrs Herbert he's out drinking most of the time.'

Swinging the car down the drive, she targeted the gap between the stone pillars on either side of the entrance.

'He also met Pamela Charlborough.'

'At the Grange?'

'No. At the church.

'Just the church?' asked Casper in that sharp, sudden way of his.

'Just the church,' she replied grimly. 'Ivor said he was there for hours three days on the trot.'

'Pretty church,' said Casper. 'I took a walk all around its perimeter.'

Honey remembered thinking the interior was a bit gloomy.

'It was dingy inside.'

'As I said, my dear, I walked around the perimeter. There's a very neat graveyard surrounded by ivy-covered walls and laurel hedges.'

'How very poetic.'

'There's also a stile behind the church and no more than two fields between it and Charlborough Grange.'

Honey gripped the wheel, her eyes shining with delight. 'So Ivor, the taxi driver, wouldn't have known if he'd visited Charlborough Grange or that he'd met Pamela Charlborough. He presumed he'd gone no further than the church.'

'Should you not be calling her *Lady* Charlborough,' said Casper in passable resemblance to Noel Coward.

Honey grinned. 'From what I've heard, she's far from being a lady!'

'You're prejudiced. Do you really think she was having an affair with our American friend?'

'Well, if he wasn't having an affair, then why else did he want to meet her?'

'The meeting could have been prearranged or it could have been by chance. Either way, there's still our missing Mr Herbert to consider. Mr Maxted is found murdered and Mr Herbert has disappeared, probably on a bender. To use detective parlance, I think it's an open-and-shut case.'

Honey shook her head. 'I can't see it's that simple. If his wife's sister was dead, what was the point?' A spine-chilling answer sprang into her mind. 'Unless he hadn't known she was dead. Unless he suspected . . .'

'Now you're talking pure fiction. You're making up the plot as you go along.'

She wasn't listening. Absorbed in what-ifs and whys, she shot past the main gate of Charlborough Grange. Casper cried out in alarm as she spun the car round on the spot.

'Sorry, I was miles away.'

Casper righted himself and readjusted his hat.

'So was I. If it wasn't for my seatbelt I would have flown through the windscreen.'

* * *

This time no one answered the front door.

Honey looked down to where she'd left the car parked on the gravel drive at the bottom of the steps. Casper looked comfortable enough, his arms folded over his chest, his hat pulled down over his eyes, but she knew he was brooding. He'd lost the clock and he was pig sick about it.

The door stayed shut. The windows looked out sightless over the warm stone terraces simmering in the afternoon sun. The shadows of trees were growing longer across the lawns and the heads of flowers quivered with honeybees. The air was heavy with floral perfume and ripe green leaves, the smell of grass gently baking in the summer sun.

She made a snap decision and followed the path along the front of the house, through an arch and into a rose bower — a tunnel of blooms heavy with scent, yellow roses vying with white ran the full length.

Through a gate and she found herself in a walled garden where fruit trees clambered over warm, red brick. Such gardens had existed in medieval times; perhaps this one predated the present house, the house itself standing on the ruins of an older dwelling.

The workmanlike surroundings, the rubbish bins, a small cement mixer, a ride-on lawnmower waiting to be put away, led her to the tradesmen's entrance. The rear of the house was as silent and bereft of human contact as the front.

'Hello?' she called out.

The sound was lost in the warmth beating against the red-brick walls, the sturdy metal objects standing sentinel at the side of the path.

She stood absolutely still, drinking in her surroundings. If you listened hard enough and were very observant, you could almost smell danger. She did just that, bringing all of her senses into play.

Nothing!

No surprised countenances appeared at the windows; no curious eyes watched as she found a back door, opened it and went in.

She found herself in a conservatory where the greenery was as virulent as in the Amazon rain forest.

'Who the hell are you?'

Even before she turned round, Honey guessed she was in the presence of Lady Charlborough.

She was sitting in a wrought-iron chair, her finger poised over what appeared to be a diary or address book. A gold sovereign hung from a chain around her neck. She wore a gold belt, gold high-heeled sandals and earrings to match. Despite the contempt in Mrs Quentin's voice, she'd still expected a mature Chelsea rather than Essex girl. It was hard to keep the surprise from her voice.

'Are you Lady Charlborough?'

The woman, whose hair was Scandinavian blonde, had a tan only obtainable from somewhere like southern Spain or a high-voltage sunbed. She was holding a glass in her free hand. The liquid in it was clear and sported a slice of lemon. Gin rather than water.

Lady Charlborough looked her up and down with the utmost disdain.

Plucked eyebrows rose, and dusky eyes opened wide with a mix of streetwise caution and upper-crust disdain.

'Yes. I'm Lady Pamela Charlborough. Who the hell are you?'

'Honey Driver.' Her hand shot forward. It wasn't taken.

Pamela Charlborough threw the book to one side and raised her eyebrows. 'Is that supposed to mean something?'

'I suppose not. I really wanted to ask you about your brother. You know he's dead, don't you?' It was the first thing to come into Honey's head, a surprising opening gambit.

'Brother?' She frowned.

'Oh. I must be mistaken. I was told he came here and spent some time with your husband.'

'I have no idea what you're talking about.'

'You don't have a brother.'

'That's right. I don't.'

'Ah! Perhaps you're not the first Lady Charlborough?' Something else she knew already, but it was best not to let on that she'd been prying.

The expertly made-up face stiffened. 'No, I'm not! I'm the second wife,' smiled Lady Charlborough. 'The trophy wife, you might say, seeing as my husband is some years older than me.'

A rather chipped and tarnished trophy, thought Honey.

Lady Pamela slugged back the remains of her cut-glass tumbler, took out the lemon and ate that as well.

'So what the hell do you want?' No hint of friendliness. Lady Pamela wasn't the sort to make friends with the lower orders — not female friends, anyway.

But Honey shot it to her.

'An American tourist was fished out of the river the other day. I was under the impression he visited you here. His name was Elmer Maxted, though he did sometimes call himself Bernstock.'

Lady Charlborough tapped her pen on the chair arm and glanced impatiently at the book she'd flung aside.

'I can't say I've ever made his acquaintance.'

'Really? I have it on good authority that you have.'

Her ladyship did not look amused.

'Whoever told you is mistaken — either that or a liar.'

'My informant is an upstanding churchgoer who told me she saw you hobnobbing with our American friend over the church wall at the bottom of your land. Or were you just passing by?'

The pink lips twisted into a snarl.

'Old Mother Quentin. Nosey cow! Time she was pushing up the daisies in that bloody church instead of putting them in pots!'

'Were you having an affair with Elmer?'

Lady Pamela's jaw dropped. 'How dare you! Who the hell do you think you are!'

'Let's just say I'm an interested party affiliated with the police. I can't help the questions being asked. The police would ask the same. Maybe it's better if you told me the truth rather than them.'

'But you're not the police!'

Honey didn't flinch. OK, it was all bluff, but bluffs baffle brains — that's if Pamela Charlborough had any.

For a brief moment the flesh beneath the expertly made-up face squirmed as though Lady Pamela's skin had tightened around her face. Telling the truth and saving face were fighting it out.

She snapped. 'I saw this bloke on the other side of the wall and we passed the time of day. Anything wrong in that?'

'There's no such thing as coincidence.' Honey bristled. 'I wouldn't have given it a second thought, except that Elmer Maxted married a sister of Sir Andrew's first wife. Now that's what I call too big a coincidence!'

Lady Pamela raised her tanned, toned body from the chair. Her botoxed lips curled back, displaying perfect teeth which Honey estimated cost the same price as a luxury car.

'That's the way out,' said her ladyship, pointing a finger tipped with apricot nail varnish. 'Now get out before I call the police!'

'You can if you like, bearing in mind that I happen to be working with them.'

'Don't care! Clear off! Go on! Bloody clear off!'

Honey paused. 'OK, Mrs Charlborough. I'm off.'

'*Lady* Charlborough, if you don't mind!'

Honey didn't hold back the sneer.

'Are you kidding? As long as you've got two nostrils in your nose, you'll never make a lady!'

The sound of smashing glass sounded as she closed the door.

'Temper, temper,' she muttered to herself, grinning from ear to ear as she made her way out.

Once outside, she tapped in Steve Doherty's number on her phone, determined to tell him all she knew. No signal. Drat.

The wall of the house was preventing her finding a signal. Surely, she could find one somewhere in these spacious gardens. Perhaps around the back?

There was a kitchen to one side, an empty place with deep white sinks, left over from the Victorian age when servants provided the cogs in the wheel and outnumbered the family they served.

Turning away from the kitchen and the house, she made her way down the path and out of a walled garden. On the other side of an arched door turned silver by centuries of English weather, she found herself in a vegetable garden. A path led back round to the front terraces, and she would have tried phoning again, but the greenhouses caught her eye.

They were huge, dominated by one that was much bigger than the others. The greenery pressed thick and dark against the glass panes. Like plants from *Day of the Triffids*, she thought, about to pull up their roots, escape and eat someone.

Like the house, the area around the structures and inside seemed deserted.

Pots of fresh earth, waiting for new bulbs or seeds for next spring, sat on tables just inside the door of the first two. There were seed trays, specimen pots, cardboard boxes of plants, packets of seeds and bulbs pulled from the earth and nestling in brown paper bags tied up with string.

The smell of turned earth mingled with the stink of a compost heap. Freshly mildewed cabbage leaves lay like a floppy hat on top the rotting pile.

Wrinkling her nose, she stepped past it and headed for the second greenhouse, then the third — the largest and most interesting.

Sandbags were heaped around the door. She remembered they used to pile them around bomb shelters and gun posts in the Second World War. They were meant to protect a place from bomb blasts. A first-aid box was nailed to a post next to a jeep covered with a camouflage net: all terribly military.

The wall of sandbags hid a Perspex door. Sacks. She wondered if they had held something else before they'd held sand. There was no way she could check. Her attention turned to the door. It had a handle, and handles were meant to be used. Like Alice, she pushed it open and entered Wonderland — of a sort.

Moist air hit her face like a damp blanket taking her breath away. The smell of vegetation, growing thickly and roof high, was too strong, the humidity too thick to breathe — exactly as she imagined a jungle would feel.

The effect was so real that she stopped and listened, half expecting the chattering of monkeys or the screech of parakeets.

'Me Jane. Where Tarzan?' she whispered under her breath. She took a few more steps and looked up. No sign of a beefcake wearing a pillowcase around his loins.

The humidity seemed to solidify as the door slid silently shut behind her.

The narrow path between the huge greenery petered out just a few feet from the door. If she was to go on, she would have to part the thick foliage Great White Hunter style; a machete would have been useful.

No, she decided, stepping back. It was too dark in there. Too real.

It suddenly occurred to her that Charlborough might keep wild animals in here. The Marquis of Bath kept a whole menagerie at Longleat; lions, tigers and leopards prowled the grounds. Who knows what you could keep in a small jungle!

'Now's the time to panic.' She uttered the words in the weeniest whisper, and even that seemed too intrusive in this strange jungle hidden on an English estate.

Was it hidden?

If so, why?

She started backtracking on autopilot. She could have turned round. Going forwards was always quicker than going backwards. But she didn't have eyes in the back of her head and she *needed* to see what was behind her. Just in case . . .

'Halt!'

Her breath stopped!

Her heart stopped!

Her feet certainly did. It was as though she'd backed into a barn door — one made of oak — big, hard and locked!

It took a big scoop of courage to make her turn round.

Facing this human barrier was worse than not doing so. Chiselled features, chiselled body, as though roughly hewn from rock. Being eye to eye with his pecs was disconcerting. Raising her eyes failed to improve matters.

'You are trespassing.' His voice was higher than she'd expected, as though his larynx had suffered a severe blow. The two didn't go well together. If her legs hadn't been shaking, she might have laughed. Instead she played her trump card, the acceptable excuse.

'I'm working with the police with regard to the disappearance of an American tourist.' She chanced a grin and a casual shake of her head. 'Just thought he might have wandered in here — you know how these Americans can be.'

She hoped he didn't detect the last trace of the accent she'd inherited from her father years ago.

'What's happening here?'

A draught of fresh air heralded the arrival of Sir Andrew. For a moment he took in the situation. Alarm flashed in his eyes then was gone. His smile was controlled.

'I thought you'd gone, Mrs Driver.'

Her heart stopped racing. A suitable excuse leaped from her tongue.

'Mr St John Gervais wished to take one last look at your clock. He's pretty upset about losing it. I said I would ask your permission. No one came to the door when I knocked, so I came around here. I thought I saw someone here . . .' She threw a tight smile in the direction of the stone man. 'And I did.'

'Trevor is my butler, gardener and anything else I require him to be.' He turned to the man. 'That will be all, Trevor. Mrs Driver is just leaving.'

Sir Andrew took a firm grip on her arm. It wasn't quite frogmarching, but not far off. She'd been aware that Trevor was carrying something, but hadn't stirred up enough courage to notice what it was. Now she saw him toss a small sack onto a pile of other sacks. It rolled off and something rolled out.

Trevor cussed.

Honey gasped.

Eyes starred up at her from a severed head.

Her legs wobbled. Her head swam. She needed air. Fresh air. Right now!

CHAPTER 21

Andrew Charlborough couldn't help chuckling at the woman's reaction to one of the many props they used in their war games. The head had been made of latex of course.

Her surprise had been prolonged, even after he'd told her it wasn't real and what it was used for.

Longleat had its wild beasts and extensive grounds in which to keep them. Most of the estate surrounding Charlborough Grange had been sold off years ago. War games complete with a pretend jungle and bodies provided a decent income; besides which, he enjoyed them. It took him back to other times and other places. He'd explained all this to Hannah Driver. He'd seen her recover, seen her blush and then seen her off the premises.

Amateur sleuths were the least of his worries. His features hardened as he watched the car pull away. Once it had gone, he went back along the corridor to the study. From his pocket he took a neatly folded cotton handkerchief, the initials LTC embroidered in dark red at its corner. Gently he wiped the handkerchief over Lance's photograph before straightening it. He fingered its frame.

'God, Lance. I do miss you,' he said, his voice trembling with emotion.

Suddenly he became aware that he was no longer alone. 'You're an obsessive! Do you know that?'

Pamela's strident voice pierced his sorrow and his skull. She sashayed toward him, hips rolling, blonde hair clipped tightly around her pronounced cheekbones.

His face reddened. 'Get out of here!'

She blew fiercely on the cigarette she was smoking.

'It's your own fault he stays away from here, you know. You're too overbearing. The boy wants to lead his own life. And why shouldn't he? What's it to you, darling? Eh? If you really, really think about it, what's it to you?'

Her husband's eyes followed her as she walked around the room purposely tapping the corner of each framed photograph so it no longer hung straight.

'You don't have an answer!' she said with a light laugh. 'I've heard how you talk to him, insisting that he toe the line or else . . . and the dear boy . . . he so loves his father . . . HIS FATHER!'

She laughed like a gurgling drain, and Sir Andrew shot daggers at her across the room.

She came closer and purposely blew smoke into his face then rested her hand on his chest. 'What if he knew the truth? I wonder how much he would love you then. Because I know, you know. I met Mary's brother-in-law. He told me what he suspected. Now,' she said, a painted fingernail tapping the matching colour on her lips, 'perhaps I should tell the police about this before I tell Lance. Or should I phone that woman and tell her?' Her expression hardened. 'What's it worth not to tell either of them, Andrew? Eh? Fifty thousand? One hundred thousand?' She shook her head. 'Chicken feed. And this chicken deserves more than that, I think.'

Andrew clenched his jaw as he gazed down into his wife's face.

'Marriage to you has been torture, Pamela.'

Her eyes opened wide with feigned surprise. 'What else did you expect? I didn't marry you because I loved you. It was all for money. For your beautiful, beautiful money! What else! And when we divorce, I'll take half of it with me.'

'Over my dead body you will!'

'Your dead body! Wonderful. Could you possibly arrange that, and I'll forego the divorce? After all, I'd much rather be a seriously rich widow than a moderately rich divorcee.' She patted his chest. 'How's your heart, darling?' She laughed. 'Silly me. You don't have one. At least, not as far as your wife is concerned. You only love your son . . . if he is your son.'

'Pamela, have pity . . .'

She stopped and pouted. 'Pity has a price, darling. Think about it.'

She was still laughing when she left the room. Andrew's face hardened as he stared after her, and thoughts of what he'd like to do to her roared through his mind.

* * *

Mark Conway looked up at the ceiling. The room held only a bed, a chair and a low table. The rest of the house was divided up into flats. This was where they always met, where he would sate his physical desires and she would tell him of her contempt for her husband, his employer. He would listen. Just listen and not make comment.

Her fingers continued to trace circles over his chest. Her voice was low and huskily enticing. He knew the sex had been good for her. She'd told him so. Now she was saying other things, things that filled him with dread.

'I wish he was dead. How easy would it be to kill him? You could kill him, Mark. Just think . . .' Her lips were full but cold on his. Strange he hadn't noticed that before. 'If he were dead, we could spend all day in bed. All day. Every day. And we'd have all his money. How easy would it be to kill him, do you think?'

'Easy,' he said, because he knew it was the truth. 'Very easy. But then, why should I? He's very good to me. He's always been very good to me.'

Her tongue flicked at his ear. 'Because, my darling, if he were dead you'd have me.'

'And you would have all his money.'

'That's right. Just me.'

'What about Lance?'

'What about Lance? No doubt he'd get something, but nowhere near what he's been used to. I'd get the lion's share.'

'You sound very sure of that.'

She smiled like a cat as her hand slid down over his loins and did delicious things between his thighs.

He moaned as though never before had he experienced such ecstasy.

'Because I know something that you don't. I know that all Andrew's money could easily become mine.'

CHAPTER 22

First, she dropped Casper off. He'd thrown his head back and laughed like a drain when she'd told him about the plastic head and the war games in the greenhouse.

'My dear, never have I see you look so pale.'

'Not a word to a soul.'

Placing his right hand across his chest and adopting a suitably serious expression, he made a promise.

'In the interests of our continuing harmony,' he added.

She was surprised to see that Doherty was waiting for her when she got back to the hotel.

Plastering a smile on her face, she trotted into the small room just off the main lounge which she kept for business appointments.

A tray of coffee, brown sugar and cream sat on a tray in front of him.

She could tell by the look on his face that this was not entirely a social visit.

'I would have preferred a whisky,' he said, jerking his chin in the direction of the untouched tea.

'You could have asked for one.'

'I did. Your mother turned me down.'

'Oh! I'll get you one.'

'Never mind.' He stood up looking grim faced. 'I haven't time to hang around.'

'Really?' she said flippantly. 'Who's been murdered?'

His expression told her that she'd hit the nail on the head.

'I told the chief constable I didn't have time for all this, but he insisted I inform you.'

His bluntness stung.

She was just as blunt back. 'So inform me.'

'Mervyn Herbert.'

'In the river?'

Doherty shook his head. 'No. In his own garden under the rockery. There'd been a gas leak and the gas company dug up the garden. And before you ask, his head was bashed in and he had a sack over his head. A spice sack, same as before.'

'Poor man.'

She'd only met Mervyn Herbert in passing and hadn't much warmed to him. But still, he was another human being and had met a pretty dreadful fate.

'Surely Mrs Herbert must have noticed some disturbance.'

'No. She sleeps at the front down in the basement. Didn't hear a thing.'

'Is she telling the truth? I'd get rid of him if he was my husband.'

'Understandable, but the lab boys tell me they don't think he was murdered there, and Mrs Herbert is in a bit of a state.'

'And there is that first husband to think about.'

'Oh yes. Loretta's father.'

Her stomach rumbled. She'd been thinking of smoked salmon salad all the way back from Limpley Stoke. No time. She grabbed a handful of peanuts from a dish on the bar. 'Mind if I go with you?'

'I'm fine with that, but I should warn you that until we've done a thorough investigation, we have to treat her as a suspect.'

'Even though the murder was done elsewhere?'

He shrugged. 'In the house, in the garage, or even outside in the alley. Who knows? A thorough search is underway.'

'I take it you've already questioned her?'

'The doctor wouldn't let me. Said she was in deep shock.'

'There,' she said, swinging her bag over her shoulder. 'All the more reason for taking me with you. It might help calm the poor woman. Even if she is your prime suspect.'

'I didn't say she was my *prime* suspect.'

'As an accessory with her first husband? Loretta's father?'

They were out on the street. He frowned. 'Are you by any chance a mind reader?'

'Only as far as men are concerned.'

'I feel the same about women.'

On the drive there, she told him about her visit to the vicar, but not about snooping in the greenhouse. She'd never live it down. She'd tell him what was relevant.

'Elmer's wife's sister was Sir Andrew's first wife. He went calling at the Grange, though everyone's denying it. Pamela Charlborough denied knowing him until I mentioned a witness who saw her meeting Elmer when he was wandering around the churchyard.'

'Is that right?'

'So says Mrs Quentin.'

'Useful person, Mrs Quentin.'

Honey made a sound of agreement and looked out of the window. The early morning rain had disappeared. A rainbow twinkled above the viaduct taking the railway line to London via Green Park. The air smelled fresh and new.

Doherty appeared to be thinking. 'And do you think he was having an affair with Lady Pamela?'

'Of course not! If he visited Charlborough Grange at all, or if he talked over the church wall to Lady Pamela, it would be something to do with his family. He was keen on what he was doing. Perhaps found an old family skeleton and got bumped off for it.'

Doherty shook his head. 'Too melodramatic. OK, so he'd planned an activity holiday — if you can call it that. Believe me, the root of the problem is at Ferny Down Guest House. Mervyn Herbert was a sleazebag — too fond of his stepdaughter, from what I can gather. I want to know where her father is. He's got something to do with this. I can smell it.'

Honey chewed at her lip rather than say outright that she thought he was talking out of the back of his head.

Doherty noticed. 'Are you worried or hungry?'

'I didn't have breakfast.'

Doherty tutted. 'The most important meal of the day!'

Honey's head turned sharply. 'Did my mother ask you whether you were married?'

'No. She asked me whether I prefer carpet or hard stone floors.'

Honey groaned and rolled her eyes.

He looked intrigued and turned his eyes from the road. 'What?'

'Look where you're going.'

A blue double-glazing van veered away into the nearside lane. The driver gestured with one hand and shouted something about getting a driving license.

They reached their destination all too quickly. Feeling as though her heart was somewhere behind her belly button, Honey held back, waiting for Doherty to get out of his car and ring the doorbell.

Two uniformed policemen were standing guard outside.

She nodded a brief acknowledgement. They nodded back and eyed Doherty as he approached them.

She'd never been present at the scene of a crime. What would she see? Hopefully the body had already been taken to the morgue. One fright per day was more than enough. She had to say something trivial to steady her nerves.

'That doorbell's been well polished,' she said.

Doherty looked at her.

'People clean things like there's no tomorrow when they're nervous or in shock.'

Wasn't that one of her mother's observations? She winced. The older she got the more she realised that one generation took on the baggage — and mundane sayings — of the one before.

Loretta answered the door. Her clothes were basically as before and she had colour in her cheeks. The numerous rings she wore glinted as she shut the front door. The expression of teenage disdain was unchanged.

'Ma's out back,' she said brusquely. 'Straight down there.'

A single solitaire diamond flashed on her index finger as she pointed in that direction.

'Nice ring. Is it new?'

Loretta blushed. 'A present. From a mate.'

A male mate, Honey decided, and intimate. Only intimacy brought that bright a red to a girl's cheeks.

Cora Herbert was sitting in her favourite spot in the conservatory. A mug of tea and an ashtray sat on the table in front of her. Beyond the door men in jumpsuits methodically moved earth from one part of the garden to another.

The thick black lashes had left traces of mascara on her damp cheeks. A pall of cigarette smoke rose and circled in the air. The cigarette trembled as she flicked the length of ash into the tray. She looked grim, tired, her eyes outlined in a red that almost matched her lipstick. Black roots ran like a basalt valley through her hair parting. The rest was dry, blonde and in need of a wash.

Honey's throat was like sandpaper. 'I'm so sorry for your loss, Mrs Herbert.'

Both she and Doherty took a seat. Tea wasn't offered. The room was stuffy and filled with smoke. The door was shut, the smoke seeking escape through a fanlight set in the plastic roof.

Cora nodded an acknowledgement.

Doherty opened the questioning. 'When did you last see your husband, Mrs Herbert?'

Honey was instantly reminded of a famous painting, the one where Oliver Cromwell's men are asking a young boy, the whereabouts of his father, Charles I.

'I've already told you that,' Cora snapped.

All resemblance to a royal painting flew out of the window. Cora was, to put it mildly, rough around the edges. She looked more like Cromwell.

'Tell me again,' Doherty said slowly.

Listening to his line of questioning decided her. She nudged his arm. 'Can I have a word in private?'

Doherty pursed his lips. Yet again this was a different Steve to the one who let loose in a local bar. This was his profession. He'd trained for it, started at the bottom and worked his way up. Whereas she . . .

He looked as though he were about to refuse. Whatever made him change his mind could be down to the old adage that two heads were better than one. Or did he really think he was in with a good chance of going to bed with her? Either way, they made their excuses and went out into the garden, shutting the door behind them.

Not that Cora seemed to care — smoking, staring at the floor and flicking ash onto the ugly carpet. She didn't seem actually upset, just anxious, as though she wanted this to be over, and the quicker the better.

Skirting the heap of dug-up earth, they made their way to the far end of the garden, where a plastic gnome peered through a canopy of rhubarb leaves.

Honey folded her arms. 'What's this all about?'

Doherty adopted a blank look. 'I don't know what you mean.'

'Liar!'

He shrugged and spread his hands. 'What?'

Honey eyed him accusingly. 'OK. Don't explain. Let me guess. Bath Hotels Association asked for a police officer within the force to work with them on their idea, you were ordered to volunteer because you didn't do too well on your last case. And then . . .'

He opened his mouth to protest.

'And then,' Honey went on, determined to have her say though it was pure speculation, 'when Elmer Maxted's body was found, you determined to hold on to the case. You saw it as a means to repair your reputation. That's why I'm here, isn't it? You don't like the Hotels Association sticking its nose in but will tolerate it for your own selfish reasons.'

He began to laugh, bending from the waist, lower arm across his belly. 'Wh . . . a . . . t?'

Honey was unmoved. 'And now we have the laughing policeman!'

The look in his eyes contradicted what the rest of his body was doing. The eyes certainly had it, and that was what she would judge him by.

'Don't ever go on the stage.' She headed back for the conservatory, satisfied that the air between them was at last clear.

All the same, she was feeling uneasy. The whole scenario had changed. This wasn't just about a misplaced tourist. It wasn't even about the likelihood that Elmer had been mugged and murdered purely by chance. Such things rarely happened in Bath. For the most part the city was peopled by the cultured, the civilized and the upwardly mobile, or that was what people preferred to believe.

On the face of it this second murder had nothing to do with tourism. This was outside her experience and made her nervous.

'I've had second thoughts,' said Doherty from behind her as they headed back. 'Mrs Herbert has to be the prime suspect. Who else would plant their husband in their own garden?'

Although tempted to slam the door on him, Honey left it open. Irritating as he was, Cora's cigarette smoke was worse.

Cora was sitting in exactly the same position as when they'd left her. Goodness knows how many cigarettes she'd consumed in their absence. She had good reason to be on a chain-smoking marathon. Her eyes were watery and had a vague look. Despite the make-up, her complexion was greasy and white.

'I didn't do it,' she said before anyone had asked her.

'So how did he get there?' asked Doherty.

Cora's eyes popped like marbles. 'How the hell should I know?'

Loretta lurked in the background, leaning against the wall, arms folded, her expression as dark as her mother's flaking mascara.

Doherty was sounding serious. 'I'm afraid you're going to have to come into the station for further questioning.'

Honey could find no words of sympathy and nothing helpful to say like, 'It's surely a mistake,' or 'I shouldn't worry if I were you.' The evidence was damning. Like Doherty had said, who else would plant their husband in the garden?

'I'll walk back,' Honey said once they were outside and Mrs Cora Herbert had been helped into the back seat of a police car.

Doherty shrugged. 'Please yourself.' He turned to Loretta. The girl's face was expressionless, as though she were still digesting what was going on.

'What about you?'

Loretta's bright eyes narrowed and her red lips twisted into a contemptuous snarl. 'I don't travel with pigs. Tell her I'll call in when I'm passing.' She stood on tiptoe and shouted at her mother. 'I'll be down to see you, Ma! You can count on it!'

Honey caught the sudden sob in her voice. 'Will you be all right?'

'I'll get down there later. Mum would want me to take care of things.' She jerked her head back at the 'No Vacancy' sign. 'We're expecting paying guests. Have to look after them, don't I?'

'You're a good daughter. It must be upsetting. I think you're very brave.'

Loretta shrugged again, causing the straps of her top to slide down over her thin shoulders. 'Not really. I know she didn't do it. There's no evidence.'

She stated this confidently, standing with her arms still folded protectively across her chest, her head held high. Was that a smile Honey could see wavering around her lips?

Her smile vanished when she saw the enquiring look on Honey's face.

'Don't look at me like that!'

'I'm sorry.'

It wouldn't do to leave on a negative note. She forced a smile.

Her eyes dropped back to the flashing diamond. At least, it looked like a diamond.

'That's a pretty ring,' she said, trusting her sudden change of subject didn't sound too contrived.

The comment lifted Loretta's heavily made-up face. 'Nice, ain't it?'

She flashed the ring. 'My dad gave me it,' she said in a strange and dreamy kind of way.

Her first thought was that Robert Davies must have come into a nice sum of money to have afforded such a flashy ring. She didn't say that. 'That's nice. Were you close to your dad?'

'Yep!'

'But not to Mervyn.'

Loretta's expression darkened into a deep scowl. 'A prime-time creep!'

Honey imagined the affect Loretta's skimpy attire might have had on Mervyn Herbert. He had the look of a lecher about him.

'Did he bother you?' It sounded ineffectual, stupid to her own ears, so Loretta's response did not surprise her.

'No,' she said, shaking her head, a sarcastic smile twitching around her mouth. 'But he was always trying it on. Couldn't keep his bloody 'ands to 'imself.'

CHAPTER 23

Honey murmured and stretched her tired body. The sound of surf brushing over a golden beach changed suddenly.

Funny, she thought languorously. *The sea sounds just like my telephone at home . . .*

Drat!

Just when a gorgeous hunk was handing her a long, cool drink, the dream was broken.

Swearing under her breath, she switched on the light and reached for her watch — 12.32 a.m. The phone was still purring. Drawing her other hand from beneath the thick layers of sheets, blankets and satin eiderdown, she eased herself up against the pillows and reached for it.

'Hope you weren't doing anything special.'

Doherty!

'Just sleeping.' Well, actually, she'd been dreaming of him, but had no intention of further inflating his ego.

'At this time of night?'

She rolled over onto her side, cuddling the phone against her cheek. 'Stephen! I do sometimes go to bed before midnight!'

'Do you?'

He sounded genuinely surprised. The truth was she was tired out after serving a party of history buffs holding their annual bash. History was sometimes viewed as dry; the historians ensured their throats were always wet. Run off her feet this evening, dreaming of him had provided a little light relief.

'Look, Stephen, running a hotel and being a sleuth—'

'An amateur sleuth.'

'Thank you . . . is quite burdensome. Anyway, what do you want?'

There was a pause. 'I've had a heavy day. You know, Mrs Herbert and all that.'

Honey pulled herself up into a more comfortable sitting position. 'Is she still being questioned?' She frowned at the thought of poor Cora ending up in a cell on a bed that wasn't her own.

'There've been developments.'

It was too much to hope that Mervyn Herbert had been a random killing.

That didn't excuse Doherty ringing her at this hour, and she wouldn't declare that she was attracted to him. Let him make the running. Let him tell her what the 'professional' detectives were up to.

'Well? Are you going to tell me?'

'Yes,' he answered in such a robust fashion that she assumed he was slightly tipsy. 'But only if you agree to meet me at the Zodiac.'

Swallowing the first jolt of excitement, she groaned as though he was the last person she wanted to see. Not true, but necessary with a man like him. Anyone could see he was vain. Even his female work colleagues drooled over him. Worse still, he knew the effect he had.

'I don't know . . .' She forced herself to sound reluctant.

'The night's still young. And so are we.'

'I don't feel young.'

'Let's live while we can.'

She thought about it. Two dead bodies in less than six weeks. Life was certainly getting precarious. Could she? Should she?

She glanced at the clock. Not yet one o'clock.

She swung her legs out of bed. 'Give me twenty minutes — no, thirty. It's a pretty long walk unless I get a taxi.'

'No need to do either. I'm parked outside.'

* * *

A pale-green silk sweater, jeans and loafers, plus a quick brushing of her hair and she was ready. She popped on pearl earrings as an afterthought. Classy.

As he drove, she blinked at the impatient city where visitors still wandered taking in the atmosphere, and late-night revellers and theatregoers headed for nightclubs or a taxi home.

Doherty was driving extremely steadily though no van drivers were honking their horns at him. Not that many van drivers made deliveries at one in the morning.

'How many have you had to drink?'

'Two small ones.'

A borderline case of drink-driving? She wasn't sure, but she wasn't chancing it.

'Can we go for a walk?' she said suddenly. 'I don't really feel like a drink.'

He gave in without a fight. 'OK.'

They headed for Pulteney Bridge, parked the car and got out. He automatically offered her his arm and she took it. Not a word passed between them. Honey was comfortable with that. She presumed he was musing over the day's events, but also enjoying making her wait for what he had to say.

They stopped and took in what they could see of the bridge and the river.

Doherty leaned on the parapet and fixed his gaze on the lights reflected in the river. 'Mrs Herbert's out of the picture. Pathology confirmed a time of death when she was out at bingo.'

'So, what next?'

'We're looking for Mrs Herbert's first husband, Robert Davies. He's a dead cert for doing it.'

'Because of Loretta?'

He looked at her blankly. Her stomach churned.

'He's not long out of prison, and he's very protective about his daughter . . .'

A breeze blowing off the river whipped her hair across her face. It was too late. He'd twigged there was something she'd left unsaid.

Leaning forward, his hands resting on the parapet, he looked up into her face.

'You know something I don't. I can see it in your eyes.'

'You can't see my eyes.'

'Do I have to beat it out of you? I can play good cop, bad cop if called upon.'

She sighed. 'Can I call upon you to buy me a coffee instead?'

'Yeah. Sure.'

His gaze wandered to the other side of the river. 'Look at the river. The current runs faster at its edges. I reckon Elmer came down on the current on this side. If the current is just as strong upstream as it is here, then the body could have been put in anywhere along that stretch. But that piece of wood came down with it.' He stood thoughtfully for a moment.

'And Mervyn Herbert?'

He shook his head. 'Seems like the same killer if the sack over his head and traces of coriander are anything to go by. That's a herb, isn't it?'

She told him it was and thought of Jeremiah. The sacks had to have come from him.

Before she had chance to mention it, Doherty stepped in.

'We questioned a spice stall in the market about their sacks.'

'The owners wouldn't have a motive, would they?'

'Not at this moment, they don't. But who knows? Something may crop up.'

Honey thought of Jeremiah and Ade. What motive would they have?

She rubbed at her forehead and tried to work out where this was going. Being dragged out of bed for midnight walks didn't happen very often. It was something lovesick teenagers did when they couldn't afford anything else after a lively night out.

'So you think Loretta's father murdered both Elmer *and* Mervyn?'

'I think so. The spice sacks link them. And Davies has a record.'

'So do a lot of people.'

'Do you?'

He looked faintly surprised, as though he were half expecting her to admit to something vaguely criminal.

'Not a criminal one. I just carry a lot of baggage — you know, failed marriage, widowed, raising a kid, mad mother . . .'

'I wouldn't say you were mad.'

'I meant my mother!'

'No need to snap.'

'Sorry.' She rubbed at her frowning forehead again.

'Right. Now, what is it you know that I don't?'

He sounded insistent. She wondered if he would drag her down to the station for questioning if she didn't spill the beans and made a snap decision. 'Blow the coffee. I reckon Loretta Davies might have been abused by her stepfather. There's definitely no love lost between them.'

Doherty raised his eyebrows and his jaw dropped. 'Christ! You've just given me the best motive in the world. Revenge. And who could blame the man?'

'Mervyn deserving what he got won't keep Loretta's father from prison. But why murder Elmer?'

Doherty grunted. 'He got in the way.'

Late-night revellers chose that moment to come skipping along the promenade like six-year-olds. Every so often they leaped up at the flower baskets hanging from the lamp posts, hitting them with their hands and sending them swinging.

Doherty waited for them to skip on by before continuing.

'Mrs Herbert told us at first that Mervyn had gone to the pub. The Green Park Tavern — a favourite of mine, so it happens.'

Honey nodded. The Green Park Tavern was a fair walk from the guest house towards the viaduct and the train station.

'She told me that,' said Honey. 'He did it quite regularly.'

'When did she tell you?'

'The first time I went there, when Mr Bernstock, as he was then, went missing. Mervyn shot off at the same time. I presumed he was avoiding me — you know, just another busybody to blight his days. Obviously, that wasn't quite the case.'

Suddenly the scene that day came back in full clarity. 'Oh my God!'

'God's not here. Just me. What's the problem?'

'He was helping some men from the council take out a large chest freezer. It was being dumped. I never saw him after that.'

Doherty flicked open his phone, punched the shortcut button and immediately introduced himself and what he wanted.

'Check the file. Where's Davies working?'

There was a pause as the lowly police officer on the other end obeyed and checked the particulars.

Something was said that she couldn't hear. Doherty didn't look too pleased.

'That's all it says? The council? Didn't anyone think to check which department?'

Obviously not. He slammed his phone shut.

'Chimps. The lot of them. Qualified by a bit of paper, and they're all bloody chimps!'

'Never mind. You already know that there's nothing in the freezer now.'

'Absolutely.'

Doherty's arm brushed around her back. She took it as a signal to resume their walk. He was surprisingly serious as he talked, his eyes now fixed on the ground in front of them.

If he was being 'fresh', as her mother used to say, he showed no sign of it apart from the encircling arm. He was into his subject, recounting what had happened — as related by Mrs Herbert.

'Sometimes, when he'd had enough of Bath and tourists, or when her former husband was threatening to bash his head in, Mervyn used to jump on a train.'

'Where to?'

'Anywhere. Two days or so and he returned. But not this time. Then Davies turned up and was more than pleased that he wasn't coming back. Offered to move back in. Loretta was all for it. Cora didn't seem opposed to it either. They could have worked in collusion.'

'What makes you think that?'

'He's scarpered! That's a sign of guilt if ever there was. Probably in Mervyn's Volvo estate. We haven't found that either.'

'The moment the body came to light.'

'That's it. And now what you've just told me about Mr Herbert possibly raping his stepdaughter . . .' Doherty only barely refrained from punching the air with his fist. 'It's him! It has to be him!'

CHAPTER 24

'Good evening.'

Honey smiled as she greeted diners arriving for dinner in the restaurant of the Green River Hotel. Most were guests, but Smudger the chef knew his stuff, so there was always a smattering of locals wanting to sample his seafood thermidor or his heaven-sent white-chocolate mousse with orange liqueur.

Mary Jane had two weeks before she went back to the US for a while. She came floating in wearing a strawberry-pink chiffon, and her long feet were encased in Roman-style gold sandals, the straps of which finished in a knot halfway up her shins. A septuagenarian, Mary Jane intended growing old outrageously.

A look of contentment suffused her gaunt features, and her eyes glittered with a far-seeing look — totally suiting a woman who claimed to number ghosts among her friends. The incumbent of her regular room had left, and she had immediately changed rooms. Once again, it was left to her and Sir Cedric.

Room 5 was spooky; there was no other way to describe it. Honey disliked the high wooden ceiling and the silly closets that were lacking in depth and had no room to hang clothes. She planned to renovate during the off-season.

Sensing her plans would not be welcome, she had not yet mentioned this to Mary Jane.

'Sorry I'm a little late coming down,' said Mary Jane in her lazy Californian drawl.

Close up, her eyes shone with unworldly brightness. Honey guessed what was coming, and it had no grounding in reality.

'I have been conversing in the most intimate terms with dearest, darling, Sir Cedric,' she said, her eyelashes fluttering and her long fingers resting on her ribcage. Her voice dropped to a whisper. 'He has confided some really scandalous family secrets.'

Honey feigned awestruck interest and adopted the same hushed voice. 'Is that so?' At the same time, she guided the elderly and very tall lady to her usual table, where her long legs and torso folded obediently into a chair.

'Indeed. He had three wives, you know!'

She tittered like old ladies are prone to do when scandals are on the agenda — though it had to be said, Mary Jane did not quite fit the image of a comfortable old lady.

Honey handed her the menu. 'He didn't chop off their heads, did he? You know, like Henry VIII?'

'Oh, no,' came the adamant reply. Her expression was deadly serious. 'It was very naughty, and I've been sworn to secrecy.'

'Then I won't pressure you,' said Honey smiling.

'But I must tell you this,' said Mary Jane, her sinuous fingers locking over Honey's arm. 'I'm going on one of these fabulous ghost walks this evening. It visits some of the places Sir Cedric has told me about. Would you like to come along?' she asked, eyes of periwinkle blue youthfully bright in her wrinkled face.

Honey eyed the steadily filling restaurant. 'I don't know whether I've got time for that.'

Mary Jane looked crestfallen. 'I quite understand, my dear. Now let me see,' she said, rummaging in her solidly square bag. 'I have a bus timetable here somewhere . . .'

Honey couldn't be mean.

'No need for the bus. I can spare ten minutes to give you a lift.'

'Oh good.' The voluminous bag was snapped shut. 'Your mother said you would.'

Honey maintained her smile through gritted teeth. It galled to find out she'd already been volunteered before she'd had chance to offer.

She might have stayed prickly if her eyes hadn't clapped on John Rees. He was wearing a smart but casual cream linen shirt with shoulder tabs. It gave him a faintly military kind of look.

'How are ya?' he said, getting to his feet and shaking her hand.

She wanted to say, *All the better for meeting you*, but she didn't.

'I'm very well. And you?'

She held the professional smile. He might be here just to sample the food. And anyway, once she came back down to earth, her gaze strayed to his partner.

The woman was slim — not just in a *thin* way, but glossy, as though a copy of *Vogue* had fallen open and the model had stepped out fully fleshed.

She was sipping water and her eyes were downcast. The latter were perfectly made-up — dark smudges in all the right places, lashes as thick as furry caterpillars.

'Miriam,' he said by way of introduction. 'This is Honey Driver, who owns this fantastic place.'

Miriam nodded, murmured good evening, but didn't look up. Honey resisted clenching her jaw. After all, what did it matter if she'd been fantasizing about their assignation at his bookshop. The stuff he'd wanted to adorn his walls beside the artworks and books had already been collected. OK, it was by invitation only, but it was still basically a public event. Anyone could go in and buy tickets, but at the back of her mind . . . well, she could dream.

'I'm looking forward to the open evening,' she gushed, keeping her smile trained on gorgeous John.

'So am I.'

There was something about his manner that was different. He smiled but his features were stiff. She guessed he was coping with tension, and Miriam, his glossy, bronzed companion with her black hair and red lips, was the cause of it.

Feeling disappointed, Honey excused herself. Waltzing around the restaurant, she was a picture of solicitous charm. And waltzing around in her head was the same recurring thought. Why were all the best guys already spoken for?

Lindsey was supervising the bar. As usual she dispensed drinks and opened bottles of wine swiftly and efficiently. She never mixed up orders and never panicked.

She was tipping a measure of Harvey's Bristol Cream into a schooner, the largest of the sherry measures. Honey knew without being told that it was for Mary Jane, who had developed a passion for the very English drink. No doubt a little spirit inside would prepare her for the spirits she might encounter on her ghost walk.

'Your friend the bookseller has company,' said Lindsey, her eyes travelling to John Rees and back to her mother.

Honey rested her elbow on the bar and sighed. 'And there was I thinking I might get the opportunity to eat him alive.'

'You don't mean that. Personally, my preference is for the rugged, silent type. I like the cop.'

'Don't let Gran hear you say that. She won't like it.'

'The fact that I'm giving my mother the benefit of my experience?' Lindsey leaned forward, arms resting on the bar. 'You need youth on your side, mother. Grandma's talking marriage; I'm talking about having fun.'

'Your grandma's old-fashioned.'

'No she's not. She's a control freak. She doesn't really want you to remarry. I've seen how she works it. Take that businessman who used to come in here. First, she pushed you in his direction, and when you did take an interest, she told you he was like a sailor — a girl in every port.'

'He was.'

'I think she lied. She likes to manipulate.'

It was strange, it was annoying and it was plain bloody cheeky. The game, then, was to keep her daughter on her toes, not to lose her to someone over whom she had no control. So, strong men were out of the question. Only the weak would prevail.

Honey asked, 'So who's the supermodel?'

Lindsey checked the restaurant reservations, running her finger down the page until she found the booking. 'Mr and Mrs Rees.'

'Oh!'

The restaurant was full, and compliments to the chef were coming thick and fast. Honey knew she should have felt supremely smug that things were going so well tonight, but John Rees had punctured her balloon. Steve Doherty was still a contender, but that ego . . . John Rees didn't have one. Or baggage. At least, until tonight.

She was almost glad when the customers thinned out and Mary Jane came tottering over to claim her lift to the ghost walk.

'I hope I'm not inconveniencing you,' she said, the weight of her bony fingers on Honey's arm as light as a feather.

'Of course not,' Honey lied, her eyes sliding sidelong to Mr and Mrs Rees. Their heads were almost touching across the table. Their expressions were intense, not with desire, but with something else. They could have been talking about their marriage; they could just as easily have been disagreeing over the colour scheme for a new kitchen.

Mary Jane folded herself into the car in much the same way as she had her seat in the restaurant. Basically, in three parts — lower legs, upper legs and torso.

A finely crocheted grey cape was draped around her shoulders and fastened with a pin at the front.

Mary Jane chatted all the way, recounting how often she'd contacted Sir Cedric in the privacy of her room. By the time they'd reached Queen Square and the Francis Hotel,

Honey knew all about Sir Cedric's wives and which one Mary Jane was related to.

'Fanny,' she pronounced emphatically. 'Fanny Millington. Bob the Job actually located a picture of her — just a sketch, but enough to tell me she was a handsome woman. She bore Sir Cedric six children. His first wife didn't have any. Apparently, she was fragile. I suppose we'd say that Fanny had good genes.'

'What about the third wife?' Honey asked, purely out of politeness.

'I don't know anything about her genes. Apparently, she ran off with the coachman and the marriage to Sir Cedric was annulled.' Beaming broadly, she shrugged her square, bony shoulders. 'Isn't family history just wonderful!'

Quite a crowd had gathered at the bottom end of Queen Square, just along from the Francis Hotel.

Crocheted cape billowing in the breeze, Mary Jane strode to join the other tourists. The merry band chattered like magpies, quivering with excitement at the prospect of seeing what few had ever seen.

Honey turned the steering wheel, meaning to head back to the hotel, when Loretta Davies emerged from Charlotte Street at the top end of the square. She was wearing a white blouse and a black skirt, regulation uniform for a hotel waitress.

Honey hit the horn and downed the passenger side window. 'Do you want a lift?'

Loretta opened the door and got in. 'Thanks. I've just finished my shift. Working helps keep my mind off things. I've made sure our place keeps going, but you just have to get out, don't you?'

Honey agreed with her.

Despite the uniform, three gold earrings dangled from Loretta's right ear. The white blouse was long enough to cover her belly button. Overall, she was fairly presentable.

It was now nine thirty. She calculated that Loretta had been on duty since mid-afternoon to be going home this early.

'Where do you work?'

'La Traviata.' She slid her feet out of her shoes.

Honey recognised the name of the upmarket Italian restaurant situated behind the world-famous Royal Crescent. 'Me feet are killing me. I've been on since two.'

'Poor you. I didn't know you worked in the catering trade. I presumed you did a bit for your mother.'

'Not bloody likely.'

The smell of trees bathed in darkness drifted into the car. So did the aroma of fast-food joints — hamburgers, kebab shops and tacos bars.

'My mum likes things done her way. She gets Marge in to clean and do the laundry and ironing when it's busy. Especially now. I've hung around and looked after things, but it's only temporary. I had to get out. Honest I did.'

Her voice seemed to nosedive on the last two words. For the first time it occurred to her that Loretta was not quite as confident as she made out. She was hurting. Under the circumstances, it wasn't surprising.

It took guts to ask the next question, but she forced herself. 'What did your mother say — you know, about your stepfather groping you . . . I presume you told her?'

'Not a lot.'

Doherty's line of questioning had turned in that direction the previous night.

'It's understandable for a father to protect his daughter and to get angry if someone hurts her. So where's Loretta's father?' he'd asked.

'How the hell should I know?'

Of course Cora knew. But she'd guessed where the questioning was going. Her first husband had a motive to kill her second husband for abusing Loretta.

She cast her mind back to that night at the Zodiac. 'She's protecting him,' Doherty said.

Honey fingered her glass. 'So if he did it, why bury him in the rockery? Don't you think that's a bit close to home?'

'As good as anywhere. Close to where the incident took place. I reckon he panicked.'

'Are you saying that Cora was an accomplice? She helped hide the body?'

'She's denying it.'

She sipped at her vodka and tonic, thought about it then shook her head. 'I don't see Cora helping her ex-husband. Bury Mervyn right under our noses and hope we don't notice?'

'That's right.' He sounded and looked as though he'd uttered the last word on the matter.

Honey rose to the challenge. 'Did you ever see that rockery? It was ludicrous. No one could help notice a change in its shape.'

He shook his head. 'Not necessarily. Trust me. I'm a policeman.'

'I think you're wrong. I think someone wanted to shift the blame.'

He chuckled and ordered himself another pint. 'You've been reading too much Aggie Christie.'

She sighed. Perhaps he was right. But Ferny Down Guest House had been taken apart for evidence that Mervyn had been murdered on site. Cora and Loretta had been questioned for hours. There was no evidence. Nothing. Doherty had been gutted — hence the call to meet him at the Zodiac Club.

Now here was Loretta sitting beside her, and she couldn't help but feel sorry for Cora Herbert. The poor woman must be suffering more than her business.

They were fast approaching the Lower Bristol Road.

'I'll come in with you if I may,' said Honey. 'Just to see how your mum is bearing up.'

Loretta looked cautious at first. She'd fully expected her to say no. But she didn't.

'I suppose so.'

To Honey's eyes Loretta was no longer the girl with the hard eyes and the blatant attempt to be sluttish. She was a vulnerable little girl.

The porch light was still on when they got there. Loretta had a key. Honey followed her along the passage leading to the rear kitchen and the small sitting room adjoining the conservatory.

There was no one there.

'Mum?'

'I'm in here.'

The response came from Mervyn Herbert's 'den'.

Cora was on her knees tidying up, repacking what the police had unpacked and putting it away. Her backside wobbled against her meaty calves as she did it.

'I hope I'm not interrupting anything.'

Cora stopped what she was doing. Her face hardened when she saw Honey. 'What do you want?'

'I gave Loretta a lift. I just thought I'd see how you were. Is there anything I can do to help?'

'Well, you could start by finding a landscape gardener. My rockery's a right shambles.'

She turned back to what she was doing. 'And these watches, Mervyn's collection thrown all over the place. Everything's a mess. Bloody coppers! Mucking my place up like this. I've got a business to run. It's got to be tidy, you know, or people will think I'm a slob.'

'Yes, I know.' It came out kind of wrong, but clearly housework didn't rate that high on Cora's agenda. She knelt down beside her on the moss-coloured carpet. 'Let me help you.'

Each watch was individually wrapped in old newspaper and repacked in a cardboard box.

They were very nice watches. Watches and clocks. Was there really a link?

'They look quite valuable.'

'I wish,' muttered Cora. 'We'll let the auctioneers tell us what they think. The whole lot's going up for sale.'

'I hope you get a good sum.'

'Load of old junk.' Cora's response was mumbled and begrudging.

'Honestly, Mrs Herbert, specialist collectors might give you quite a bit more than you'd get at auction. I can ask around if you like. In fact, there's a certain name that springs readily to mind. You might know him. Or perhaps Mervyn knew him. He's called Casper St John Gervais?'

Cora shook her head in a vague manner. Not only didn't she know, she didn't really care.

'Never heard of the bloke.'

Honey wondered what Casper would say. *I collect clocks, not watches*, probably. He'd also remark that he never frequented establishments along the Lower Bristol Road.

Honey pressed on. 'Do you think your husband might have known him?'

Cora shrugged and pulled herself up onto her feet. 'I don't know and I don't bloody care!'

The flaps of the box were slapped firmly into place.

Cora averted her eyes.

'I've got things to do,' she said with an air of finality.

Honey got to her feet. 'I'll see myself out.'

She paused in the porch outside the conservatory. Loretta was standing there swigging Coke from a can and staring out into the garden. There was something deeply vulnerable about the girl. There was also something about Cora's behaviour that made her ask a further question.

'Your mother was surprised that you told me about your stepfather and his assaults. Why was that?'

That teenage shrug again, the sort that's meant to signify indifference but in fact conveys deep pain.

'She didn't want me to mention it.'

It was like a gate closing. Not much of an answer, but she sensed it was the only one the teenager was prepared to give.

Outside the night sky had blurred to slate grey, that time in June and July when darkness never quite takes hold.

Honey took deep breaths and looked upwards as she tried to clarify the clues and the people. Some said that a crime was like a jigsaw puzzle; one bit fitted into another.

It was just a case of gathering up the right bits and putting them into the right place. Trouble is, she thought, you have to find the bits in the first place.

For a start, there was Loretta's father. His motive for killing Mervyn Herbert was understandable. But Elmer Maxted? Everything began with the lone American here to trace his family tree. Surely Davies could not have had anything to do with killing him, could he? The watches and clocks situation was also puzzling. Was it just a coincidence that Mervyn collected one and Casper the other?

Loretta's natural father was still nowhere to be found.

She flicked open her phone and dabbed at Casper's number. It rang and he answered — quite quickly, as it happened.

'How well did you know Mervyn Herbert?'

He sounded taken aback at first, but quickly recovered. 'My dear girl, as I've already told you . . .'

'I don't believe you. So! Who are you going to speak to? Me or the police?'

This was all instinct, a long shot. She sensed his unease. She'd asked quickly even before he'd had chance to say hello.

There was a pause, a period when she felt she could almost hear his brain ticking over. If she closed her eyes, she could even see his throat tightening.

'You'd better come on over,' he said.

'I will.'

CHAPTER 25

Pamela Charlborough drank deeply from a lead-crystal wine glass and eyed her husband over its rim. The wine tasted good but did nothing to make him look more appealing.

Once again, she imagined him lying still and white instead of sat at the same table with her, his hair almost white, his face mottled with broken veins. At least if he were dead she would get to keep the lifestyle and the wherewithal to maintain it. In her mind she blessed Merry and Singh Life Insurers. What a boon they were to modern living and the plight of the recently widowed.

Unfortunately, she wasn't widowed. For better or worse — mostly worse — she was still tied firmly to Andrew.

She breathed deeply as the after taste of the wine tantalized her taste buds and fumed upwards into her brain. She opened and closed her eyes as she took deep breaths. Each time she opened them her gaze alighted on things in the room she would keep and things she would throw out once he was dead. It was something she'd done a thousand times, her mind changing as things were added or taken away from the house according to Andrew's dabbling in antiques — most notably clocks.

The stuff from the Far East would be first to go. Whoever would want those dreadful bits of bamboo that threatened to fall over if you brushed too close? There was a table made of it, a coat stand and a matching umbrella stand complete with bamboo-handled umbrellas and walking sticks. She sighed. It was really all too much. The only flimsy things she adored were made of silk, edged with lace and extremely expensive. She still looked good in silky underwear. She smirked to herself. She looked pretty good out of them too.

She poured more wine as the pristinely white porcelain clock on the sideboard struck eight. Both her eyes and those of her husband went to it before looking at each other. A slow smile crossed her husband's face. He was laughing at her, crowing because he'd got it back and grabbed the money from her luggage.

Pamela simmered then snapped.

She raised her wine glass in a mock toast. 'All right, darling! You've got it back. Well, bully for you!'

Andrew was drinking brandy. He swilled the amber liquid around his glass as he regarded her. His smile was contemptuous.

'Really, Pamela. You have no taste and your propensity for seeking out the more seedy side of society is really phenomenal. Fancy selling it to a second-rate clock dealer like Simon Tye. The man's a crook.'

'Necessity!' she snapped. 'You keep me too short of cash.'

'You spend too much.'

Eyes wide and angry, she gripped her wineglass more tightly. 'You give me too little!'

Andrew's gaze went back to the newspaper he'd been reading. He usually read a newspaper when they sat down for the evening meal. It saved having to converse with her.

'My dear, I must have been mistaken. I thought it was cheap to live in Spain. That's why it suits cheap people.'

Pamela sprang up from her chair, sending it toppling backwards.

'I'm not cheap, Andrew! I'm normal!'

Her husband raised his eyebrows over the day's headlines and tutted. 'Don't lose your temper, darling. It emphasises your wrinkles.'

The lead-crystal wine glass flew down the table. Andrew ducked.

'You bitch!'

Pamela stood her ground on four-inch mules, the soles made of cork, the uppers of interwoven pink and blue silk.

Andrew was on her before she could run. The back of his hand hit her face and sent her flying across the table. Hair tousled, eyes blazing and blood trickling from her lip, she glared up at him, her fingers gripping the table edge.

'Why did I marry you?'

Andrew was disdainful. 'Hah! Why did I marry you, more to the point?'

Slowly, she righted herself and pushed her hair back from her eyes. 'But I know why you married me. I was the barrier between your first wife's family and you and Lance. If they probed too close, they'd find out the truth. As a widower you would still have attracted their attention and occasional visits. You remarrying kept them at a distance. And I know why, Andrew. He told me. Elmer Maxted told me!'

His face paled. She knew she'd hit the mark. Clinging to the table edge, she arose from the floor, her eyes shining. Now she was the one with power.

'I know what you did. I know about Lance and who he is — who he really is.'

Andrew's jaw tightened.

Blood trickled into Pamela's mouth when she smiled. For once she was winning.

'I can ruin you any time I like. But it won't cost you much to keep my mouth shut. I like Lance. I wouldn't want to ruin his life.'

Andrew said nothing, his pale eyes darting between her, the drinks cabinet and Mark Conway. Unheard by his wife, Mark was standing in the doorway, listening and waiting. Andrew threw him an unspoken message to stay. Pamela, slightly the worse for drink, carried on with her tirade.

'Lance, the real Lance, bled to death. Haemophilia. It's passed on to them by their mothers: the American told me

Lance had it — or at least the Lance he knew. But our big, grown-up Lance doesn't have it, does he? Oh no, most certainly he does not. In fact, he's an extremely healthy young man. I wonder what his DNA would prove if they took swabs from you and him? But then, you already know the answer to that, don't you?'

'You're drunk,' Andrew said contemptuously.

Pamela laughed. With half a bottle of Château Talbot sloshing around inside her, she staggered to the door. 'Spain, here I come! And I don't give a hoot if I've got to crawl there!'

Gripping the banister, she dragged herself up to her room. 'Spain, sun, sea and sex! Here I come!' She turned round when she got to the top. 'The sex especially!' she shouted, her eyes glittering with the desire to hurt. 'Good sex happens with young men, not old has-beens like you!'

She turned away from him and came face to face with Trevor, her husband's batman and jack-of-all-trades, standing at the top of the stairs. His look was inscrutable.

'What the hell are you staring at?' she shouted, waving her arm in an effort to slap his chest.

'Nothing, madam.'

'*Nothing, madam,*' she mimicked. '*Nothing, madam!*'

Andrew stood quietly at the bottom of the stairs waiting for her to have the final word. He knew she would.

She swayed slightly. He wished she would fall.

She didn't. She hadn't finished yet. She smiled at him over her shoulder. God, but he hated that smile.

'Be a good little husband, Andrew, and transfer some money into my account. Fifty thousand to start with.'

'I don't have adequate funds.'

A cruel smile twisted her lips.

'Then sell a few things. Especially that clock! Yes! I insist you sell that clock in order to buy my silence. Now! Immediately.'

Although her vision was blurred, she saw the hatred on her husband's face.

So what?

She began to laugh then tapped Trevor on the shoulder. 'Your master awaits you — Fido!'

She swayed more unsteadily before staggering off to her bedroom.

The door slammed. Sir Andrew beckoned Trevor to follow him. 'I need to talk to you.'

The two men went into the dining room, closing the door behind them and Mark Conway who then turned and went upstairs.

* * *

'A rare example of a late eighteenth-century mantel clock. Can we start the bidding at one thousand pounds?'

The middle of an auction room was not the best place for asking questions and getting answers. Honey assumed Casper had done it on purpose, especially when their meeting coincided with lot 75.

To her eyes the clock looked incredibly plain, but the tense atmosphere in the saleroom confirmed its importance.

'Its provenance is indisputable,' whispered Casper as though he were in pain.

'It's plain.'

The auctioneers voice filled the room. 'Four thousand three, four thousand four, four thousand five . . .'

Casper was bidding. He did it casually, as though he didn't really care whether he bought it or not. But anyone who knew him was not so easily deceived.

'It is said to have belonged to Jane Austen's father, sold to pay for his burial.'

'I didn't know the church charged that much, seeing as he's buried next to the road.' The graveyard had been peaceful back then, of course. Now visitors could almost do a drive past, it was that close to the A4.

Casper hissed at her to be quiet.

'Sorry. I'll wait for you outside.'

She slipped into the store opposite and purchased a chocolate muffin. Casper wasn't into eating in company so it was a case of grabbing what she could and eating it before he came out.

The traffic was heavy around Queen Square, and the bin hanging from a lamp post received her food wrappers. By the time she was finished, Casper came strolling out of the auction house looking mighty pleased with himself.

'I take it you were successful?'

He nodded. 'Did you doubt that I would be?'

'I wouldn't dare.'

'Now. This fellow Herbert. He is, or rather was, very friendly with a clock and watch dealer named Simon Tye.'

'You never met him yourself?'

He shook his head. 'Absolutely not. I asked Simon Tye. He's had dealings with him once or twice.'

Honey thought of the watches and described them to him. 'Do you think they could be stolen?'

He shrugged. 'Ask the police.'

'There's Simon,' Casper said, pointing to where two men were manhandling a grandfather clock — more accurately named a long case — into the back of a dark-blue Volvo estate. 'I'll introduce you.'

CHAPTER 26

'Is this your car?' she asked the man introduced to her as Simon Tye.

Simon answered her a split second before Casper could butt in, presuming she was going to ask about watches.

'As matter of fact, no. It belongs to a friend.'

'Mervyn Herbert?'

He grinned. 'I know, I know. I should 'ave give it over to the coppers, but I was after this clock and me own jalopy is off the road.'

His blatant honesty astounded her.

'I wanted this clock,' he said on seeing her expression. 'The price was right, and for the mo I had the transport. OK?'

It sounded reasonable enough. But clues were stacking up. He'd known Mervyn. He'd known he'd collected watches. He also knew that his body had been found.

He caught her eyeing him with curiosity. 'Tell them I'll drop it round.'

His cheek amazed her. Her first priority had been to tell Doherty about the watches. Now it was also about finding Mervyn's car.

* * *

The desk sergeant at the police station showed her into an interview room. He also provided her with tea and biscuits.

Honey sucked on a chocolate digestive that she'd just dipped into her tea; not the healthiest diet in the world, but snatched on the hoof.

Through the window she could see the Georgian buildings at the back of Manvers Street. Her eyes travelled slowly over the backyards where weeds grew and stray moggies mated and fought with each other. Down under the houses were deep cellars. Some stretched out under the road and had rough workshops in them behind iron grills. Some were damp, dark and musty. Others had been transformed into rather nice basement apartments, workshops and studios. The best, abutting the main thoroughfares, had become trendy wine bars and upmarket restaurants. The Zodiac Club was one of these.

Doherty breezed in. 'What's up?'

'I saw Mervyn's car this morning.'

He stopped dead in his tracks. 'Where?'

'A chap called Simon Tye said he was only borrowing it and that he would bring it in when he'd finished. He knew Mervyn and Mervyn let him borrow it when he needed to move something big.'

'You're kidding!'

She shook her head. 'A bloody nerve. You'll catch him unloading a clock on the double yellow lines closest to his shop.'

He immediately gave orders to have both the car and Simon Tye picked up.

'I take it from your lack of excitability that he wasn't too nervous about the murder.'

She shrugged. 'No, he wasn't. You can never tell though, can you? After all a Volvo estate is big enough to take a body as well as a long case clock.'

He looked thoughtful. 'Have you got a cellar under your hotel?'

'Yes. I have to store wines somewhere. That's what cellars were originally for.'

He scratched at his stubble which made a reassuringly rasping sound. 'I'm wondering about this piece of wood. The number could very well be the number of the cellar of a house with access to the river. Anyway,' he shrugged, 'might as well follow it up. I've got sod all else to go on, but then that all depends . . .' A flash of triumph lit up his eyes, but he said nothing. Curious, she ploughed on anyway.

'Does Simon Tye live close to the river?'

'I don't think so, but we'll check.'

'Mmm,' she muttered. 'You sound as though you know where he lives.'

'He's known to us. A bit too sharp for his own good at times.'

'Is that all you've got to say?'

He grinned. There *was* something. 'I wondered whether you were free next Wednesday evening? Who knows, we may have a reason to celebrate.'

She shook her head. 'I've been invited to an open evening at a bookshop.'

She sensed that he wanted to ask her if she was going alone, but had curbed himself. However, something was brewing, and it wasn't just tea. He was rubbing his hands together, and his eyes were unblinking when he looked at her. It struck her as odd that he wasn't showing that much enthusiasm for pursuing enquiries regarding Simon Tye and the Volvo estate. And there was that triumphant look again.

'You look as though you scored with a supermodel last night. What's up?'

'We've got him,' he blurted. 'Loretta's real father.'

'And this is a celebratory tea?'

She raised her mug. The motif on the side read *I love Bath*. She flashed that side at him.

'Nice to see that the police are promoting tourism, if only in a small way.'

'I'm being serious. Robert Davies is in custody. We found him living with a girlfriend on a narrowboat at Bathampton.'

'I'm pretty serious too. Why do you think the Hotels Association are getting involved in police work? It's not because we've got nothing better to do.'

Doherty took another slurp and sighed with satisfaction. It could have been as much for the tea as for the case in hand.

'We can't celebrate just yet,' he explained. 'Not until I've got a full confession.'

Honey frowned. 'You haven't got any evidence. You can't have anything on him if you're still thinking of going after this house by the river thing.'

His cheeks did a funny sucking in and out, as though she'd slapped him on both.

To her great surprise, he slammed his mug down on the desk. 'Well, I think I'm the best judge of that,' he said, folding his arms more tightly than usual, pressing his bulging muscles more noticeably against his shirt. 'We're the professionals. You're only a liaison personage.'

Her eyes opened wide. 'A personage, am I!'

Now it was her turn to slam the mug down on the desk. She got to her feet, leaning on her knuckles so she was halfway across the table that stood between them.

Doherty flinched.

Honey had a husky voice at the best of times. Now it rasped out like the rattle of a machine gun.

'Why would Robert Davies kill an American he didn't know?'

Doherty's cheeks sucked in and out — like bellows — but less effectively.

'We don't know for sure that he killed both of them. That's what we're going to ask him about. Mervyn Herbert and Elmer Maxted were about the same build, same height. We think the first killing was a textbook case of mistaken identity.' The smugness returned.

Honey sniffed. 'A bit overdramatic, in my books! You're clutching at straws.'

'Look,' he said, mimicking her stance. Both now rested their knuckles on the desk so that their noses were only inches apart. 'He's number one in the frame.'

'He's all you've got in the frame.'

He grunted. His eyes were pools of misty blue that too easily betrayed his irritation that she'd ridiculed his judgement.

Honey straightened. 'Let's think this through. What about the watches. Were they stolen?'

'We've no record of them.'

'You haven't checked.'

'There's no need to!'

He spread his hands and shrugged. Beyond him the backs of Georgian buildings glowed like honeycomb, one building very much like another. That was how they were built: beautiful crescents, squares and terraces apparently erected to be absolutely identical and in pleasing symmetry. But they weren't. They were only similar at the front, with alterations done in the years hence. The rear edifices of each and every building differed quite starkly from their neighbours.

'Steve, it doesn't make sense. How could one be so easily mistaken for the other? OK, I know they were the same height and build, but their features were so different. Their hair colour for a start.'

Honey considered it quickly. She'd only seen a passport photograph of Elmer Maxted, but she'd seen Mervyn Herbert. There were more differences than similarities.

Doherty wasn't to be put off.

'They may have been wearing similar clothes.'

She shook her head reproachfully. 'It's been warm this month and neither would have been bundled up in coats. People can disguise themselves if they're dressed for winter, wearing scarves and mufflers and thick padded jackets, but — hi there, just in case you didn't notice — it's summer.'

His face crumpled as though it was made of paper and she'd just bashed it. The hurt look turned to male petulance, a noisy agitated affair compared to the petulance of a woman.

'That's it! This is the end of our liaison. This is a murder enquiry and I don't need to tell you *anything*!'

She folded her arms. 'We'll let the chief constable decide that.'

'Blow him!'

'You're being childish.'

'I am not!

'You're not thinking.'

'Look! If you're a copper you get a nose for felons like Davies. Believe me, he did it. The first victim was a case of mistaken identity. The second — well, I think we all know the reason for that. The bloke had it coming to him.'

'And the piece of wood? And the spice sacks? The wood had to come from somewhere, a house close to the river. And why spice sacks? Whoever killed these men had to have had access to a source. Otherwise, why not coal sacks or hay sacks, or even plastic bags?'

She could see from his expression that he really didn't want to go down that route at all.

'We'll cross that bridge when we come to it. I expect Davies got hold of them somehow.'

Honey had heard enough. She headed for the door.

He shouted after her. 'I'd really like to see you again!'

She hesitated, wanting to turn and say, *OK. When?* But her pride made her keep heading for the exit. He wanted results. Quick results. She wanted the truth, even if it took some time. That, she supposed, was the amateur coming out.

CHAPTER 27

Honey knew what was coming. She found her mother in the restaurant trying to fold table napkins. They weren't very good. If she deigned to help out, it would only be as an excuse to interfere.

'Lindsey didn't come home last night.'

'Who told you that?'

Her mother pursed her lips disapprovingly. 'I went in to make her bed this morning, but didn't need to. It hadn't been slept in.'

Her mother had her own flat but stayed over from time to time. Fortunately all the rooms were taken at present.

'She slept at Sam's,' said Honey.

'Sam? Who's he?'

'She. Samantha.'

She wasn't too sure whether it was true. Lindsey had called and left a message on the answerphone saying she was sleeping at Sam's place. She didn't know of a female friend named Sam: no way was she telling her mother that.

The pinched lips straightened. 'That's all right then.'

Her mother's next subject was that Mary Jane was organising a séance in the hope that Sir Cedric would manifest himself on a more visual plain.

'I think she's nuts,' said her mother. 'But there. What can you expect from a woman of her age?'

Honey glanced at her mother. If the truth be known, she was only five years or so behind Mary Jane.

The phone burbled against her hip. She eyed the caller's number, didn't recognise it, but pressed receive anyway.

'Hi. This is John Rees.'

Flip went her heart. The day was turning brighter. What was it Lindsey had said? Better to be desired by two men than one.

'Just a minute.'

Her mother tilted her head quizzically. 'Who's that?'

'It's private.'

She took the phone outside. Sun-dappled leaves rustled against a powder-blue sky. Even more perfect.

'I thought we needed to finalize things.'

His voice reminded her of the southern guys in Elvis Presley's backing group: the sort of huskiness that comes down the nose rather than out of the mouth. Her legs turned to jelly.

* * *

They arranged to meet at the George in Norton St Phillip, an ancient and very large hostelry a few miles outside the city and famed for its huge portions.

Founded by monks who brewed their own ale, it had been an inn for over six hundred years, the place was a living museum. Leather harnesses, old flintlocks, rusty farm implements and bright brass lanterns hung from every beam, every spare bit of ceiling space. A pile of leaflets about its long history were readily available. A Japanese group were in, faces full of enthusiasm. One after another they went to the bar, scrutinised the leaflets and took what they wanted.

North American accents blended easily with those from Canada, Australia, New Zealand and South Africa. French, Italian, German and Dutch gabbled alongside Japanese and Spanish. The place was busy — as usual.

'Wow! Can you beat this!' John exclaimed, head back and eyes wide with wonder. 'Everything is so . . . old! Don't you just love it?'

'It's been here a long time,' said Honey, then felt guilty for making such a trite remark. She'd so badly wanted to make an impression, but what sort of impression was that?

'Are you interested in history . . . ?' She stopped herself. 'Sorry. Of course you are. That's the whole point of the exhibition, isn't it?'

If she'd been younger, she would have blushed. The thought was whimsical and fluttered around her mind, pushing aside her thoughts about Elmer Maxted — at least for now. They wouldn't go away completely. She felt an affinity with him. He'd come looking for his roots. She understood that. Being the daughter of an American father and an English mother, she floated between the two worlds not knowing quite where she belonged at times. Once he'd blotted his copybook, her mother had blocked out her father's memory.

Like Geoff and me: could behaviour towards men be hereditary? She shuddered at the memory and likely consequences of her departed husband.

John was ordering food. She'd been running on autopilot when she'd told him what she wanted: king prawn salad in Cajun spices.

They were both driving, so they stuck with soft drinks. Once that was done, they got down to more serious conversation — or as serious as it needed to be.

'So how long have you been running the hotel?'

It was the question he was bound to ask.

'Two years now.'

'You must enjoy it.'

'Sometimes I enjoy meeting people. Sometimes I want to hide away from them.'

'Understandable. I suppose you don't get too much time off.'

'Not nearly enough. At least this police thing gets me out of the place. It's an interesting other dimension to the hospitality trade.' She surprised herself by burbling on about the murder case, about what Steve had said, and what she had said. She stopped herself before her obsession became overwhelming.

John didn't question whether she was married, divorced or widowed.

'I met your mother and your daughter.'

Honey grimaced at her drink. 'The sugar and spice in my life — though don't ask me which is which.'

'Your daughter looks like you. Your mother . . .'

She held up a warning finger from the side of her raised glass. 'Don't mention anything about broomsticks! OK?'

'I wasn't going to. I was going to say that she's quite a character.'

'That's putting it mildly.'

'Oh come on. You make her sound like Cruella de Vil.'

'No, my mother would never make a coat out of puppies, though she might make a stew.'

He eyed her speculatively. Speculation and truth-seeking about her family were all she needed.

'Only joking. She's just getting old and cantankerous,' she said lightly, lowering her eyes as she sipped her drink. Heaven help her if Mum ever found out she'd said that.

Over plates of magnificently pink prawns speckled with spice, their conversation turned to the exhibition. She watched his lips move as he told her about the guest list. They were strong lips, yet supple. *Kissing*, she thought. *I bet they're good at kissing.*

He told her the names of the wines he'd chosen and the fact that his sister-in-law had taken charge of the catering. She wanted to ask why his wife, the ice queen he'd brought into the restaurant, wasn't doing it, but it was none of her business. Keep to the facts, she thought to herself.

Be a pleasant girl, Hannah! Her mother's voice again. On this occasion she decided to take her advice.

'So what other historical artefacts have you managed to get hold of?'

He finished swallowing a particularly fat prawn before answering. 'A suit of armour, a sedan chair and a clock: each represents a certain aspect of history. The suit of armour represents military history, the sedan chair represents the history of transport and the clock represents industrial history — the crowning glory of the Industrial Revolution.'

Tilting her head to one side so that her hair tickled her shoulder, she asked, 'So where do Queen Victoria's unmentionables fit in?'

'Simple,' he said, confidence emanating from him like a halo. 'They represent women's rights, the march towards emancipation.'

Honey coughed into her drink.

John looked surprised. 'Have I said something funny?'

In danger of blowing her drink out through her nose, Honey pinched her nostrils quite fiercely. It took a few seconds before she could answer.

'I can't quite see the connection.'

It was difficult to control the giggles. She sensed he'd meant to make her giggle. Was her preoccupation with the Elmer Maxted case making her a Dolly-dull-drawers?

If it was, he didn't refer to it, but went on to explain.

'Big underwear. Big skirts. The women's movement was restricted by their clothes. Then came the twentieth century and — WHAM — everything changed.'

'Though not very quickly.'

'OK, no. Not very quickly. Well, not until the twenties, the Charleston and the flappers. But it happened. Women finally escaped big skirts, tight corsets and big underwear.'

It was strangely comforting to watch as he wiped up the juices with a piece of granary bread. 'Imagine all the things you wouldn't be able to do if you wore a big skirt.'

Honey shook her head and finished her meal. As she raised her glass to down the last drop, she caught sight of a familiar face. Loretta Davies saw her, pushed back her chair and marched over.

The smell of wine escaped from her mouth and her eyes were bright with too much of it.

She was wearing an embroidered tunic and green leggings. Rings still adorned her fingers and dangled from her ears. Honey gave silent thanks that her pasty belly was covered.

'We came out 'ere to get away from the likes of you. Are you following us?'

'No. Certainly not.'

Loretta looked about to make a scene, but her mother intervened. 'Don't make a scene, luv. It ain't worth it.'

Loretta shrugged her mother's restraining hand from her shoulder.

'You know they've arrested my father.'

Honey half rose. 'Yes, I'm so sorry, Loretta.'

'He didn't do it.' She shook her head as she said it, each individual movement coinciding with each spoken word. 'He didn't,' she added defiantly, as though those two last words confirmed everything not contained in the evidence.

Her voice carried. People cast looks in their direction.

Her mother intervened. 'Come on, Loretta. You're making a scene.'

Cora pointed an accusing finger inches from Honey's face.

'They've told me not to touch any of Mervyn's stuff until you lot take another look at things. Robert didn't do it. I know he didn't.'

Honey's eyes narrowed as she watched her go. The question of number six or number nine resurfaced in her mind. The merry moment between her and John was over — at least for this evening.

She wasn't aware at first that his eyes had narrowed and he was studying her.

'Judging by the look on your face, I guess we'd better call it a day,' he said.

'Yes.'

Her gaze strayed to the heavy oak door shutting behind Cora and her daughter.

She felt sorry for them and wished she hadn't suggested to John coming out here. It was sheer coincidence and regrettable. They needed support. She'd try to give it, but first things first. She had to go back to Charlborough Grange and ask if Elmer Maxted had visited the house more than once. Not this afternoon. She still had a business to run. Tomorrow would do, and she didn't need to go alone.

'Are you doing anything tomorrow?'

John shook his head.

'Fancy a drive in the country?'

'Sure. Where to?'

'Charlborough Grange. Do you know where it is?'

'Sure. Of course I do. That's where the guy lives who's loaning me the clock.'

CHAPTER 28

A summer shower had come and gone. The sun came out and the A36 that ranged out of Bath and up through Freshford was as wet and shiny as a docile river.

A rainbow stretched from one side of the valley to the other. The road, the valley, the river and canal snaked towards it.

Honey felt a bit fraudulent telling him this was nothing but an afternoon drive. John explained that he was happy to take the opportunity to finalize arrangements for the loan of the clock.

Her phone rang just as they pulled up outside. It was Steve Doherty.

'Guess where Davies has been living?'

She didn't want to guess. From the moment she'd squeezed into the bucket seat in John Rees's Austin Healey, the real world and her concerns had folded in on itself — a bit like the way she'd folded into the seat.

At this moment in time she didn't care who had killed who. The warmth of John's thigh was pressing against hers. Who cared that the day was warm? A little more heat of this type was perfectly acceptable.

She thought about hanging up. Doherty pre-empted her.

'Honey? Are you there?'

Too late!

'Go on. Hit me.'

'Prior to the narrowboat, Davies was living in a flat in Charlotte Terrace. Right next to the river. Number *six*, Charlotte Terrace! We've got him!'

She could imagine his face, the wide-open eyes, the smile fixed like that of a painted clown. No. Clown was wrong. He was a man doing his job in a strait jacket. He had rules and guidelines, the media and a demanding public to deal with.

'Did you find any evidence?'

That she had the audacity to ask the question surprised her. She could imagine his lips pursing as though he'd just sucked on a lemon.

'Circumstantial, but enough. See? I told you he was the right man.'

Doherty was cock-a-hoop that he'd found the culprit. Either he hadn't latched on to the note of misgiving in her voice or he'd ignored it. The inclination to tell him she was still unconvinced played second fiddle today. He deserved support.

'Yes. You did.'

The connection was terminated.

'All set?' said John.

The young man named Mark Conway listened attentively as John explained why he was there.

'Ah, yes sir. I'm aware of the arrangement.'

They were shown into the conservatory and invited to sit on Lloyd loom chairs. Gratefully they sank into cushions covered in heavy cotton on which huge roses flourished. Mark went off to alert Sir Andrew.

'It's pretty hot in here,' said John, wiping the back of his hand across his forehead. He looked around popeyed. 'I suppose this is unchanged since Queen Victoria's time.'

'This place gives me the creeps. Don't you think those plants look like triffids?'

'They are a bit tropical.'

His voice deviated from the calm tone that she was used to.

'You don't like this place either, do you?'

He shook his head and gave her a direct look.

'I'm instinctive about places. I pick up vibes.'

'Please. No paranormal stuff. One professor of the paranormal is more than enough!' She told him about Mary Jane. 'She's from California.'

'That explains a lot.'

Charlborough made an impressive entrance just as John finished laughing, striding towards them, hand offered, his face a picture of patrician bonhomie.

He obviously favoured wearing the same colour from top to toe. Today he was casually dressed in a pale-green lamb's wool sweater and matching trousers. The collar of a checked shirt showed above the V neck of his sweater.

'John. How are you, my dear fellow?' There was warmth in his welcome.

'Fine, sir. I thought I would drive out and go over the final arrangements with you — if it's not inconvenient, that is?'

'No, no, my dear fellow! Not at all!'

Perhaps it was the way John said it, or perhaps the way he looked, but Charlborough seemed unable to say no.

When Charlborough's eyes turned to her, his smile tightened.

'This is Honey Driver. She collects antique clothes,' John explained.

Honey saw no point in denying the obvious. 'We've already met.'

They shook hands. Recognition clouded his eyes then was gone. His smile was tight, his grip limp.

'I came here in my capacity as liaison officer for the Bath Hotels Association. I asked you about Elmer Maxted.'

'Ah, yes,' he said with a stiff nod of his head. 'You'd mislaid an American tourist.'

The terminology irritated.

Her smile was as stiff and cold as his. 'He was not mislaid. He was murdered.'

'Ah! And the police have arrested the perpetrator?'

She couldn't help thinking he already knew this. News travelled fast — the 'old boys' network was rife with senior police chiefs and crown court judges.

'They have arrested someone. Whether they make the charges stick is, as always, a different matter.'

'Quite so.' He turned immediately to John. 'Now, about my clock . . .'

Honey's gaze wandered to the gardens and grounds beyond the thick foliage and the stifling conservatory. A church spire pierced the sky above a row of rustling poplars. The humidity, all for the benefit of the monstrous plants, was unbearable. She began dabbing at her glistening cheeks with the back of her hand.

'I'm sorry,' she said, interrupting their conversation, 'would it be all right if I went outside for some fresh air?'

For a moment she detected indecision on Charlborough's face, as he weighed up the consequences of granting or refusing his permission.

'Sorry for boring you,' John said as casually as you'd like. 'We're rambling into the realms of history.' He grinned across at Sir Andrew. 'Not everyone is as fascinated by the subject as we are.'

Charlborough's expression veered between arrogance and pained forbearance. 'Of course.' He turned to Honey. 'Please keep to the garden area. I have projects underway in the rest of the grounds.'

She didn't ask what projects, but the fact that places had been forbidden made her curious.

Her sweat cooled once she was out in the fresh air. Steps led down from the raised area outside the conservatory. Red and orange nasturtiums trailed from weathered urns. A balustrade of moss-covered stone ran around its perimeter.

Manicured lawns of epic size and decorous design swooped between the flowerbeds and trees, like a river running towards the sea. Unlike a river, these lawns ran up against a red-brick wall. The mortar joining the bricks was white and smeared, the bricks uneven and irregular, signs of age and ageing. An arched wooden door, the sort found in churches and medieval castles, dissected the wall just before it disappeared behind a laburnum. Although not a gardener, she vaguely remembered that laburnum flowers were poisonous. She made a mental note to check this, though goodness knows what for. Poison had not been used in the recent murders.

The door might not have beckoned so strongly if Charlborough hadn't ordered — yes, *ordered* — her to stay within the garden. But there it was, a cast iron ring hanging there, waiting to be touched, turned and pulled.

It's probably locked, but it wouldn't hurt to try. The door opened. There again were the huge greenhouses thick with greenery, far more profligate than the huge specimens thronging the conservatory. And the size . . . a football pitch? At least. It was huge!

The roof curved like those on wartime structures, those now disintegrating under the onslaught of the years and the weather. Sandbags piled a dozen or so high protected its entrance. A shovel stood upright in a pile of sand beside a wooden fruit box — the sort used for storing oranges.

Just like the last time, no one was around. She wondered when they actually held these war games that people paid to fight in.

The only sounds were of birds and bees. Just as she'd hoped, there were a few loose sacks on the ground next to the sand.

Sacks! *The* sacks?

She grabbed one and shook out the sand.

Holding it with both hands, she scrutinised its size. It looked too big. Just to make sure, she took a deep sniff. It smelled of new sacking.

Just as she thought about leaving, the door to the greenhouse made a wheezing sound. Humid air poured out to taint the freshness of a day after rain.

The fact that someone had come out with the tepid air did not register as quickly as it should have done. The sandbags were piled high and hid him until they were facing each other, each taken off guard, each unsure of how to proceed.

'You.'

The same man as before. The man Sir Andrew had referred to as Trevor. Some kind of butler. Some kind of nightmare.

She brazened it out. 'Yes. I got a little hot in the conservatory. Sir Andrew said I could go outside.'

He had a square face, a downturned mouth, deep-set eyes and shoulders that, although wide, totally lacked muscle definition. It was as though they had been welded from sheets of steel, thus having no rounded corners. His eye colour was hidden in the dark hollows beneath his brows.

She held the sack behind her back, letting it fall slowly to the ground.

'I'll make my way back now. I was promised a pot of tea.'

Not the entire truth, but close enough.

The man shifted his weight onto the opposite leg; either his tension was dissipated or he was about to make a grab for her.

Discretion immediately became the better part of valour. Her legs propelled her back to the door and the manicured lawns, the house and the overpowering heat of the conservatory.

Hiding behind a sweet-smelling bush, she took the opportunity to catch her breath, daring to look behind her to ensure no one was following.

Sir Andrew had said that he was just a gardener tending the greenhouse. But the unease remained. Was it really only for war games, or was it something more sinister? Drugs were the obvious answer, if she cared to take a jaundiced view of Sir Andrew. But what sort of drugs grew to that height?

'Better now?' asked John when she returned.

She forced a casual smile, the sort that worked well with pink cheeks and being slightly breathless.

Sir Andrew's eyes bored into her. 'I'm so glad you feel better.'

'Yes. Thank you.'

She wondered if he had guessed that she'd disobeyed his orders, but wasn't given chance to find out.

The sound of a woman's voice seemed to splinter the beams of weak sunlight that had managed to shine through the canopy of plants.

'Darling, I didn't know we had visitors!'

Pamela Charlborough wore a red silk dress that rustled when she walked and her perfume smelled of money. Her bare arms were covered in freckles and her toenails were painted the same colour as her dress and the high-heeled mules she wore. She was swaying slightly and carrying a very full wine glass.

'Another of your little soldier friends?' she asked in a raucous voice. 'My, but he's out of uniform! You should reprimand him at once, darling. Bend him over your lap, pull down his trousers and smack his tight little bottom!'

She burst out laughing but stopped on noticing Honey.

'Oh! A little woman soldier, perhaps?' Her features screwed up like discarded paper. 'Don't I know you from somewhere?'

'Pamela!'

The broken veins in Charlborough's cheeks spread over his face like a raging forest fire.

Lady Pamela, who was obviously a bit tipsy, looked surprised. 'Have I got the wrong end of the stick, darling?'

Sir Andrew's face was like thunder. 'Go away, Pamela!'

John looked embarrassed.

Honey merely observed, feeling almost ashamed at belonging to the same sex as the sun-tanned blonde.

Lady Charlborough's eyes narrowed once she was within range to see Honey's face more clearly. 'Didn't you come here with that charming young detective? Yes! I'm sure you did.' She turned to Sir Andrew. 'Oh my dearest, darling, what have you been up to now?'

These two were far from being dearest, darling to each other.

Sir Andrew seethed. 'Nothing! You're drunk!'

'Oh, am I, darling? Then I'd better stop at once.'

She laughed, took a few steps forward then poured her wine into a potted plant. The wineglass followed its contents, the bowl breaking from its stem.

Her husband was far from amused.

'Pamela! For God's sake, that's Waterford Crystal!'

Smirking stupidly, Pamela Charlborough hid her mouth behind her hand.

'Silly me. Should not have said those dreadful things, should I? Naughty, naughty things.' She laughed again.

Although Charlborough looked thoroughly embarrassed, Honey found it hard to pity him. He was too smooth. Being lord of the manor was ingrained in him. This was hardly the first trophy wife to end up feeling trapped and disappointed with the older, richer man she had married.

'I apologise for my wife's rudeness.' Sir Andrew's voice dropped an octave or two and his apology seemed sincere.

'We get on best when we're apart,' said Lady Pamela. 'In fact, I'm off to Spain tonight. My husband is footing the bill. Aren't you darling?' It was a statement, not a question.

'That's nice for you. I hope you have a lovely time,' said Honey, her smile and tone as sarcastic as she could make it.

Pamela wagged a perfectly manicured finger. 'Aren't you the woman playing detective? I seem to remember you mentioned it when we met before.'

'Yes.' Honey maintained her smile. 'I probably remember it more clearly than you do.'

The inference was obvious but took a while to sink in. Once it did, the insincerity of her ladyship's smile was echoed in her eyes.

'Well, that's the way it is with trade, isn't it? I presume one has to do everything one can to make ends meet.'

Just when she was ready to floor her ladyship with a swift right hook, John stepped in.

'Where do you stay in Spain?'

His tone and smile were enough to charm the pants off a nun — and Lady Pamela was far from being that.

* * *

They left with arrangements fully made for the loan of the clock, and Lady Pamela invited John to stay at her private villa if ever he came to Spain. Honey was ignored.

'Bitch,' muttered Honey once they were in the car and heading back to Bath.

'I think her husband is of the same opinion,' said John.

'A divorce in the making?'

'You bet. I've been lucky in that respect. My ex-wife is very convivial.'

The slim, gorgeous creature? Honey had to find out.

'Was that her . . .'

'In the restaurant the other night? Yes.'

Honey breathed a sigh of relief. He was just her type — and available.

'She sounds like a lady — which is more than I can say for Lady Pamela Charlborough.'

CHAPTER 29

There were garages converted from the original stabling at the rear of Charlborough Grange. The doors had been widened to take cars.

Mark Conway was servicing the engine on Pamela Charlborough's Mercedes Sports. He was slick with sweat, his T-shirt sticking against his skin and emphasising his muscular build.

His hands worked quickly and efficiently. He knew what he was doing. Was absorbed in it.

He smelled her perfume before he saw her — expensive perfume, of course.

'Darling, you're coming to Spain with me, aren't you?'

The bonnet was up and threw a shadow across his face.

'I'm wanted here,' he said without turning round.

He heard her heels clicking on the concrete, knew her hips were swaying provocatively as she sashayed towards him.

His blood raced when she ran her hands down his back, tracing his muscles beneath the thin fabric of his T-shirt.

'I want you in Spain,' she said. 'I want you every which way in Spain.'

His bare biceps were hard beneath her hands. She sucked in her breath. 'You have such a beautiful body, Mark.'

'I'm busy.'

He tried to shrug her off. She clung on.

Her lips brushed against his neck.

'Imagine making love on a deserted beach or high on a clifftop overlooking the sea.'

Thoughtfully he wiped his hands on a piece of rag. 'Your husband might not like that.' There was contempt on his face both for her and her husband. Not that Lady Pamela noticed.

'Never mind him. I would like it,' she breathed. 'You know I would.' Her fingers travelled up to his jaw. 'I thought you loved me.'

He smiled. 'I've made love to you.'

'Whatever. It's enough for me. And I thought we'd agreed . . . you know . . . that afternoon. You agreed to get rid of him.'

'You weren't serious, were you? How would I do that?'

'Fix his brakes,' she whispered. 'Make it look like an accident.'

He stared at her. 'You really mean it.'

'Of course I do. You look appalled, my darling boy.'

She sounded surprised.

He shook her hand from his arm and continued to stare at her, as if seeing her without the gold that made her glitter. His expression was grim, his tone muddied with emotion.

'No. Not me. I can't do it.'

She flounced off, slightly wobbling on heels too high to cope with the loose gravel of the drive.

'What did she want?'

Mark turned, startled by Trevor's sudden appearance. 'She's crazy.'

'Still a good screw though? What's the price on your ongoing relationship?'

Mark laughed and shook his head. 'She's crazy. She wanted me to fix the brakes on the Roller.'

Trevor nodded silently but said nothing. He walked off towards the house. His loyalty was to Sir Andrew. Without him he had no job. Without her his position was secure.

* * *

Honey checked herself in the mirrored doors of the dining room. This evening she'd chosen to wear a white linen suit with a blue-and-silver rope belt. Casual but classy, her favourite words when it came to fashion.

'These earrings,' said Lindsey, who had insisted on choosing her clothes with her, had made up her face and was now choosing her accessories. 'And this bracelet.'

'Whatever you say.'

Having someone else make all the decisions was wonderful.

'And remember to be home before twelve,' said Lindsey with a crafty grin. 'You won't change into a pumpkin or anything. I was just going to remind you to take your key, just in case.'

'I promise I won't sleep over.'

Lindsey shrugged. Honey sensed her backing off. She knew what was coming.

'So, who's this Sam?'

Lindsey tutted and shook her head. 'You couldn't resist, could you? You had to ask.'

'Please,' Honey whimpered. 'I worry about you.'

'Don't. Sam is a great guy. There's a lot between us. Just how much, only time will tell. I think that's enough information for now.'

Honey held up her hands in mute surrender.

'I'm off now.' Her smile disintegrated on seeing her mother's reflection over her shoulder. She was dressed in Donna Karan and smelled of Chanel No. 5.

Her pert little nose was upturned, her hands flapping about. 'And what shall I tell Mr Paget?'

That tone of voice! School reports came to mind. *Must try harder!*

'Mother, who is Mr Paget?'

'I've already told you. He's a dentist!'

'I'll look him up when I need a tooth pulled.'

Pouting her apricot lips, her mother said, 'And what about Mary Jane's séance? Seven thirty, she said.'

Honey closed her eyes. Typical of her mother and totally without warning, she'd leaped from one subject to another. 'I forgot!'

'Yes, you forgot, Miss Know All!'

Mary Jane was a delight, a truly valued guest, but in comparison with gorgeous John?

Lindsey took hold of her shoulders and guided her to the door.

'You're off. Never mind the séance. Grandma and I will go, won't we, Grandma?'

Gloria Cross glanced from daughter to granddaughter.

'You're conspiring against me. In cahoots, the pair of you!'

'Grandma! Come on, let's go to the séance. We'll have fun. Let's see if Grandpa comes through.'

Her grandmother rolled her eyes. 'Heaven forbid!'

Grandma was hesitant. Honey felt obliged to add weight to Lindsey's offer.

'Mother. I have to go to this presentation. This is important. I've accepted the invitation and have to attend. See?'

Retrieving the embossed card from her purse, she waved it in front of her mother's face.

Her mother's expression was unaltered. 'You don't fool me. I know why you're going.'

'But, Mother, I thought you wanted me to catch myself a man.'

Her mother sniffed. 'That doesn't excuse you. Mary Jane will be *very* disappointed.'

'I have to go,' Honey mumbled and headed for her precious exit through the bar, leaving her mother grim faced and muttering about the evils of drink.

* * *

Union Passage is a traffic-free thoroughfare of specialist shops with narrow frontages, some unchanged since Beau Brummel was a lad.

Street musicians and jugglers rub shoulders with tourists looking for a bargain and office workers after a lunchtime sandwich. Despite the shops selling PlayStations, mobile phones and smart TVs, it has retained its Dickensian charm.

Ideal for a bookshop, thought Honey, walking with confidence through a gathering dusk on a balmy July night.

John Rees had been lucky enough to lease a shop still retaining an old-fashioned frontage of Art Deco design. The theme of the framework supporting the window was taken across the glass in the form of a transparent Beardsley woman. Typically, she had flowing tresses and gown, her willowy arms framing the central display.

The shop door was open. A hum of conversation and the tinkle of glasses drifted out. Hopefully the night air would drift in. Few shops boasted air conditioning, and although linen was cool it creased easily.

Making up in depth what it lacked in breadth, a throng of people jostled like a queue, wine glasses held tightly to chest. Cut-glass voices droned on about the meaning behind an author's work or the reasons why women were forced — *forced* — into wearing corsets.

'It was a man's way of keeping a woman submissive,' the dreaded Audrey Tyson Dix was imparting to a politely attentive John Rees.

Honey stood on tiptoe to ensure that their eyes met.

He smiled, swiftly introduced Audrey to someone else and eased himself in her direction. He managed to grab a glass of wine en route.

'Glad you could come.'

'It's a tight squeeze,' she said. As she said it a woman with a bookshelf bosom and belly to match squeezed between them. Despite the fact that she'd eased through sideways, Honey still ended up with her wine glass pressed against her nose.

John grabbed her hand. 'Follow me.'

Holding her wine glass high, she did as she was told.

'There's steps here,' he said over his shoulder.

Three steps.

'And some more.'

Another three.

Eventually, they were at the back of the shop and had room to breathe.

John nodded to where the crowd was thickest. 'Never mind the culture, you can see what they've really come for.'

Sadly, he was right. The wine and food had been placed on a table at the front of the shop on the lowest level. That was where the crowd was thickest.

She smiled up at him and clinked her glass against his. 'There are always exceptions.'

He smiled back. 'I'm glad to hear it. Would you care for a look at the exhibits?'

'OK.'

First stop was her own property.

'Yours, of course.'

'Not literally,' she said, shaking her head. 'They might have been OK for Queen Victoria, but I wouldn't be seen dead in them.'

'Passion killers.'

'Definitely. I barely saved them from one of my foreign waitresses who presumed they were a tablecloth. My mother calls them 'harvest festivals'. All is safely gathered in.'

'Can't say I'm surprised.'

Her eyes strayed to Sir Andrew's clock. John followed her gaze.

'He insisted I insure it.'

Honey frowned. 'I've only met the owner a few times, but already I get the impression that it's the love of his life.'

John tilted his head to one side as he observed it. 'Not exactly. Apparently, he idolizes his son, Lance. So I hear.'

'Is that so? I haven't met him.'

'I get the impression he's at Harvard, though unwillingly. It was his grandfather's wish and a provision in his will that Lance finish his education there. The old man left all his money to his daughter, but when she died everything went to him. Seems he was only a kid at the time, not much more than a baby.'

'I wonder what she was like in comparison to Lady Pamela.'

'A bit more of a lady?'

'I would think so.'

'I understand wife number two has now left for Spain. Sir Andrew phoned me earlier. He's promised to show up later.' He shrugged. 'Whether he will or not . . .'

Honey's gaze slid sidelong to the horde of hungry guests. 'He'll have to squeeze himself in.'

John looked at his watch. 'He did promise.'

'Well, I doubt that he's accompanying his darling wife to Spain. I think he must hate Spain as much as he does her.'

John shrugged and took a slug of wine. 'He was living there when his wife died in a car crash. Head on, just her and the boy. Luckily Lance survived.' He frowned. 'So I understand. Though I've never met him.'

They moved slowly along the exhibits — the books, memorabilia, lace mittens, bonnets, old tools and so on.

'Look at these,' he said. He indicated a few sheets of newspaper preserved behind glass. 'Do you know it's only in the last hundred years or so that newspapers were available to everyone? Facts were shouted out by town criers and passed mouth to mouth. Truth could be heavily distorted between source and target audience back then.'

Honey squinted to read the tiny print of the oldest newspaper he had there. 'It's a wonder any news ever got through.'

John nodded. 'Great battles, politics and only respectful articles about the royal family. My dad kept old newspapers covering the war years: he used to bring them out now and again just to remind himself of what he'd gone through.' John's voice took on an aura of sadness. 'It's surprising how reading an old newspaper can jog the memory.'

'You're right. They're not just for using as cat litter or wrapping up rubbish.'

'Only the tabloids,' laughed John. 'And definitely not old newspapers. They can teach us so much, old news and old photos. Forgotten histories.'

John regarded them as a treasure trove of information. And suddenly so did she. Her mind went back to Cora Herbert wrapping up her husband's watches in newspaper. Old newspapers. American newspapers? Had they belonged to Elmer Maxted? Had they been part of his investigation into family history? And incidents. Newspapers, both print and photos recorded incidents that could be clues to his research and much more besides.

'Yes,' she murmured, squinting to read the tiny print at the same time as evaluating what was going on in her mind. 'Old newspapers can be . . . That's it!'

John frowned at the glass she'd shoved into his hand.

'I have to go.'

'Was it something I said?'

'Yes,' she groaned, touching his face with her fingertips. 'John, would you think I was too forward if I told you that I wanted to take you to bed?'

He shook his head. 'No.'

'Oh, that's wonderful. But I can't hold you to that just yet. There's something I've got to do. Can you keep it warm for me? I can't say I'll be back tonight, but imminently. What do you say?'

'That's good for me.'

He looked happy when she kissed him on the cheek. It was all she could do for now.

Every step to the shop door was painful, not just because it was slow but because business was overriding pleasure.

She had to get to where it had all began and clocks had nothing to do with it. A few steps along Union Passage and she almost flipped at how forward she had been coming on to John Rees like that. *You're a mature woman*, she told herself. *You can do anything you want.*

* * *

She didn't hear him following her. She wasn't meant to. That was the good thing about wearing trainers. OK, your feet might end up stinking, but no one heard you following.

He saw her take her phone from out of her pocket and tap in a number. Judging by the brief moment the phone was next to her ear there was either no signal or the battery was flat.

He'd expected her to return to the hotel. Instead she headed for the taxi rank outside the abbey.

Swearing beneath his breath, he eyed the amount of people still strolling around.

His eyes wove with her through the crowds and watched as she got into a taxi.

A text came through to him on his own phone. He read the message quickly. He was wanted. It wouldn't take long. He'd catch up with Honey Driver later.

CHAPTER 30

Lady Pamela Charlborough snapped shut the clasp of her Gucci handbag and summoned all her bravery. She turned to her husband.

'My car's broken. Mark will have to drive me to the airport. I've booked a hotel. He can stay overnight.'

Her husband took quick strides across the room, caught her wrist and squeezed hard.

Fear creased the pumped-out flesh around her botoxed lips as she struggled.

'Stop it! Stop it! You're hurting me.'

He tightened his grip.

'Good. I want to hurt you.'

He smiled at the thought of her feeling pain, the discomfort as her veins filled up with trapped blood.

He brought his face close to hers.

'Let me go!'

'Darling,' he said between grinding teeth. 'How can I let you go, my little darling? You who think you have the right to dispose of my possessions even before I am dead, things that I prize, things that have been in this house for years.

'I needed the money!'

She was frightened.

His face closed on hers. His hand encompassed her neck. His thumb pressed on her windpipe. She began to choke and tugged with both hands at his fingers, eyes wide with fear.

Sir Andrew still held his brandy glass in his other hand. The feel of her squirming against his strength excited him. Her mouth was open. He knew she was trying to scream but no sound came out. He held her neck far too tightly for that.

The wineglass snapped in his hand.

Pamela's eyes almost bulged out of her head, partly through lack of breath, partly through fear.

He brought the jagged edge of the stem close to her face. She closed her eyes. When she found nothing had happened, she opened them again.

She mouthed all the most profane words she knew yet no sound came out. But he understood. She could see from his eyes that he had understood. It had been years since she'd looked up into his eyes at this close a range. He looked as if only part of him was in the room. The rest was somewhere else.

He relaxed his grip on her neck and she found herself free again. Staggering and gasping for air, she ran for the stairs.

Once the bedroom door was safely locked, clothes and shoes and toiletries flew into her luggage. Lingerie was wound into balls; shoes were shoved haphazardly among delicate laces, silks and cashmere.

Luggage straps and locks were fastened. Passport and essentials were thrown into a tan leather bag with the famous Gucci symbol on the side. Her mobile phone fell onto the silk and satin counterpane.

Chest heaving, she stared at it. Revenge was like an ice-cold knife between her ribs. It was not in her power to destroy Andrew, seeing as she needed him to carry on supporting her, but she could make things difficult for him — swine as he was.

She phoned the police, asked for whoever was in charge of the case and told him that the murdered American *had* visited Charlborough Grange.

'It would be very worth your while if you questioned my husband.'

Doherty sounded unimpressed. 'We do already have someone helping us with our enquiries. I'll let you know if we need to speak to you or your husband again.'

Frustrated by his answer, she slammed the disconnect button. Someone had to be interested.

Her! The hotel liaison person! She'd left her card.

Honey answered on the fourth tone.

'My husband lied. The American was here,' she said once the initial introductions were taken care of.

'That's interesting. Thank you very much.'

Lady Pamela's mouth remained open. This was not the response she'd hoped for — from either of them.

'Interesting? Is that all you can say?'

'Look, I'm a bit busy at the moment, but if you'd like to jot down all you remember . . .'

'Surely what I know deserves a little time?'

'Alright. Tell me something.'

Pamela paused. 'Elmer Maxted. Do you know where he died?'

'As far as the police are aware he was killed in the cellars of one of the houses with access to the river. They think the house he was murdered in was numbered six or nine.'

'Never mind. I'll put it in a letter.'

She slammed the phone shut. Razor thin, it slid from her hand and into her suitcase.

Nothing was going quite as she'd wanted it to. Even her car was refusing to start. 'Give me an hour and I'll take a look at it,' Mark had said.

'Half an hour!'

He'd turned his back on her temper. 'An hour!'

'Mark, I think you should come to Spain with me.'

She'd pleaded with him. He'd said nothing.

She'd wanted to say so much, but couldn't. He might not approve of what she was about to do.

The maid had left today's *Bath Chronicle* on the dressing table. The headline caught her eye: SUSPECT RELEASED. She read on. The police had raided the wrong house, the wrong terrace. What was more, the suspect they had arrested had been released due to lack of evidence. She shivered.

Her room was an oasis of tranquil pale lime and deep pink. She sat herself at her desk, took out a pad and began to write. Once finished, she read what she had written. Her fine eyebrows arched with satisfaction. Yes. This would do the trick.

Frances Tolly, the housekeeper, came in to tell her that Mark had failed to fix her car.

'Then tell him to get the Rolls out, and tell him I need a driver,' she added. 'I'm not driving that bloody great thing! He'll have to stay overnight at the airport hotel.'

And come with me. Yes, he must come with me!

Pamela smiled at the prospect. Perhaps it was just as well that the sleek little Mercedes would not start. The thought of Mark's youthful body sent a shiver of excitement down her spine. There was so much potential in that young man. Tempting him into having sex with her was easy. Now she must apply more pressure in order to persuade him to get rid of Andrew.

Frances turned to go.

'Wait a moment. Can you post this for me, Frances? It needs a stamp.'

'Of course.'

After sealing the envelope, she passed it to the maid.

That, she thought, closes the last chapter in a loveless marriage. They'd get divorced and she'd get her share of the money and that would be that.

Her luggage was transferred into the trunk of the Rolls Royce. Trevor, her husband's most loyal servant, who served as butler and did anything else her husband required, was driving. She would have preferred Mark, but was told when she'd asked that he'd gone on an errand. She didn't look back as they drove off. She never wanted to see the place again.

The main gate loomed up before them. Suddenly, Trevor stopped the car.

'What's wrong?'

'The brake drums are binding. Dust I expect. Not too much of a problem, but best checked. We'll have to go back.'

She shivered. Had Mark really fixed the brakes as she'd asked him to? She'd immediately regretted it — once she'd sobered up that is. Thankfully it was Trevor driving.

He swung the car round and headed back down the drive, stopped and got out.

He left the car running while he went into the garage to find what he needed.

When he got back out the car was gone. He ran round to the front of the house. Nothing. No car to be seen.

Arms hanging listlessly at his side, he shrugged and walked back to the house. She'd probably wanted to drive herself. It wouldn't be the first time she'd shot off to meet a secret lover. Either that or someone from the house had taken over.

He didn't care which it was. He had the greenhouses to contend with. He had war games to prepare.

CHAPTER 31

Cora's hands shook as she placed the cereal packets along the sideboard in the dining room, the granola next to the bran flakes, the cornflakes next to the Rice Krispies, then the Weetabix, the Shreddies and the Sugar Puffs.

Things wouldn't be done like this at the Green River, but in a guest house it was perfectly acceptable. The lines were straight, the crockery gleamed and the cutlery sparkled. None of this seemed enough for Cora. Again and again she realigned the packets. Her hands shook, and for once her fingers did not reach for cigarettes.

Honey tried to contain her excitement. She could be wrong about the newspapers being the key to everything, but her instinct told her otherwise.

'It must be very difficult — losing your husband and trying to keep things going.'

She didn't add anything about Mervyn having abused his position as stepfather to Loretta. *How would I feel?* she wondered.

'Our Loretta's a help. She's given up her other job to give me a hand.'

'That's good of her.'

Cora stopped the obsessive moving of cereal packets and glared at her. 'She's a good girl! I won't have anyone saying anything else. Neither will Bob.'

Robert Davies! The impression came over loud and clear that she and her former husband were shoulder to shoulder in this.

'You don't think he killed Mervyn?'

'Of course he didn't! He was tempted, mark you! So was I, come to that.'

Honey shook her head. 'No, I don't think he did either.'

'That copper does.'

Honey knew Cora was referring to Doherty.

'You have to admit your first husband did have a motive for killing your second husband. But why the American? It doesn't make sense to pin that one on him as well.'

Cora shook her head emphatically. 'He didn't do it! Neither of 'em!'

Sitting at a table with an instant coffee she had no intention of drinking, Honey watched as Cora resumed her fussing along the sideboard, straightening servers, smoothing the lace-edged cloth covering the polished wood. The intricacies of the case slid around in her head — a bit like pieces of scrabble — a bit like Cora rearranging the cereal packets.

Move that bit there, this bit here, and approach from another angle. She could have come straight out and said, 'Hey, can I have a look at the old newspapers those watches are wrapped in?' Best to tread softly, she'd decided. *Softly, softly, catchee monkey*, or in this case, a motive and a murderer.

'Do you think Mervyn was capable of murder?'

The question was out before she could put on the brakes.

Cora was like a figure on a TV screen when someone hits the pause button on the video. She didn't seem surprised, more confused, as though the thought had never, ever entered her bleached-blonde head.

Eventually, she came to herself. 'Mervyn was a first-class creep. And that's putting it mildly! Bob was never like that. Never!'

She picked up a duster and began flicking it at imagined specks around the bay window. The windows rattled as a heavy truck trundled past, heading towards Bristol.

'But him murder that nice Mr Bernstock? No. Like our Loretta said, Mervyn invited him into his den. He didn't do that very often, I can tell you. Even me and our Loretta weren't allowed in there.'

Something clicked in Honey's brain. Cora had just called her first husband Bob. No! Could it be Mary Jane's Bob the Job?

'Did err . . . Bob . . . meet Elmer?'

Cora stiffened.

'Bob the Job?'

Cora leaned on the sideboard when she turned round. Her doughy figure turned doughier.

'So, you know about it. That was his interest, you see? He started doing it in prison years ago. He'd put adverts in magazines about helping people trace their roots, and they'd write to him. Got hundreds of replies, he did.'

Though her mouth was dry with excitement, Honey curbed her enthusiasm. She didn't want to alienate Cora. The poor woman had gone through enough.

'Is there any chance that you and Bob might get back together?'

Cora shrugged. 'There may be — if we get through this bother, that is.'

Honey put down her coffee mug. 'So, tell me about Mervyn's watches. He was quite a collector.'

'That's right. Rubbish, most of them — from car boots and junk shops. But that was his hobby. Mended them and got them going, he did.'

Honey tapped thoughtfully at the rim of her coffee mug as though a road through all this had only just come to her.

'Do you think I could have another look in there?'

Cora made a whistling sort of noise as she drew in her breath. 'The police said it wasn't to be disturbed. I got told off for clearing it up.'

Honey played her ace. 'You never know. I might pick up on something that the police have overlooked. Who knows, it might help your first husband get off the hook. And then, the two of you might have a future together.'

Cora pursed her lips as she thought it through. 'Why not?'

'But we won't tell the police, right?'

'Coppers! What do they know! Come on.' She flung down her duster.

Mervyn's den smelled of dried rubber and stale beer. The blink of a computer terminal caught her eye. The unit was old and smudged with dirty finger and palm prints. Having a frugal attitude to energy waste, she turned the screen off and looked for the box.

Cora had placed it beneath the ancient desk on which the computer sat. She pulled it out. As she unwrapped the contents from their newspaper, she became aware of Cora watching her from the doorway.

She placed each one on top of the desk. None of them looked particularly valuable, but you could never tell. She got out her phone and took a photograph.

Pretty soon she'd done the lot. The idea was to show them to Casper. He would know if they were valuable, and Cora could do with the money.

One of the newspapers tore as she started to rewrap each watch. Just as she'd suspected, they were old and not just published in England. Various headlines caught her eye. They were interesting, some downright dramatic, but what exactly was she looking for?

The tragedies of the world were there in black and white. Robberies, murders and children left motherless following a fire. She read on. One of the boys who survived the fire had been abducted and never seen again. The other had been given a home by a wealthy landowner in the Southwest.

Honey sat back on her haunches and sighed. 'These newspapers are next to useless. They're so old. Fancy keeping them this long.'

Cora sniffed and lit up. 'The Yank left them behind. I just made use of them.'

As far as she could see, the newspapers said nothing. The sudden idea at the bookshop wasn't as good as it first seemed. It couldn't have been them that had led to the murder of two men of two different nationalities, and probably two different dispositions. Except . . .

There was a son . . . he'd survived an accident in which his mother had died. *Like these two loves*, she thought, eyeing the orphans whose mother had died in a fire.

An odd feeling came over her, a sense that she was seeing something here that made sense, that Mervyn had also seen. One of the boys looked quite a bit older than the other. The younger one looked to be about the same age as young Lance would have been when his mother died.

She frowned. And this means something. But what?

Another newspaper. A later one. Another photograph. Father and son. The face of the father was familiar. Could it really be…?

It was all too fantastic. A child orphaned by fire, adopted by a wealthy landowner. Charlborough!

Once the watches were rewrapped, Cora went with her to the front door.

'It's a nice night,' said Honey.

Cora sighed. 'It'll be a better night once all this is sorted out. It's unsettling having people think you've done away with yer 'usband. Bad for business.' She was referring to her second husband of course.

Honey wasn't so sure. Finding dead bodies in the back garden attracted the ghoulishly curious. A murdered American was a different matter. The national press had got hold of the story, and before long it would be international news. She thought about this more deeply as she walked back along Bristol Road. She got a taxi as far as Widcombe Basin.

'I'll walk from here,' she said, and got out and paid the driver.

She took a left along the towpath enjoying the smell of water, the colours of a narrowboat moored in the lock. Lights from the restaurant of a nearby hotel lay like fallen stars on the water.

The night was clear, veins of purple stretching from the western sky, the air just cool enough to invigorate the brain without chilling the skin.

She passed a troop of tourists undertaking yet another ghost walk. The tour guide, a leggy chap wearing learned glasses above an acne-covered chin, was sounding awestruck.

'There are many legends and many buildings supposedly haunted by a "Grey Lady". One of the most famous has to be the one who haunts Bath's Theatre Royal.'

A low murmur of interest rustled through the listeners. 'Have you ever seen her?' someone asked.

'I didn't exactly see her,' said the guide. 'But I did feel her presence. It's a bit like turning round quickly and fancying you've just seen someone out of the corner of your eye.'

Perhaps it was the tone of emphatic belief that made Honey do just that. Someone ducked into a doorway. A ghost? No. She'd caught a glimpse of white trainers. Ghosts didn't wear white trainers, did they?

Swiftly she joined the crowd following behind their guide like a clutch of spring ducklings.

Someone nudged her elbow. 'Have you ever felt someone was trying to get in touch with you from the other side?' The woman spoke with a thick New York accent.

Honey grimaced. 'Mostly my bank manager when I've gone on the wrong side of my overdraft facility.'

CHAPTER 32

The sun streamed into the dining room of the Green River Hotel. The clattering of cutlery against crockery clashed with the sound of butter knives grating against toast. Guests conversed across white damask tablecloths and the smell of grilled bacon and fresh coffee drifted like a friendly wraith around the room.

Mary Jane sat at her usual table in the farthest corner — her favourite spot. From there she had a panoramic view of the breakfast room and everybody entering it.

Her head bobbed to one side when she caught sight of Honey, and a starburst of wrinkles spread out from her lips as she smiled.

Honey raised the coffee pot. 'Coffee?'

Mary Jane's smile remained as she nodded. Her eyes stayed unblinking on Honey's face.

'He's been watching you,' she said in a hushed voice.

Honey had been about to ask her what she wanted for breakfast; Mary's statement pulled her up with a start. Her first inclination was to ask if he wore white trainers. Instead she kept it simple.

'Has he, now?'

'Yes. I think it's you he's interested in. Do you ever notice him?'

She guessed where this was going: Mary Jane's long-dead ancestor.

Mine host must grin and bear it. And dead residents were so much less trouble than the living ones!

Olga, the new breakfast waitress lately arrived from Czechoslovakia, had not turned in for work that morning. Neither had Rosie, a stalwart of the fifty-plus generation who had rarely, if ever, let her down. She wanted to believe both had good excuses for not coming in.

Rosie phoned in pretty sharply. She'd slipped the length of the stairs on her backside and had gone to see her chiropractor. Anna had stayed too long in the bar with Smudger the night before. Logic told her that she was still in bed — probably with Smudger. Unfortunately, being able to work out the mysteries occurring in the lives of her staff didn't get the breakfast out. Dumpy Doris was cooking breakfast while she and two girls on work experience waited on tables. Such was the glamour of the hotel trade. Flying by the seat of your pants was about the size of it!

Mary Jane's chirpy take on the paranormal was amusing but sometimes irritating — like now.

'I saw you waltzing along the Royal Crescent the other day. He was right behind you.'

'If you mean Sir Cedric, I thought he never left the ancestral home.'

Honey waltzed off to the next table with the coffee pot.

Mary Jane leaned backwards, cricking her head to an awkward angle. 'I don't mean Sir Cedric. I mean the guy who looks like that film star who ended up getting butchered in *Gladiator*.'

Being hit with a baseball bat couldn't have been worse. She just about controlled her shaking hands. Smiling, she put the pot down on the next table. 'Help yourselves,' she said to the four Australians sitting there.

Pulling up a chair, she leaned over the table and looked up into Mary Jane's wise old face. 'Make my day. Am I being pursued by Russell Crowe? If so, I'll slow down and let him catch me.'

Mary Jane went all vague. 'It might have been *Spartacus* I was thinking of. You know, fair-haired and a broken nose.'

Honey's elation vanished. Kirk Douglas and a Zimmer frame came to mind.

'He wasn't wearing trainers, by any chance?'

As she considered the question, Mary Jane's pink lips pursed on the rim of her coffee cup. A perfect pink imprint was left behind.

'I didn't notice his feet. Just his face.'

'Ugly?'

She meant ugly as in dangerous. Visions of police mug-shots zipped through her mind.

'Bland,' said Mary after much consideration. 'But then, I might not have noted his features in detail. I wasn't concentrating too much on him. I was watching the sheep feeding on the grass in front of the Royal Crescent.'

Honey frowned. 'I don't think sheep are allowed to graze on the Royal Crescent.'

Mary Jane's expression of total belief was undiminished. 'Not now, but there used to be.' She nodded at a picture on the wall depicting the Royal Crescent as it had been in the eighteenth century.

'See? If you go to the Crescent and narrow your eyes, you can see them gambolling there just as they used to.'

'Amazing.'

Mary Jane caught her arm before she could leave. 'Before you go,' she said, her voice falling into a deep whisper. 'I thought you should know that Sir Cedric reckons your life is in danger. He saw blood and a lot of trees — like a forest, he said, only worse.'

'Really?'

'The other night at the séance. He came through, you see. He was terribly specific. You should have been there.'

In the past she had always taken Mary Jane's prophesies with a pinch of salt, but recent circumstances had taken a toll. Suddenly she felt vulnerable.

'Perhaps that's what comes of being a detective,' she said with a hint of sarcasm. 'Jane Marple survived all her cases,' she added, with a laugh that she thought sounded convincing.

'I'm sure that's got something to do with it,' said Mary Jane. 'And that's why I've decided to assist you.'

Visions came to mind of Mary Jane dressed head to toe in a pink kaftan and silver sandals, floating into Manvers Street police station.

'I think I'm supposed to do this by myself. Do excuse me. I need to help clear away the breakfast things.'

Her mother floated in accompanied by an overabundance of French perfume. 'Hannah,' said her mother. 'Mr Paget tells me you have not returned his calls.'

Each time her mother's dentist had called, she'd got someone to tell him she was out. The Eastern European girls were quite wonderful at it. Trying hard not to giggle, they adopted thicker accents than they actually had and pretended that their knowledge of English was very poor. Amazing how obliging they could be for the sake of unrequited love.

'Mother, I'm rather busy at the moment.'

'You sound just like your father. He was always busy.'

'That figures. He ran a multi-million-dollar industry,' she muttered while scraping bits of sausage and bacon rind into the bin.

'And left me almost destitute!'

'Hardly that. He allowed you what he could. After all, he only *managed* the company.'

Her mother grimaced. 'Keep your voice down. Think of my image.'

Honey rolled her eyes. Rumours that her mother's former husbands had all been millionaires were exactly that — rumours, carefully created rumours put about by Gloria Cross herself. Image, as she insistently reminded her, was everything.

'Well, there you are! No one could blame me for finding solace in the arms of another man! Nothing can beat good and frequent sex for keeping a woman looking young. You should do more of it yourself.'

Honey blushed.

At the sink, the jaw of Clint, their part-time dishwasher, dropped like a lump of lead. A soapy plate slid from his fingers. The sound of it smashing made Honey jump. The top plate from the greasy pile followed it.

Gloria Cross jerked her chin at the smashed plates. 'Two plates. That's bad luck. Everything should come in threes.' A hand encompassed in pink rubber reached for a plate.

'No!'

Before the deed could be done, Honey had grabbed it with both hands.

'Plates cost money.'

'Yer mother may have a point,' said Clint, his shaved head wreathed in steam from the dishwasher. 'It's Friday the thirteenth today. Unlucky for some,' he said with a smile and winked.

Accepting she was surrounded by weirdos, she shook her head and left the kitchen.

Making out bills in reception and dealing with the morning mail should help restore her sanity.

Everything in the morning mail was ordinary — though only up to a point. The quality envelope smelling of perfume intrigued her. It did more than that once she'd opened it.

Honey stuffed the letter back into the sweetly scented envelope and addressed the girl on reception. 'The bills are done, the phone's quiet and I'm off out.'

'And if anyone wants you?' asked a surprised-looking Olga, her cheeks pink with youthful energy.

'If they want to reserve a room or a table in the restaurant, write it down. If it's a man and he sounds reasonably endearing, give him my mobile number.'

'And Mr Paget? Your mother told me he wishes to marry you.'

Honey saw the grin on Olga's face.

'Tell him I've gone to work in a leper colony.'

CHAPTER 33

A stilted silence hung over the incident room, and the aroma of stewed coffee clogged the air. The coffee grew cold in half-full cups, and no one seemed to have even a corny gag or dry pun to break the ice.

Clutching the letter from Lady Charlborough, Honey peered in through the glass door at the glum expressions and lacklustre postures. Some personnel were slouched in their chairs, others bent over their desks, heads resting on arms. Steve Doherty was using a pencil to tap at a Santa Claus mug.

Now was the time to take the plunge. The door swung wide open. A few pairs of eyes looked up to see what noisy so-and-so was disturbing their grief.

'Our person from the Bath Hotels Association,' said glum-looking Steve, his chin still resting on his hand, his elbow resting on the desk.

He flashed a grim reaper grimace before shifting his glance onto something less unsettling. He chose the paper-clip dispenser.

'Don't tell me. You've had to let Robert Davies go and you're peed off about it!'

Steve's mouth twisted into a snarl. 'You came to gloat?'

'No.' She held up the letter. 'I've come to give you this.'

'What is it?'

'A letter from Lady Pamela. It explains a lot.'

He eyed it suspiciously.

'It won't bite you,' exclaimed Honey. 'Though she might sink her teeth into you, given half the chance.'

A wave of sniggers circled the room.

Doherty glared. 'You lot got nothing else to do? How about a bit of door-to-door? Better still, traffic duty. Savvy?'

The others in the room turned back to their individual tasks, sieving evidence files, playing spider solitaire and drinking tea.

Doherty straightened as he took the letter. As his eyes devoured the words, his dour expression brightened.

'So! She's accusing this bloke Trevor Spiteri of being a psycho.'

'Hmmm.'

'What's *hmmm*, supposed to mean?'

'I thought she'd accuse the person she hates most.'

'Her husband?'

As she noted Spiteri's address, she made that *hmmm* sound again. 'Instead it's someone dedicated to her husband. And with the right address.'

Doherty waved the letter. 'This is enough for me!'

Sensing a shift in mood, a few of his team eyed him like dogs about to be let off the leash.

'Braden,' he barked.

A dark-skinned woman with shiny black hair bolted upright.

'Get a fix on Trevor Spiteri.'

'Yes, guv.'

Her fingers pounded the computer.

'Fleming?'

The man named Fleming was already on his feet, hanging over Doherty as though ready to snaffle up every word.

'Get a warrant!'

The excitement was tangible. Honey could almost taste the change in mood. It was as though she had entered a different room, certainly not the one she'd come into just a few minutes ago. Everyone was animated, keen to replace one arrest with another.

She glowed in their praise.

'You're one of the team!'

'We got him now!'

'You're a doll.'

The corners of Doherty's mouth went sunny side up. 'You'll be wanting a job here before long.'

She smiled coquettishly and tossed her head. 'Let's not get silly. Though I did prove myself right.'

'Don't rub it in.'

'You owe me.'

'Dinner?'

'OK. But more than that. I want to come with you. I want to be in on the arrest.'

He hesitated.

'You owe me,' she repeated.

He hesitated before nodding. 'Hopefully he'll be there.'

His attention jerked to the glossy-haired detective. 'So what do we know, Braden?'

Braden leaned back from her desk, fingers still on the keyboard. 'Grievous bodily harm — ten years back. He's ex-army. Born in Warminster . . .'

Doherty jabbed a finger in her direction. 'Print it off!'

Doherty read the details before passing it to her.

Honey gasped.

Charlborough's batman, Trevor Spiteri, lived at number six, Rathbone Terrace, a stone's throw from Charlotte Terrace, where Robert Davies had lived. As with others in the city, its cellars went under the road and had doors opening onto the river. In the past the wealthy owners had moored shallow leisure craft here. They were gone now, the elegant houses divided into equally elegant apartments, rented at roughly the same price per month as each house had cost to build way back. She wondered if Trevor Spiteri wore white trainers.

'Got it!' Fleming shouted, an arrest warrant flapping in the air. Up went the cheer. Cars were organised. The plan discussed. Honey ran out behind them, her heart thudding with excitement. Without waiting for a specific order she clambered into the back seat of Doherty's car.

With a screech of wheels they were out of the car park and onto Manvers Street, Doherty aiming the car like a missile homing in on the target.

Charlotte Terrace was not as elegant as some in the city, its architecture originating at the beginning of the nineteenth century. Gone were the Palladian pillars each side of a wide door, the carved pediments over long, light-filled windows. The refined features had been replaced by the more business-like style of a swiftly moving industrial age. Aprons of black-and-white quarry tiles sloped from threshold to pavement in front of each house, worn down by a thousand footsteps.

Car doors slammed in unison. Uniforms and plain-clothes officers tumbled out of cars.

'I'll take the front door with you two.' Doherty pointed a finger at two of the passengers of another car. He turned to Honey. 'You get around the back with these two. And keep out of the way.'

Hair flying and face flushed, Honey followed the two policemen, the heels of her black suede boots scattering gravel behind her.

They came face to face with a blank wall. The two policemen looked baffled. One lifted his helmet and rubbed at the redness left behind on his forehead.

'The guvnor must 'ave got his facts wrong, miss. There's no entrance round here.'

The river bounded the rear of the houses. The side wall prevented them from going any further. There was no back alley, no way of slipping from one backyard to another.

Honey glared in the direction of the river. Doherty hadn't wanted her to come. He'd got his way.

Words were unnecessary, which was just as well. Doherty's name was mud.

Back at the front of Rathbone Terrace, heads were appearing at windows, figures at doors. As insistent as plague, speculation crept from one flat, one house and one doorway to another.

By word of mouth, it passed the black railings protecting the drops to narrow basements. Sash windows shaded with Venetian blinds or the braids and tassels of traditional design flashed past.

She barged through the cordon at the entrance to number six. Four uniformed bods were plenty enough to keep the curious at bay.

'Nobody's allowed in,' said a young fella with a ginger moustache.

'I'm not a nobody.'

He threw out his arm and inadvertently brushed her bosom.

'That's sexual assault!'

He went beetroot red.

'I didn't mean . . .'

At that moment Braden came running out, and Honey homed in on her. 'What's going on?'

'Spiteri's barricaded himself in his flat. Steve . . . DS Doherty is talking to him. He says that until this is resolved, no one is allowed inside.'

The sound of a sash window being pulled up preceded a head appearing out of a third-floor window.

The two women looked up.

'I suppose that's him,' said Fleming.

Honey agreed.

'I'll jump if you smash my door in,' Spiteri shouted.

Honey recognised the hushed voice coming from a broken voice box.

'We only want to talk to you,' Fleming shouted back.

'If I jump and hurt myself, I'll claim police harassment,' Spiteri shouted back.

Honey couldn't resist. 'You wouldn't be able to claim a single penny.'

'Name one reason why not.'

'The fall would kill you. Your head and guts would be splattered on the pavement, or you could be speared on the railings.'

Even from this distance, Honey perceived his perplexity, the horror of having reality spelled out to him. To jump or not to jump. No contest.

Feeling slighted, Honey tackled Braden. 'Doherty sent me round the back purposely.'

'Um . . . Yes,' said Braden, fluctuating between loyalty to Doherty and disgruntled sisterhood.

'He's a pig!' growled Honey.

Fleming managed a lop-sided grin. 'We all are, aren't we?'

Honey folded her arms. 'That isn't what I meant.'

'He's miffed,' said Braden.

'He's toast,' grunted Honey.

After confirming that she was definitely not to be allowed in the house, Braden summoned more assistance through her radio.

Honey found herself melting into the small crowd of watchers as though she never had been of any consequence. Mentally she was sticking pins into a real-life Doherty. He was pushing her out.

She hardly noticed the dusky young woman in the business suit come out of the house next door. Only when she spoke did it occur to her that the woman moved like a panther — silently, swiftly and with deadly precision. She came beside her that quickly.

'What is going on?'

Her voice was as dark as her hair.

Honey turned and took in the details. The crisp white collar of a starched blouse lay flat against the lapels of a navy-blue business suit. She carried a briefcase — or perhaps it was a laptop. The heels on her shoes were businesslike, built for daywear. It was easy to believe that at night those long legs appeared even longer in four-inch heels. She was beautiful.

'The police are trying to arrest the man next door.'

'But not very successfully.'

'Par for the course.'

'Do excuse me for saying so, but I got the impression you were with them.'

Honey grimaced. 'So did I. I think they'd decided that I'd outlived my usefulness.' Blurting all to a stranger seemed ridiculous, but she couldn't help herself.

The lovely lady from next door tutted and shook her head.

'Poor Mr Spiteri. And only just back from visiting his family.'

Honey's response was offhand. 'Really?'

'Yes. He was away most of the summer and has only been back two weeks.'

Two weeks?

Honey turned to face the informant. 'Is that a fact?'

The young woman's complexion was to die for. Honey felt a tinge of jealousy for her youthful skin, dark eyes and confident manner.

The perfect teeth flashed pearl white. 'I was told this by a nosey parker that I know. My own grandmother, in fact.'

Thick lashes flickered as she checked her watch. 'If you wish to confirm this, go into my house and up the first flight of stairs. My grandmother is home. The rest of the family are out at work all day. Don't tell her that I called her a nosey parker, but I assure you she knows everything that happens in this street. Her legs are bad, so she doesn't get out much and therefore sees everything.'

Out of gratitude, Honey felt a need to show interest in this helpful young woman.

'Your family is in business?'

'My parents, along with other members of the Patel family, run various businesses. My brothers and I have professions.'

'And what is yours?' Honey asked, adopting the warmest of smiles.

'I'm a tax accountant.'

Honey's smile froze.

The young woman saw her look. 'I said tax accountant, not tax inspector.'

'Ah, yes,' said Honey taking a deep breath and fanning her face with her hand. 'Thank goodness for that.'

'Please. Tell my grandmother that Zakia said you should speak to her. Like a lot of elderly people, she has an obsession with security but does like to talk.'

Honey thanked her and took her advice.

Like most Georgian houses, the property had once been home to just one family and their servants. Now it was divided into individual homes for the members of one family.

After the third knock at the Patels' door, it opened a couple of inches and a pair of dark eyes appeared over the tight restraint of a brass security chain. The perfume that wafted out through the gap was instantly recognisable. Chanel. Exactly like her mother.

'Mrs Patel? I'm working with the police. Your grand-daughter, Zakia, suggested I speak with you.'

'Will she get to work on time?'

'I see no reason why not.'

'Oh. That's good.'

Her dark eyes darted from Honey's head to her toes and back again before the door closed, the chain rattled and the door reopened.

'Please. Come in. I'll put the kettle on. You'll have to excuse the mess. I'm researching my thesis for a degree with the Open University.'

'Oh, really? What subject are you studying?'

'Computer science, though I'm not sure I've picked the right module. I think I need to enrol for a City and Guilds qualification. I'm more interested in stripping them apart than understanding the mathematics.'

Surprised, Honey raised her eyebrows. 'You mean you can actually take a computer apart and put it back together again?' Technology was not Honey's forte. To her mind you couldn't beat pen and paper. Anyone who understood the things was a genius — a saint if they could strip them apart.

Mrs Patel grinned. 'Oh yes. I can strip it down now, thanks to my grandson's instruction.' She frowned as a thought occurred to her. 'The trouble is that neither of us are any good at putting it back together again. That's what I need to learn.'

Mrs Patel was dressed in a swathe of rich green silk banded with gold. Grey hair spread out like a halo framing her face. She was elegant and oozed confidence, all in all a formidable woman. Nothing, thought Honey, had ever been allowed to stand in the way of anything she'd ever wanted to do.

'Come. Follow me. We'll make ourselves comfortable.'

She limped towards the right as she led her to the back of the house overlooking the river.

'This is my private little flat where I go when I wish to be away from the family,' she explained.

Her eyes shone as she spoke. Arm outstretched, she indicated a row of family photographs, including one of Zakia wearing mortarboard and gown, and clutching her degree. Pride shone from Mrs Patel's eyes.

Honey guessed she wasn't often in this room — at least, not when the family were home.

'Sit here. I'll make tea.'

She shuffled off into the adjoining kitchen. The sound of a kettle being switched on and crockery being laid out rattled into the living room.

The Georgians had liked high ceilings and big windows to let in the light. This one was no exception. A Bentwood rocker packed with silk-covered cushions was placed in front of the high window. Beyond the yard was the river.

'There is where I sit and watch the world at the back of the house,' Mrs Patel explained on coming back with the tea. 'Sometimes I sit at the front of the house. I have another chair just like this one in front of that window.'

'You have very nice views. I bet you see all that goes on.'

Mrs Patel sighed, her fine wrinkles deepening as they appeared to fold layer on top of layer.

'I see a lot. Sometimes it's very interesting. Sometimes it's tiring. I sit here a lot, you know. It's my hip, you see. The pain it causes interferes with my studies. I'm waiting for an operation. If I haven't got an appointment by the end of the month my son says he'll pay for me.' She rubbed her hip as she said it.

'I hope you get it sorted soon,' said Honey politely. 'Let me help you with the tea.'

'That's very kind.'

Mrs Patel made herself comfortable as Honey made the tea and brought the tray into the room.

On crossing the room she again glanced out of the window. There was a clear view between the trees to the parapet at the rear of the yard and the river.

'I wish I had a view like this.'

Mrs Patel smiled and nodded as she eased herself back into her chair after taking her tea.

'It is a joy. I see all life from here, even though I have difficulty getting around nowadays. There's little I miss.'

She suddenly looked worried and the smile dropped from her face.

'No one has complained about me being a nosy parker, have they?'

Remembering her promise to Zakia, Honey smiled and sat on a leather chesterfield, which was faded red and a bit saggy in the middle. A blue-and-red silk shawl with soft gold fringes was thrown across its back.

'No, Mrs Patel. In fact, you might be of some help in solving a murder.'

'A murder!' Mrs Patel's face brightened. 'A real one? This is a real case, not just for television?'

Honey thought of poor Elmer Maxted and Mervyn Herbert. 'I'm afraid this is for real.'

Mrs Patel clapped her hands. 'All the years of watching murder mysteries and now I'm actually witness in a real-life murder.'

'That may be so.'

'So,' said Mrs Patel, her face beaming. 'How can I help you?'

Leaning forward, Honey rested her elbows on her knees and clasped her hands together in front of her.

'I understand that Mr Spiteri next door has just come back from abroad. Is that right?'

Fearing she might frighten the old girl, she spoke softly but clearly.

'Is he a suspect? What did he do? How did he do it?'

Mrs Patel, despite her obvious age, didn't appear to be deaf, frightened or put out by the possibility that a murderer lived next door. On the contrary, she seemed to relish the prospect.

Honey had to disappoint her.

'I actually think that his guilt or innocence rather depends on what you've got to say.'

Mrs Patel's mouth dropped open. Her brown eyes glowed with excitement.

'Do go on, do go on!'

Mrs Patel was the witness a good policeman dreamed of — clear headed and totally committed to giving a good account of all she knew.

'Was Mr Spiteri away for some time?'

The correct answer would win Spiteri his freedom and Doherty a big wad of mud on his face.

Mrs Patel was quick to reply. 'He came back about two weeks ago on a Thursday at about five in the morning. I don't sleep that well, you see? That's the trouble with getting old.'

'And how long was he away?'

Her heart thudded against her ribs. Everything depended on the answer. If Spiteri had been away at the same time as the murders were committed, then he was in the clear. Doherty was not. She found herself praying for the right answer.

'He was away for about two months visiting his relatives on some island in the Mediterranean. It's near Sicily, I believe.'

A map of the Med surfed through Honey's mind. 'Malta?'

Mrs Patel nodded. 'I think that is the name of it. He did tell me, but I was never very good at geography.'

'Two months?'

Mrs Patel confirmed that it was so and Honey knew for sure that she was telling the truth. He hadn't been there on her first visit to the Charlboroughs, his position temporarily filled by Mark, the younger man. A true hunk of a butler, it had to be said.

'Fantastic!' Honey clapped her hands. She couldn't wait to slap Doherty's dumb face with the details.

Mrs Patel smiled. 'I'm so glad I was able to help. Although he looks a little intimidating, he's really quite a nice man. So friendly. Not like the other man who used to stay in the basement flat. You would never think that they worked together for the titled gentleman.'

Honey's feet had been itching to be up and away, confronting Doherty with the fact that Spiteri could not have murdered the two men. But Mrs Patel's nosiness was reaping rewards beyond belief. Her legs turned to lead. Her voice sounded far away.

'What other man was that, Mrs Patel? Would you recognise him again?'

'Of course.'

'You definitely saw him arrive next door?'

'Most definitely.'

Honey got to her feet. 'I have to tell the policeman next door. Will you come with me to confirm this?'

For someone with a dodgy hip, Mrs Patel got to her feet in double-quick time. Her enthusiasm had more effect than state-of-the-art robotics.

'I'm right with you!'

'I'll take these into the kitchen for you,' said Honey, reaching for the tray.

'No! No!' Mrs Patel pushed the tray back onto the table. 'Never mind that. This is the most exciting thing that's happened to me for years. Come on. We must hurry.'

Honey paused. 'Mrs Patel, I can't thank you enough.'

The dark eyes sparkled impishly. 'I used to be a journalist, you know. I would gather and write factual features on a freelance basis. That's why I'm so sure about times and dates and the comings and goings. Besides, I keep a diary.'

Honey stiffened, her eyes round with hope.

'A diary?'

She nodded. Her smile returned but was coyer than it had been.

'I like to write down what I've seen. Sometimes I write a line or two of poetry about the night scene — you know, the lights and everything, people hurrying by, lovers strolling, the river. Anything that catches my eye.'

'May I see it?' Honey asked. She rubbed her palms together. They were clammy and stuck together.

'If it helps at all. There,' she said. She pointed to a book bound in pink plastic. Red plastic lips stood proud of the cover. It sat on a brass-topped table, the sort that's no more than a big plaque on turned legs. 'If you don't mind getting that for me,' said Mrs Patel.

Honey did as she was told and passed the diary to Mrs Patel, who found the page and passed it back to her.

Honey took it with both hands. She noticed Mrs Patel was frowning.

The fluidity of her writing was far more beautiful than what she had to say. Her entry for that date read almost like a shopping list.

There were times of the comings and goings of her son, her daughter-in-law, the postman and even the traffic warden and what colour cars he'd booked. The entry for Mr Spiteri coming home was entered.

Just as she had stated, there were a few lines of poetry added that reflected what she had seen that day.

> *Green leaves, black road,*
> *Grey river swirling swiftly by.*
> *People walking, people talking,*
> *Green, green grass and crisp blue sky.*

'Thank you,' said Honey, giving it back to her.

Mrs Patel followed her down the stairs. At the bottom Honey turned to make sure she was all right.

'I'm fine,' said Mrs Patel, her face glowing. 'Just wait until I've locked my door.'

Having been at the back of the house, it came as something of a surprise to see that the police presence next door had diminished.

Honey addressed a remaining constable. 'Where is everyone?'

'Gone back to the station with the accused.'

Honey swore under her breath. Doherty and everyone of importance had flown the nest.

'Just the lab boys left,' the constable added as a man in a white jumpsuit pushed his way across the pavement.

After finding that her phone batteries were flat, Honey sighed and turned to Mrs Patel. 'I'm sorry, but we'll have to go to the station and report this.'

'No worries,' Mrs Patel said brightly.

'Can I keep the diary?'

'Of course you can.'

Honey's gaze slid between the two front doors, the number six of next door, and the number seven of Mrs Patel. She frowned. After that, the numbers leaped from seven to nine. Number nine had a 'For Sale' notice outside. The frontage of seven was wider than each of the properties to either side.

'Where's number eight?' she asked.

'We are six, seven and eight,' answered Mrs Patel.

The door of number six was still open to allow the comings and goings of the forensic people.

'I would dearly love to look inside that basement flat,' said Honey, eyeing the stone steps leading downwards.

Mrs Patel began rummaging in the tan leather handbag she had insisted on bringing with her. 'I have the keys.'

'You do?'

Though of short acquaintance, nothing about Mrs Patel should have surprised her, but the old girl was still capable of springing the unexpected.

'My other son owns next door. He lets it out. I keep the spare keys.'

At this juncture it occurred to Honey that rather than press a judge to issue a warrant, Doherty would have better served his purpose by knocking next door at granny's place. Mrs Patel was a matriarch of the highest order.

After deliberating about whether they should impede the legitimate key holder, the police watched as they descended the steps.

'It has its own private entrance,' said Mrs Patel. She winked. 'Very discreet.'

The basement flat consisted of two bedrooms, a bathroom, a kitchen and a ground-floor living room. A pair of French doors opened onto a tiled patio at the back.

Even after modernization and damp treatment, some basements retained a mouldy smell. Not this one. Painted white and lit by recessed spotlights, the flat was crisp and clean. Perhaps too crisp, too austere. There were no books, no magazines, no television or the slightest evidence that anyone sometimes lived here.

Honey sniffed. The smell was familiar, not greasy bacon or chemical cleaners like you find in old bedsits: perfume, very expensive perfume hung in the air. She'd smelled it before.

'What was the name of the man who used this flat?'

'Mr Conway. Mark Conway. He made models.'

Honey recalled the polite young man who'd brought the tea. Models. Modelling clay. Heads? Like the all-too-lifelike one she'd encountered out at Charlborough Grange?

'Did you ever see him here with a woman?'

Mrs Patel rolled her eyes suggestively. 'Oh, yes. Very blonde and trimmed with gold. Expensive, though slightly less than tasteful. Best described as brassy.'

Honey took a deep breath. 'I couldn't have described her better myself.'

Lady Pamela Charlborough. It couldn't be anyone else.

'So! It was a love nest.'

'Indeed.' A concerned frown crossed Mrs Patel's cheery face. 'Just the one woman, of course. It is not a knocking shop, as you call it.'

Honey shook her head and controlled the grin. 'No, of course not.'

'He didn't always come with her. Sometimes he came alone.'

'What did he do there — when he came by himself?'

'Mostly he used the workshop. Through there.'

She pointed to a door beneath the stairs. 'It leads to the cellars. My son said he couldn't do his modelling in here.' Spreading her arms, she indicated their pristine surroundings.

'I shouldn't think so,' said Honey agreeing with her.

'I do not like dolls,' Mrs Patel said suddenly.

'He made dolls?'

Mrs Patel jerked her chin like a duck prodding at a suspicious weed. 'Heads. He made latex heads for his boss.'

Honey suppressed a shiver.

She managed to keep her tone pleasant, as though she hadn't thought of the heads in the greenhouse, which of course she had.

'How come you managed to get a look at them?'

'He wanted something to cover them with. He asked my son if he could save him the small sacks the spices come in. My son, who imports spices, brought a few home and asked me to give them to him.'

Sacks! So, whoever made the latex heads for the war games used spice sacks to keep them clean. And got them from Mrs Patel's son who imported spices — the same spices no doubt that Jeremiah Poughty sold in the market.

Honey shivered. She'd been barking up the wrong tree thinking the sacks might have come from Jeremiah's market stall. And they hadn't come from the pile outside the greenhouses either. They'd come from Mrs Patel's son who had access to hundreds of them and disliked the smell of latex coming up from the cellars. Perhaps the murderer had got so used to covering latex heads with the sacks, that he'd not been able to resist doing the same with his victims.

Finding out the truth about something as perplexing — and stupidly simple — as those sacks, was like breathing frosty air. It wasn't just refreshing, it invigorated.

'So,' she said, trying hard to control her racing heart, 'when's he expected back?'

'He's not. As you can see from the board outside, my son is selling both this house and number nine. Mr Spiteri has agreed to move out at the end of the week. He's been offered accommodation with his employer, who's moving abroad. In the meantime, my son offered Mr Conway the basement of number nine in which to keep his heads. I didn't see him move his things there, but I presume he did.'

'Like rats leaving a sinking ship,' Honey murmured.

She phoned Doherty from Mrs Patel's landline before leaving but was told he was interviewing.

She should have guessed. 'Tell him he's got the wrong man.'

'I wouldn't dare,' said the female voice on the other end.

No, thought Honey. Stubborn Steve had to find things out for himself.

CHAPTER 34

DS Doherty was being stubborn.

'You need a search warrant for number nine.'

'No, I don't. I've got our man.'

'No, you haven't. He was abroad at the time.'

'He'll have to prove it.'

'There are witnesses. Us for a start. He wasn't there when we first called at Charlborough Grange.'

'That doesn't mean to say he wasn't in England.'

'It kind of leads that way, wouldn't you say?'

'No. Not necessarily.'

She hoped the sound of the phone being slammed down burst Doherty's eardrum. Stubborn cuss!

For the rest of that day, she played the same game, refusing to take his calls, pretending she was out, doing anything rather than speak to him.

Lindsey caught her cleaning the glass in the front door.

'You don't have to do that.'

'It's surprisingly therapeutic.'

'You're taking long enough.'

'You bet I am.'

Three times she'd sprayed the glass, and three times she'd pushed the polishing duster around.

'How's Sam?'

Lindsey grinned. 'Coming on nicely. By the way, I told Grandma you were practically engaged.'

The polishing stalled. 'Why?'

'She wouldn't stop asking me questions about the other night when I slept at Sam's.'

'So you threw me to the lion.'

Lindsey looked contrite. 'I needed to. She wouldn't let it go.'

Honey smoothed Lindsey's hair back from her forehead. 'Poor darling. I'm sorry about that.'

'Don't be. It's not you giving me hassle. It's her. Grandma would have been great in the days when young girls were presented at court.'

'Debutantes.'

'That's the word.'

Honey shrugged. 'You had to guard your back.'

'Thanks for understanding. She's still on about the carpet though. There was nothing I could do about that.'

'Ignore her.'

'OK.'

Honey's gaze went through the glass to the white trainers standing on the other side of the street.

Her stalker was getting braver, though doing his best to hide behind a green wheelie bin.

'Does he look familiar to you?' she asked Lindsey.

Lindsey took a bite of the cold toast she'd snitched from kitchen leftovers and shook her head.

'What's he doing?'

'Following me. I think.'

Lindsey frowned. 'Perhaps he's a hotel inspector from the tourist board or something.'

Honey blew a mental raspberry. 'Hotel inspectors don't wear Lee Cooper jeans and white trainers.'

Lindsey peered out of the window. 'How do you know they're Lee Cooper? Have you seen his bum?'

'They just look that kind of quality, and no, I haven't seen his bum.'

'By the way, Doherty called.'

'Was he apologetic?'

'I wouldn't say apologetic. Try contrite.'

Honey glanced at the gilded face of the long case clock. 'Isn't it a bit early in the day for an English lesson?'

Lindsey took on a mature expression. She wore it well. 'I was in early last night. I suppose *reflective* might be a better word.'

Honey punched a fist into the air. 'He's let Spiteri go. I win!'

'He asked you to phone him. He'd brought Sir Andrew in for questioning and following something Trevor Spiteri said was now looking for Mark Conway.'

'Ah!' Honey tapped her smiling lips. My, but it was good to be right. She became aware that Lindsey was giving her the incisive *What have you been up to, Mother?* type of look. Honey knew it well. She often used it to stump her own mother.

'He wanted to solve this case all on his own,' said Honey.

'But he didn't.'

'No. His call means that he's been out to Charlborough Grange, but Mark Conway wasn't there.'

'Right. And you know where he is. Yes?'

'No. But I'll find out.'

In her mind she was the Lone Ranger hunting down the baddy alongside a bumbling lawman. The truth was that crime wasn't quite like that at all. Leave it to the professionals, said a small voice in her mind, you know it makes sense.

The trouble was that there were *two* small voices. The other one was feeding her ego, telling her, *Sure, babe, of course you can do it. You're cleverer than him!*

Was someone lying or was it sheer pride and arrogance urging her on? Whatever! She was game for it.

'What are you doing now?' asked Lindsey. Not for the first time in her life, she sounded nervous of her mother's intentions. The way her chin was jutting reminded her of the time they'd lived in a brand-new house in a village. The locals had opposed the development. They'd also insisted that a footpath still ran through the backyard of the house they'd bought. One day Honey had caught their ringleader relieving himself against a bush she'd just planted.

He did it three days on the trot, insisting he was entitled.

On the fourth day her mother had been ready with a piece of brown paper smeared with thick, dark molasses.

Taking him unawares, she'd slapped the brown paper onto his exposed loins. The stuff was a devil to remove without help. His wife would have to help him. Likely as not, he'd also had to explain how molasses had got tangled in his pubic hair.

The footpath problem went away.

Honey was heading for the door and the man across the street.

'I'm staying here until you get back,' Lindsey called after her.

Somehow Honey felt warm about that. Lindsey cared as much for her mother as Honey did for her daughter. She was also patient, staying on board no matter what madness her mother pursued. That included running a hotel.

'I want a word with you,' she called out as she ran across the road, weaving in and out of the cars.

Horns blew. Brakes screeched to a halt.

She ignored the truck driver whose expletives did nothing for cultural heritage.

Her attention was fixed on the man in white trainers. She'd half expected him to leg it, but he didn't. Instead he seemed to come all undone, shifting his stance and drawing his hands from his pockets.

Flight or fight, that was the choice he was facing. Flight meant darting off through the evening rush-hour traffic. Fight was facing a middle-aged woman who'd obviously made her choice.

'You've been following me,' she said, fists curled over sweaty palms and resting on her hips.

He had chocolate-brown eyes and corn-coloured hair. Mid-twenties and made to be admired. What was more, she'd seen him before. It would come to her, but first the explanation.

He was dithering, still thinking about legging it.

She stiffened her stance. 'Well?'

'I didn't mean to frighten you.'

'So! Apologise!'

'I'm sorry.'

He looked into the distance. That was when she realised who he was — a little older now, but definitely the young man in the photograph hanging on the wall at Charlborough Grange.

'You're Lance Charlborough.'

She frowned. Why would he follow her? Why had she never seen him in person at the house?

'I found out,' he said plaintively, as though those three little words answered everything she might wish to know. 'I found out that my real mother died in a fire.'

Suddenly she knew what he meant, or at least where this was leading. It was pure guesswork, but her unspoken hunch about the article in the old newspaper had pointed in the right direction. What had seemed vague was now a certainty.

'How?' she asked.

'Mark had always tried to keep the truth from me. He's older than me. He wouldn't let anyone hurt me. No one.'

'Mark Conway?'

He nodded.

The truth dawned. 'Don't tell me.'

'I will anyway. We're brothers. He's older than me. When our mother died, he looked out for me. I was too young to understand. But I do now. I really do.'

There was an intense look on his face. Mark Conway's character was melding together like layers of papier mâché.

He'd *lived* for his brother. And anyone who hurt him? The opposite, she guessed.

'So! What happened?'

Lance swallowed as though he were having trouble coming to terms with what he'd learned and what he wanted to say.

'Our father couldn't cope when our mother died. He abandoned us. Sir Andrew took us in. He'd lost his son. He wanted another. A lot of money was involved, but it wasn't only that. He was devastated. His real son was a haemophiliac. He died young in a road accident miles from anywhere.'

Honey drew her hand across her breast. She had been going to give him one hell of a tongue lashing. But not now. His pain was tangible.

'How did you find out?'

'She told me. My stepmother. She got it from the American. Apparently the first Lady Charlborough was his sister-in-law.'

'And your father? Sir Andrew? Does he know that you know?'

He nodded. 'He does now. I think there's a lot of money involved. It would have gone to the real Lance. I became Lance so it could come to me. That's how Sir Andrew wanted it.'

'I bet he did.'

'When I left home a few weeks ago, my father — Sir Andrew — cried out after me that he'd make everything right. That there was no need to worry about my inheritance.'

He shook his head. His eyes seemed to melt with moisture. 'But it isn't my inheritance, is it? Not really.' He shook his head. 'I never knew anything about it until she told me. Mark knew, but he'd kept it from me. He'd protected me. He's always protected me.'

Despite his age, Lance Charlborough had a waiflike quality and she felt instantly sorry for him. In his formative years, he'd been lulled into the false security of a different identity.

She had an urge to comfort him, just like she had Lindsey as a child.

'Come and have a coffee.'

Over a Starbucks cappuccino, he told her that he'd got a job as a voluntary prison visitor. That was when he'd met Robert Davies, Bob the Job, who had developed an interest in family trees while in prison. It was him that did the tracing and came up with Elmer Maxted, related by marriage to Sir Andrew's first wife. Lance had contacted him. He'd insisted on coming over right away. Lance had begged him not to use his real name, just in case his adoptive father sussed what was going on.

'I wish I hadn't started this. I feel so guilty about Elmer getting killed.'

'Do you think your father did it?'

The chocolate pools looked into hers before he nodded. 'But I couldn't turn him in. I love him as a father, so I couldn't do that, no matter what he's done.'

She thought of her mother and nodded. 'I know what you mean.'

'I wanted to know what was going on, so I followed you.'

'Why not follow the cops?'

He shrugged. 'They're the professionals. They might have noticed me.'

It hurt. *But never mind*, she told herself. *You're proving them all wrong.* The professionals adhered to strict guidelines. Her enquiries were less stringent and carried out between the shenanigans of a domineering mother and a dozy dishwasher.

They parted company once she'd promised she would let him know when someone was arrested. He gave her his phone number, but no address. 'Just in case you cave in under torture. I don't want my father — my adoptive father — to know where I am.'

'OK.'

After he'd gone, she felt a need to talk to someone about the nuances of the case, but not the police. They were busy looking for Mark Conway, Lance's brother.

She phoned Casper. He answered within seconds.

'What now?'

'I thought you'd like to know what's going on in the world of crime fighting.'

'Not really, my dear. I just want things tidied up for the sake of next year's profit ratio. I trust you're swiftly putting this problem to bed. Are you doing that, Hannah?'

Only a man like Casper could sound so like her mother. Her mood was reflected in her tone. 'Well, you know what they say, Casper. If you want a man to do a good job, get a woman to do it.'

He made a snorting sound. Disdain was Casper's middle name.

She carried on, wanting to tell someone involved — even if only on a moderate level — all that was going on.

'The police arrested a Trevor Spiteri.'

'That's a foreign name.'

'Being foreign isn't a precursor for guilt.'

'That's a matter of opinion.'

'He's innocent and could prove it. Anyway, I think I should tell you I'm being followed.'

'A psycho?'

She paused. Lance was far from being a psycho, but he was insecure, a little sad.

She explained about the basement flat and the expensive perfume. She also explained about the newspapers that the watches were wrapped in.

'It all ties in. Lance wrote to Elmer, who was murdered because he knew it was virtually impossible that his nephew was still alive. The real Lance died in a road accident way out in the Spanish interior, far from any city. Drugs to speed blood clotting weren't so widely available then. Elmer left behind newspapers that he'd collected some years back. They contained a report of a house fire, the death of the mother and the escape of her two sons. Being a detective he must have investigated further, and found a photograph of the Charlboroughs in the press. The youngest boy was a ringer for the younger of the two boys whose mother had died in the fire. Elmer used to drink with Mervyn in his den. I think a bottle of whisky loosened his tongue and he told Mervyn more about what had happened and what he was here for. I think Mervyn tried a touch of blackmail.'

'And now?' Casper's tone was only slightly less disdainful than it had been.

'I'm going to try and speak to Lady Pamela. She's a cow, but I think she'll be willing to drop her husband in it.'

'I suppose you're right. It wasn't a happy marriage.'

'Far from it.'

After that, she phoned Doherty again. 'The next-door neighbour kept a diary of the comings and goings in Rathbone Terrace.'

'And?'

'I think I know where Mark Conway is.'

'I want that diary.'

'I'll bring it to you, but not yet. Not until I'm satisfied that every stone's been turned.'

CHAPTER 35

It might have been sheer instinct that made her swerve into the car park in front of the church. On the other hand, it could have been fear. Confronting Charlborough filled her with dread.

She watched while two women armed with bunches of gladioli, roses, lupins and delphiniums disappeared through the arched doorway. Keeping the church clean and placing flower displays in dark little alcoves took on a sudden — and safe — attraction.

Why do you suddenly want jam and Jerusalem? she asked herself. *Because being a detective isn't like doing a crossword puzzle.*

Summer was in full swing, the trees groaning in the breeze with the weight of dark-green leaves, the grass bowing in waves.

Once the coast was clear, she got out of the car, locked it and followed the path through the churchyard.

Passing along the side of the church and around the back, the grass was longer and the earth lumpy, as though those buried were trying to sit up.

Wispy heads of uncut grass tickled her legs. She shivered, and not just because of the grass.

As she ventured further into the older part of the churchyard, marble gave way to pockmarked stone. The names of the departed had flaked away. Lichen blemished the faces of granite angels and ivy smothered the last breath from a rose bush planted on a child's grave.

In the distance sunlight flashed on the windows of Charlborough Grange.

Honey took a deep breath. 'Let's go beard the lion,' she murmured.

Swiftly, before she could change her mind, she climbed over the stile. The footpath led her beside the canal before veering off towards Charlborough Grange.

The smell of wood smoke curled lazily up from a well-stacked bonfire. There was no one in sight.

The huge greenhouse lured her onwards. She remembered the heads, the very ones Mark Conway made from wax.

The sandbags were still piled around the entrance. The door made a sucking sound when she opened it. The humidity gushed out like a warm wave.

Outside was bright daylight. In here it was dark and smelled of rotting leaves.

Within seconds her clothes were stuck to her back.

'Anyone here?' she called.

There was no neat path down the middle, no trays of seedlings waiting to be planted. Huge leaves fanned out from plants whose more natural habitat was Borneo or Sumatra, anywhere further south and east than North Somerset.

This was a jungle. It was the only word to adequately describe it. The sudden sounds of insects, the calling of monkeys and all the other strange noises associated with a tropical rain forest burst into being.

Her hair clung stubbornly to her face as she looked this way, that way, half expecting something monstrous to leap out from between the fronds of tropical lushness.

'Is anyone there?' she shouted again. She told herself not to waste her breath. Who the hell was going to hear her above the din?

Bravely she made her way beneath huge leaves, the thick foliage closing behind her.

Perhaps it was a tree root she fell over, or perhaps a stone. Whatever it was threw her off balance. She fell heavily to the ground.

'Damn!' she muttered.

She peered up through the thick vegetation. There was no movement of monkeys or birds. She tried to listen for anything other than the animal sounds. But they couldn't be real. She could see no animals. The sounds were on tape and someone had switched them on.

With trembling fingers, she parted the leaves and peered out.

She saw him at once.

He crept low, his footsteps not making a sound. His face was blackened. He wore fatigues, carried what looked like an AK47 under one arm. His hand rested on a long leather sheath hanging from his belt.

Honey swallowed. Good God, had she stumbled into a real war game?

She couldn't be sure who it was. She assumed it was Charlborough.

Discretion being the better part of valour, she melted into the undergrowth.

The soil she slid into was soft and damp. She inwardly groaned at the obvious. Footsteps would be seen.

She sank back as far as she could without making a noise. What would Charlborough — if it was Charlborough — do if he caught her?

Swallowing her fears was like swallowing cornflakes without milk. They stuck and were sharp in her throat.

But should you be afraid? she asked herself. Was it for certain that Charlborough had done the dirty deed? He was protective of his adoptive son. And Mark Conway had been having an affair with her ladyship. She guessed Lady Pamela had made the running. She was that type.

She advised herself that she was condemning without good reason.

More rustling ensued around her. Another figure joined the first one.

She heard someone sigh. 'Christ, I've had enough of this.'

Peering cautiously through the undergrowth, she saw the recent arrival take off his balaclava.

'Still, it has been a good team-building exercise,' said the other man.

This was great! She didn't recognise either of them.

'Gentlemen!'

They looked taken aback to see her emerging from the bushes.

'Are you with us?' asked the Johnnie-come-lately.

'No. I'm with the tourist board. We're doing a survey on customer satisfaction. Are you totally satisfied with your weekend here?'

She dragged Mrs Patel's notebook out of her bag just to make the lie look a little more authentic. It was conspicuously pink, and she tried to hide the plastic lips on the cover with her hand.

'I'll just make a few notes,' she said as more weekend soldiers tumbled out of the bushes. 'How do you rate the course on a scale of one to ten?'

She pretended to note down the series of numbers called to her.

'Thank you,' she said, shoving everything back into her bag. 'You've been very helpful.'

All thoughts of confronting Andrew Charlborough went out of her head. Hot and sweaty, she ran all the way back to the canal.

The sobbing branches of a willow tree dipped into the water. The grass beneath it looked soft and green. Heart pounding, she flung herself beneath its shade. As she did so, Mrs Patel's notebook fell out. The red plastic lips looked incongruous with the greenness.

Having been invited to read Mrs Patel's poetry and diary entries, she'd forgotten to do so. Birdsong and the sound of a brightly painted narrowboat heading towards Bath made her want to linger.

Castles, roses and impossibly blue birds decorated the vessel's full length. The bright colours even outdid the cover of Mrs Patel's diary. But the cover made her smile. It was fun, just like the diary.

'Nice day,' she called out. 'Lovely boat.'

'Thank you.'

She looked in the direction the narrowboat had come from. There was a white yacht moored fifty yards away. The sign fastened to the wooden decking it was fastened to said, 'PRIVATE MOORING. CHARLBOROUGH GRANGE'.

Sir Andrew owned a luxury riverboat, all shiny fibreglass and stainless steel. It must surely have a large engine, another mechanical device for Mark Conway to look after.

She picked up the diary and began to read. It was strong stuff — at least as far as the case was concerned.

Mrs Patel reported Mr Conway coming in but not going out. She also mentioned activity at the river's edge, someone clearing out their cellar and boats coming and going.

The dates were clear. Honey frowned. Mrs Patel was very observant. She described what looked like a rolled-up carpet or a piece of furniture being turfed out into the river. Her phraseology reflected her obvious indignation. It looked to come from number nine, she had added.

'But number nine's empty,' murmured Honey.

She lay back in the grass. The peace of the old canal was disturbed by yet another boat. It didn't sound like a narrow boat. Opening her eyes, she raised herself onto one elbow and looked. The river cruiser was white and long. Its owner-captain stood proudly at the wheel. A blonde woman accompanied him. They were both in their fifties, just about the right age for indulging their dreams. Of course, if you were rich enough . . .

Suddenly she sat upright. Sir Andrew Charlborough could afford to indulge himself. The canal, not the river, ran through the grounds of Charlborough Grange. Via a series of lock gates, the canal led into the river . . .

She dialled Steve Doherty's number.

'Have you interviewed Mrs Patel?'

'Honey!'

He sounded pleased to hear her voice.

'Yes, I have. Very interesting, but we need a bit more. Best of all would be finding Mark Conway.'

'He's our man. I told you. He killed both men.'

'We confirmed with Sir Andrew that his wife had been having an affair with Mark Conway. He didn't seem unduly worried about it.'

'Did she deny it?'

'She wasn't there. Her husband says she's gone back to Spain.'

'And he's not worried about that either.'

'You're not surprised?'

'You only met her once. I met her twice.'

'She wasn't that bad.'

'She was blonde, Steve, and you're a man, which means you're biased.'

'We're trying to find Mark Conway,' said Doherty.

'He's in number nine! It's empty! Mark Conway was used to slipping in and out unnoticed, and I know how he was doing it. Sir Andrew has a boat. Mark Conway maintains it just like he does the cars. Anything mechanical, he said.'

At the other end of the phone, Doherty shouted, 'Get hold of the key holder!'

CHAPTER 36

It was eight o'clock in the evening and Mrs Patel was not at home. The alternative was to track down the agent selling the property.

A mist was rising from the river when they eventually got the keys. The estate agent, annoyed at being dragged away from potential clients, had insisted on accompanying them.

'Go carefully! This is a very valuable property,' he cried as they pushed against the door once the key had turned. 'It has great development potential!'

'Search the whole house,' Doherty ordered. Four burly detectives rushed into the ground-floor hall.

The estate agent had a shiny tie and a surly attitude. 'I hope you don't expect me to accompany you. There's no electricity on. You'll be in pitch darkness in some parts of the building,' he added.

Doherty grabbed Honey's arm. 'Not you. This is police business.'

'No way! I've been with this case all the way through. You can't blank me out now.'

'Yes, I can. I'm a policeman.'

Doherty was about to follow them until he noticed Honey leaning over the railings, looking down into the basement courtyard. The gate hinges creaked as she pushed it open.

'Oi!'

Instead of following the uniforms, Doherty raced after her down the slimy green steps. The small courtyard wasn't big enough to swing a cat — even a kitten, but it still smelled of cats pee.

The door to the cellar area had glass panels of multi-coloured diamonds.

It wasn't locked. Doherty pushed it open.

'I say again, the electricity is not switched on,' said the estate agent, leaning over the railings above them.

Doherty switched on his flashlight. 'No need to concern yourself, sir; boy scouts are always prepared.'

'So are girl guides,' said Honey and did the same.

They passed into the gloom. The light from their torches revealed that whoever bought the place had a lot of work to do. Nevertheless, they were likely to make a fortune. This was probably the last house on the block ripe for conversion to flats.

A passageway led to the rooms at the back. He opened a latched door and discovered the steps down to the lower level. They moved silently, surprised at hearing so little evidence of the big-footed men exploring above them. At the bottom of the steps was a small hall. Honey raised her hand to her nose. The smell of damp and mould was overpowering.

Doherty moved off to her right. Just as they'd supposed, there was an opening in the stonework between number five and number seven.

Doherty motioned for Honey to stay behind. She did as she was told, though not because he'd ordered her. She'd heard something and fancied he had not.

The light from Doherty's torch moved away. Her own began to dim. Drat. Why hadn't she thought to recharge it? She turned it off to preserve energy.

Telling herself that she wasn't in the least bit nervous, she moved sideways, thought she passed through a doorway, but couldn't be sure.

It was dark now. Doherty and his flashlight were far away.

She guessed she was in one of the small, square cellar rooms close to the river. This was where provisions were kept in years gone by. Not now. Now there was only decay and damp and darkness.

Like a cloak it surrounded her. She moved sideways thinking she heard someone, something.

The smell of mud and a rush of air told her she wasn't far from the river now. There was still ground under her feet so she couldn't possibly fall in, she told herself. All the same, she took great care. Not until she could see the orange lights shining from the other side of the road did she sigh and switch her torch back on. It was probably only a rat she'd heard earlier. She flashed her torch in front of her and sucked in her breath. Were those rats she could see moving about on the river? If they were, they were a strange shape and very large.

Her foot brushed against something. She flashed her torch downwards and her mouth went dry. The flashlight caught a pair of staring, dead eyes. This was not one of the plastic heads she'd found in the war games greenhouse. This was real, the flesh blackened and falling away from the face. The earrings were gold.

Pamela Charlborough was not in Spain!

Her stomach churned. She put her hand over her mouth and almost dropped her torch. Just then the sound she had heard earlier revealed itself. Despite her height, his arm was around her neck. Her legs buckled as he jabbed his knees into the backs of hers.

'Let me—' she began. It was all she could say. He was holding her so tightly.

'Do you see them?' he asked, his voice excited, his whole body seeming to tremble. 'Do you see my trophies? My father told me how to kill. That was the other reason he stepped in when our mother died. Our father served with Sir Andrew in Malaya. Did you know that? The Gurkhas used to cut off their enemies' heads. My dad learned how to do it from them. And Sir Andrew. Him too.'

She gagged. His arm was tight against her throat.

A cold chill ran down her spine. Even before she felt it against her neck, she knew it was coming.

'This is my friend,' he said.

Because the steel blade rested on her neck, he loosened his grip on her throat. Obviously, he guessed she'd be too scared to do anything silly. He was dead right.

'I'm not a police officer,' she said, trying not to sound frightened. 'My name's . . .'

'I know what your name is. You're just like the others. You want to upset everything. Can't have that, can we?'

She closed her eyes, prayed it would be over quickly, then thought of her mother and Lindsey. Which one would have to identify her?

She fought the terror.

YOU ARE NOT GOING TO PANIC.

Easier said than done.

'Please!' Her voice sounded small.

She managed to peer over his arm. She could see the river and the waning light of sunset glowing around the opening and the city lights across the river. She prayed for Doherty to come. He was *bound* to come.

* * *

Fifty yards away, Doherty's flashlight had failed. Muttering to himself, he edged his way back over the slimy flagstones.

The walls crumbled silently as he felt his way back to where he'd left her. The muted light from the world outside was shining ahead of him. He saw them silhouetted against the light and held his breath.

Was that his own heart he could hear?

Be quiet, he wanted to say, but no words came.

Frozen to the darkness, his heart went out to her. His first thought was to rush Conway. No! She'd be dead by the

267

time he got there. Somehow, he had to catch Conway off guard and get him away from her. But how?

He locked eyes with Honey and knew she'd seen him. Hopefully, Mark Conway had not.

In the little light there was, he looked for anything that might help him push the pair apart. There was nothing on the walls, nothing on the floor. There were iron hooks and bars ranged along the ceiling. Before refrigeration this was where meat was hung. One of the bars hung from the ceiling like a giant pendulum.

Doherty was only of average height. Would he be strong enough? He felt the sweat running down his face as he calculated its weight and how hard he'd need to swing it.

Conway seemed oblivious to any small noise, even the sound of heavy footsteps above his head. Doherty looked from the hanging iron to Conway. Everything depended on him getting it right.

* * *

Honey had been watching what Doherty was doing. She knew that somehow she had to swing Conway round so he'd get the full impact. Too short or too far and she could be hit. Meanwhile she listened as Conway muttered about Charlborough and what he'd done.

'He was my brother, you see. Our mother was dead. Our father didn't want us. That's what hurt the most, but Andrew made up for that. He gave us a home — as long as Shaun became Lance. That was the deal.'

'And he paid your father off,' she said, looking beyond him and praying she'd get the timing right.

'That's right. Very handsomely, but then, look what Sir Andrew was gaining.'

Honey swallowed. The knife was sharp against her throat. The tiniest movement or the wrong word and her crisp white shirt would be the wrong shade of pink. And yet she had to move, and not just a little. Violently, so that he was facing Doherty.

She braved herself to ask a few more questions.

'Do you hate him for that?'

'Of course not. He's treated us well.'

Honey thought of the crisp, clean love nest. 'Yes. Of course you did.'

'First that American trying to upset the applecart, and then that slimeball Herbert begging for money.'

'He tried blackmail?'

'Yes. That's the only way his sort ever gets money, by leeching off others.'

'So you buried him in the rockery hoping that Mrs Herbert's first husband would be blamed.'

'That's right! That's right. Lance had been having a fling with that little slut Loretta. He told me all about it.'

His laughter echoed off and around the damp ceilings.

'Bob Davies deserved to be blamed. It was his fault that the Yank came visiting in the first place. Him and his stupid hobby. Maxted had the money to check things out. Detecting was his hobby. He didn't need to do it. But he wanted to see the boy, and then that stupid bitch told him the truth.'

Mark told it all. The gaps in the jigsaw began to fall into place. The real Lance had inherited haemophilia from his mother. He had died in the same car accident in which she had died. Sir Andrew hadn't been too well-off at the time and was determined to hold on to the fortune his wife had brought to the marriage. Without an heir it would have reverted back to his wife's family. So he'd bought — it was the only way she could describe it — *bought* Shaun from his father. The deal was struck on the condition he took Mark as well.

'So a kidnap was contrived, the boy never found.' Her voice sounded shaky.

Mark continued to be forthcoming. 'That's how it worked. Shaun — Lance — never knew any different.' He paused. She felt his body tensing and guessed what was coming next. 'And he's not going to know. Not now. Not ever.'

'But you killed Lady Pamela. Surely she was trying to protect you?'

'And make sure she got her husband's money. That's why she accused Trevor and not him. Bitch! Dishonest bitch!'

She saw Doherty reaching out, trying to get hold of the bar without being seen.

Honey licked the sweat off her lips and tensed her muscles. Doherty was almost ready. His fingertips touched the rough metal before gripping it tightly. He heaved on the iron bar, pulling it back as far as possible before he let it go.

It was now or never.

The pendulum swung. Just as it reached its farthest point, Honey jerked from the waist. Conway was taken off balance. To regain his hold on her, he had to face Doherty.

The iron swung and hit him full on.

Honey was flung sideways as the force of the iron sent Conway crashing towards the water.

She lay winded, breathing in dust and dirt, feeling soreness on her cheek.

Doherty ran to her.

'I'm all right,' she kept saying in a squeaky voice that sounded nothing like her own. 'I'm all right.'

'She's all right,' he called out to the other figures moving in the gloom.

'Is he dead?' Even to her ears, her voice hadn't quite gone back to normal.

Doherty glanced towards the dark bundle lying still on the floor. 'With the side of his head missing? I should think so.'

Honey rejected his offer to help her to her feet. 'I'm OK.' She looked down at her favourite suit and groaned. 'Why did I choose white?'

'Because you're contrary and won't be told anything.'

'Luckily for you! If we still had the death sentence, poor old Bob the Job would have swung by now.'

He frowned. 'Who?'

She shook her head. 'Never mind.'

CHAPTER 37

A guy wearing a lop-sided toupee and a carnation in his buttonhole smiled in her direction and headed her way. His course altered the moment John Rees appeared.

'Have you had a good day?' he asked once the drinks were on the bar.

She nodded. 'Good enough. My daughter hasn't told me she's pregnant, the chef hasn't sliced off a customer's ears, and no one's set the curtains alight with a double sambuca.'

He nodded affably. Being affable as well as good-looking was definitely one of John's things. She told herself he was exactly what she needed — nothing too macho, too cocksure and too much of a lad with the ladies.

'You seem good, you know. Kind of relaxed.'

She licked a dewdrop of wine from her bottom lip. She couldn't stand wastage.

'I am. Tonight I'm wearing my relaxation hat.'

'Do you have many?'

She counted them off on her fingers. 'There's my father confessor hat — people tell you all sorts of details about their private lives over the bar. Then there's my 'the customer is always right' hat. That's the one I reserve for the loudmouth who insists on his consumer rights when a greenfly lands on his salad. Then there's . . .'

'Whoa! And what about your amateur detective hat?'

The sound of her sigh seemed to echo through her body. It was lovely to feel relaxed from top to toe.

'It was a case of brotherly love and family fractions.' She lifted her glass. 'It's all over now.'

'So how do you intend to celebrate?'

'My favourite would be to buy something really old, silky and outdated from auction. There was a clothes auction yesterday, but I couldn't make it. Shame. There were some good items going under the hammer. But never mind. I'll catch the next one.'

John smiled. 'It was a good auction.'

'You went?'

He nodded.

'Lucky dog!'

'I was. I bought you a present.'

He reached down to the gap between their bar stools.

'Here,' he said. 'I saw this and thought of you.'

She started to undo the black plastic bin bag he'd handed her.

'Stylish wrapper,' she mused.

He shrugged. 'It was practical.'

Her fingertips touched something familiar. A thrill shot through her. Honey smiled. Whalebone running through crisp lace and soft silk feels like nothing else in the world. She peered in and saw red satin trimmed with black lace — probably French, just like the one she'd missed on the morning when Casper had summoned her to his office.

John's hand covered hers. 'Best if you didn't get it out in here. People might get jealous.'

She grinned. 'A corset. Should look nice encased behind glass with the rest of my collection.'

The look he gave her was almost serious, certainly unsmiling. 'In my opinion it's the corset that should do the encasing. What do you think?'

A slow smile spread across her face. 'Read my mind.'

The hollow sound of a phone ringing in the deep recesses of her favourite Gucci handbag cut the conversation short. But the inclination remained.

'Mother!'

Her smile was stiff and barely patient.

'Hannah, I've arranged for Mr Paget to meet you in the bar of the Francis Hotel at nine o'clock. Are you far from there?'

'I'm sorry, Mother, I'm not. I'm in Bradford on Avon,' she lied. 'I'll have to take a rain check, I'm afraid. Can you tell him that?'

The response was grumbled.

An echo of another phone trilled from the other end of the bar. The guy with the toupee answered the call, shoved the phone away and ordered a double whisky.

'Do you know him?' asked John.

'Heaven forbid.'

'So!' said John. 'A bottle of champagne is very well deserved.'

She leaned closer to him. 'A bottle of champagne, a four-poster bed and a red satin corset.'

Her phone rang again. This time it was Doherty.

'Hi! We're partying, having a right humdinger of a celebration. Fancy joining us?' He hesitated before saying the words she wanted to hear. 'After all, you put so much into this. I need to show my appreciation.'

'I'm sorry, detective. Not tonight.' She smiled at John. 'I'm inspecting the facilities at a prominent Bath Hotel.'

'Never mind. Another time? Just the two of us?' He sounded disappointed.

She overcame the lump in her throat. 'Always willing to oblige the police.'

She snapped the phone shut. Blue eyes and stubble. Why was that so attractive? She also liked the way his hair flopped over his forehead, and that lop-sided smile. He also looked pretty good in jeans. Some guys just didn't fill them as they should be filled. She hadn't realised she was so deep in thought until John's voice broke through.

'Shall we take a rain check too?'

She jerked her head up. 'What?'

He smiled at her. 'Look. I wouldn't want to rush anything . . .'

She bent her head, fiddling with her phone as she thought things through. Suddenly the four-poster and all the trimmings didn't seem quite as attractive as they had done.

'I'm sorry.'

'Don't be. I wouldn't want to rush things.'

But Doherty would, she thought, as she left the bar. Damn him for phoning, for being lustful, masculine and annoyingly attractive. Damn her feet for heading towards Manvers Street and a party that she just had to be a part of.

Her phone rang again. 'Are you coming?' It was Doherty.

And damn him for being so sure that she'd come.

THE END

Thank you for reading this book.

If you enjoyed it please leave feedback on Amazon or Goodreads, and if there is anything we missed or you have a question about, then please get in touch. We appreciate you choosing our book.

Founded in 2014 in Shoreditch, London, we at Joffe Books pride ourselves on our history of innovative publishing. We were thrilled to be shortlisted for Independent Publisher of the Year at the British Book Awards.

www.joffebooks.com

We're very grateful to eagle-eyed readers who take the time to contact us. Please send any errors you find to corrections@joffebooks.com. We'll get them fixed ASAP.

Printed in Great Britain
by Amazon

11236168R00161